praise for

THE KITCHEN DAUGHTER

"Pick of the Week"

—*Boston Globe*

"Tantalizing Beach Read"

—Oprah.com

"Debut Book to Watch"

—SheKnows.com

"McHenry writes passionately about food and foodies. . . . While Ginny is wonderfully single-minded about cooking, her fresh, sharp story has as many layers as a good pâte á choux."

—*O, The Oprah Magazine*

"An intelligent and moving account of an intriguing heroine's belated battle to find herself."

—*Publishers Weekly*

"Skillfully rendered from Ginny's point of view, McHenry's debut novel is a touching tale about loss and grief, love and acceptance."

—Kirkus Reviews

"Readers looking for good family-themed women's fiction will enjoy this novel, and the magical element of the cooking ghosts will appeal to fans of Sarah Addison Allen."

—*Library Journal*

"An outstanding debut . . . especially attractive as a book group choice."

—*Huntington News*

"A unique voice, richly drawn characters, and a dash of magic—all the right ingredients!"

—Lisa Genova, *New York Times* bestselling author
of *Left Neglected*

"For Ginny Selvaggio, the protagonist of Jael McHenry's captivating debut novel, food is a kind of glossary and cooking provides its own magic, whether it's summoning the dead or softening the sharp edges of a world she finds neither comfortable nor familiar. *The Kitchen Daughter* is sweet and bitter-sharp, a lush feast of a novel about the links between flavor and memory, family and identity."

—Carolyn Parkhurst, *New York Times* bestselling author
of *The Nobodies Album*

"Magical, strong, and compelling, *The Kitchen Daughter* asks what is normal, how well do you know your family, and where does grief go? Jael McHenry blends seemingly unmixable ingredients into sustaining answers. I read this book in one satisfying gulp and smiled in comfort when I'd finished this distinctive, nourishing, and wise novel."

—Randy Susan Meyers, internationally bestselling author
of *The Murderer's Daughters*

"A delectable family drama, *The Kitchen Daughter* whips up a sumptuous blend of suspense, magic, and cooking. A nourishing debut."

—Allison Winn Scotch, *New York Times* bestselling author
of *The One That I Want*

"Jael McHenry's debut is a blast of fresh air, featuring an utterly original heroine who filters her view of an unpredictable world through her love of food. A fresh premise, terrific writing, and memorable characters blended beautifully—and made me devour *The Kitchen Daughter*."

—Sarah Pekkanen, author of *Skipping a Beat*

This title is also available as an eBook

the

KITCHEN DAUGHTER

a novel

JAEL McHENRY

G

GALLERY BOOKS

New York London Toronto Sydney New Delhi

G

Gallery Books
A Division of Simon & Schuster, Inc.
1230 Avenue of the Americas
New York, NY 10020

First Gallery Books trade paperback edition December 2011

GALLERY BOOKS and colophon are trademarks of Simon & Schuster, Inc.

For information about special discounts for bulk purchases, please contact Simon & Schuster Special Sales at 1-866-506-1949 or business@simonandschuster.com

The Simon & Schuster Speakers Bureau can bring authors to your live event. For more information or to book an event contact the Simon & Schuster Speakers Bureau at 1-866-248-3049 or visit our website at www.simonspeakers.com.

Designed by Renato Stanisic

Manufactured in the United States of America

10 9 8 7 6 5 4 3 2 1

Library of Congress Cataloging-in-Publication Data is available.

ISBN 978-1-4391-9169-9
ISBN 978-1-4516-4850-8 (pbk)
ISBN 978-1-4391-9196-5 (ebook)

For my parents,
Karl and Lynnea McHenry.
All the best parts of me are you.

Acknowledgments

So many generous and wonderful people have contributed to *The Kitchen Daughter* in countless ways. I could have filled every page of this book with your names. Instead, here is a shorter list of some of my larger debts.

Huge thanks to my brilliant agent Elisabeth Weed and my remarkable editor Lauren McKenna for reading the manuscript that was and recognizing what it could become. I see your patience, diligence, and insight on every page. I'm also immensely grateful to Megan McKeever, Jean Anne Rose, Ayelet Gruenspecht, and everyone else at Gallery Books for their expertise and assistance as I did this whole publication thing for the first time. Many thanks to Kathleen Zrelak, Jenny Meyer, Blair Bryant Nichols, Stephanie Sun, and Samuel Krowchenko for their help with publicity, foreign rights, speaking engagements, and much more. If any of you are reading this without homemade brownies in hand, give me a call and we'll fix that.

For reading, editing, brainstorming, fact-checking, naming, suggesting, taste-testing, inspiring, advising, and when I needed it, just listening: Michelle Von Euw, Erin Baggett, Heather Brewer, Joan Cadigan and the St. John's Book Club, Robb Cadigan, Russ Carr, Linda Cambier, Pam Claughton, Keith Cronin, Karen Dionne, Chris Graham, Dan Hornberger, Lynne Griffin, Tracey Kelley, Derek Lee of The Best Food Blog Ever (bestfoodblogever.com), Juli McCarthy, Derek McHenry, Heather McHenry, Randy Susan Meyers, Amy Sue

Nathan, Joe Procopio, Kennan Rapp and Rocio Malpica Rapp, Margaret Schaum, Dr. Ariane Schneider, Therese Walsh, and Barbara Yost.

My critique group, for dead-on insight and never-ending encouragement: Ken Kraus, Shelley Nolden, Kelly O'Donnell, Rick Spilman, and Bruce Wood.

My writers' strategy group, for support and ideas and good company: Camille Noe Pagán, Emma Johnson, Maris Kreizman, Siobhan O'Connor, and Laura Vanderkam.

For writing brilliantly about Asperger's syndrome, from the outside and the inside: Dr. Tony Attwood, Gavin Bollard, John Elder Robison, and the women from all over the spectrum who contributed to *Women From Another Planet?: Our Lives in the Universe of Autism*.

Everyone at Backspace (bksp.org), Intrepid Media (intrepidmedia .com), and Writer Unboxed (writerunboxed.com). I'm honored to be a part of some of the best writing communities online. Thank you, thank you, thank you.

Friends and family everywhere, from Philadelphia to Petoskey and Westwood to Wasilla, for your love and support. I owe you all more than I can say.

And of course to my husband Jonathan, with whom I share everything, including a brain, and all the credit.

The discovery of a new dish does more for the happiness of mankind than the discovery of a star.

—BRILLAT-SAVARIN

Eat what is cooked; listen to what is said.

—RUSSIAN PROVERB

the

KITCHEN
DAUGHTER

CHAPTER ONE

Bread Soup

Best Ribollita

Olive oil — 4 pieces garlic smashed — 1 onion coarsely chopped — 1 lg can tomatoes — 1 lg can beans — 1 bunch Kale — 1/2 loaf bread in cubes

Brown garlic and onion in oil, not too brown — add tomatoes crushed by hand with their juice, then water 1/2 way up the pot — bring to simmer — drain & rinse beans twice & add to soup — cut bread in cubes and add to soup — cook a few minutes — salt & pepper to taste

Bad things come in threes. My father dies. My mother dies. Then there's the funeral.

Other people would say these are all the same bad news. For me, they're different.

The cemetery is the easiest part. There's a soothing low voice, the caskets are closed, and I can just stand and observe like I'm not there at all. The man in the robe talks ("celebrated surgeon . . . loving mother . . .") and then Amanda does ("a shock to all of us . . . best parents we could have ever . . ."). I keep my eyes on the girls, Amanda's daughters, Shannon and Parker. They're younger than I was at my first funeral. This, at twenty-six, is my second.

It's cold. They must have heated the ground to dig the graves. The soil wouldn't yield to a shovel otherwise. Not in December, not in Philadelphia. I know that from the garden.

After Amanda finishes talking, she walks back toward us and leans against her husband. She makes a choking sound and I can see Brennan's arm reaching out to hold her. She bends her head down, leaning further in, until she's almost hidden. Held in Brennan's other arm, Parker drops a Cheerio and makes a little O shape with her tiny mouth. Dismay, surprise, something. I hope she doesn't start crying. Everyone is crying but me and the girls. They don't because they're too young. I don't because I don't feel like this is really happening.

A new voice, a man's voice, goes on. I don't listen to the words. It doesn't feel real, this funeral. It doesn't feel like I'm here. Maybe that's a good thing. Here is not somewhere I want to be. Dad's gone. Ma's gone. I'm not ready.

I look at hands clutching tissues. I watch feet shifting back and forth on the uneven ground. All the toes point in the same direction until, by a signal I miss, they don't. I walk slowly so I don't trip. Amanda reaches back and gestures. I follow her to the car. We travel back home by an unfamiliar road. I stare down at my black skirt, dusted with white cat hair, and feel the pinch of my narrow black shoes.

But at home, things are worse. There isn't even a moment for me to be alone before the house fills up. Strangers are here. Disrupting my patterns. Breathing my air. I'm not just bad at crowds, crowds are bad at me. If it were an ordinary day, if things were right and not wrong, I'd be sitting down with my laptop to read Kitcherati, but my laptop is up in my attic room on the third floor. There are too many bodies between me and the banister and I can't escape upstairs. This is my only home and I know every inch of it, but right now it is invaded. If I look up I'll see their faces so instead I look down and see all their feet. Their shoes are black like licorice or brown like brisket, tracking in the winter slush and salt from the graveyard and the street. Dozens.

Without meaning to listen, I still hear certain things. I catch *Isn't she the older one?* and *Not standing up for the people who raised you right, I just can't say* and *Strange enough when she was a girl but now it's downright weird* and *Caroline always did spoil her something awful.* I keep moving around to escape attention, but these conversations fall silent around me, and that's how I know it's me they mean. When people aim their condolences at me, I say "Thank you," and count to three, and move away. Once I find myself in a corner and can't move but Amanda comes to move the other person instead. I feel rescued.

It gets warmer, worse, like they're not just inside the house, they're inside my body. Stomping around on the lining of my stomach. Swinging from my ribs. They're touching everything in the house, pale fingers like nocturnal worms swarming over picture frames and the doorknobs and the furniture, and if they get to me they'll crawl and cluster all over my skin.

I look up, away, searching for something reassuring. These things are the same as ever, I tell myself. These things have not changed. The ornate plaster molding, a foot-wide tangle of branching, swirling shapes, lines the wide white ceiling. Tall doors stretch up twice as tall as the people, twelve thirteen fourteen feet high. There's plenty of room, up there. It's my home. These are its bones. Good bones.

Then I feel warm breath and someone's solid bread-dough bulk, only a couple of feet away. It's one of the great-aunts. I recognize the moles on her throat. She says, "I'm so sorry, Ginevra. You must miss them terribly."

Her hand is close to my arm. My options are limited. I can't run away. I can't handle this.

I lose myself in food.

The rich, wet texture of melting chocolate. The way good aged goat cheese coats your tongue. The silky feel of pasta dough when it's been pressed and rested just enough. How the scent of onions changes, over an hour, from raw to mellow, sharp to sweet, and all that even without tasting. The simplest magic: how heat transforms.

The great-aunt says, "You miss them, don't you?"

I want to respond to her question, I know that's the polite thing to do, but I don't know what to say. It's only been three days. Missing them won't bring them back. And what difference does it, would it, make? I haven't seen this woman since I was six. I'm not likely to see her again for years. What's it to her, how I feel?

In my mind, I am standing over a silver skillet of onions as they caramelize. The warmth I feel is the warmth of the stove. I've already salted the onions and they are giving up their shape, concentrating their flavor. In my imaginary hand I have a wooden spoon, ready to stir.

"Ginevra, dear?" the great-aunt says.

"Auntie Connie," interrupts Amanda's voice. "Thank you so much for coming."

Connie says, "Your sister seems distraught."

I nod. Distraught. Yes.

Amanda says, "Ginny's having a tough time. We all are."

I see her hand resting on Connie's shoulder, cupped over the curve of it, her fingers tight. I peek at Amanda's face and her eyes are still red and painful-looking from the tears. I wish I could comfort her. I concentrate on her familiar gold ring. It's the color of onion skin. Yellow onions aren't really yellow, it's just what they're called. Just like dinosaur kale isn't made from dinosaurs and blood oranges don't bleed.

"It's a shame what happened. Terrible shame. You should sue," Connie says.

"We're thinking about it," says Amanda.

"They were so young," says Connie.

I say, "They weren't that young," because they weren't. Dad was sixty-five. Ma just turned fifty-nine. We had her birthday two weeks ago, right before they left. She made her own cake. She always did. Red velvet.

"We miss them something awful," says Amanda, not to me. Her voice is unsteady. "We're so glad you and Uncle Rick could come, Connie. Do you want to come meet your great-nieces?"

"Oh, yes please, we don't get up here very often anymore," says Connie. She lets herself be ushered away. But in the next moment there's another someone coming toward me and I just can't stand this, all these shoes, all these bodies. There are only so many times my sister can rescue me. Two, three, five—have I used them up already?

Crowding my right shoulder is a man with no hair, his head as pale and moist as a chicken breast. His breath smells like bean water.

"Ginny of the bright blue eyes! The last time I saw you you were so small! So small! Like this!" he exclaims, gesturing, his hand parallel to the floor.

"Got bigger," I mumble. I have to escape somehow, so I excuse myself without excusing myself and head for the kitchen. Five steps, six, seven, praying no one follows me. When I get there, I'm still shaken. I pull the folding doors closed.

Breathe. This is home, and it feels like home. All rectangles and squares. The kitchen is a great big white cube like a piece of Ma's Corningware. Tall white cupboards, some wood, some glass, stretch up toward the long leaded glass rectangles of the skylight. Next to the fridge we have a step stool because only Dad is tall enough to reach the top shelf of the cupboards without it. One whole wall is lined with shelves of cookbooks, bright rectangles of color sealed behind glass-paned doors, which protect them from kitchen air. Ma's books on the left, mine on the right. A floor of black-and-white square tiles stretches out toward the far wall, where there's a deep flat sink, itself made up of rectangles. The wide white counters are rectangles, and so are the gray subway tiles of the backsplash above them. In the center is Ma's butcher block, which was once her own mother's, a rectangular wooden column with a slight curve worn down into the middle over the years. The single square window has an herb garden on its sill, four square pots in a row: chives, mint, rosemary, thyme. Any wall not covered with bookshelves or cupboards is rectangular brick. Other people call it exposed brick but I don't. It is painted over white, not exposed at all.

I kick off my shoes and feel cool tile under my bare feet. Better.

The hum of strange voices creeps in through the folding doors. I imagine Dad at the stove in his scrubs, shoulders rounded, hunched over and stirring a pot of Nonna's bread soup. He is so tall. I take the hum of the strangers' voices and try to shift it, change it into a song he's humming under his breath while he stirs.

All those people. All those shoes. I need to block out their bulk, their nearness, their noise.

Nonna's books are on my side of the cabinet, which is alphabetized. I reach down to the lowest shelf for a worn gray spine labeled *Tuscan Treasures.*

When I open it a handwritten recipe card falls out. At the top of the card *Best Ribollita* is written in loose, spooled handwriting. I never learned Italian. The first time I knew that bread soup and ribollita were the same thing was at her funeral. I looked it up afterward in the dictionary. It was on the same page as *ribbon* and *rice* and *rickshaw.*

My heart is still beating too fast. I dive inside the recipe and let it absorb me. I let the instructions take me over, step by step by step, until the hum begins to fade to silence.

I draw the knife from the block, wary of its edge, and lay it down next to the cutting board while I gather the garlic and onion. The garlic only has to be crushed with the broad side of the knife and peeled. I lay the blade flat on top of the garlic clove and bring down my fist. It makes a satisfying crunch.

The onion has more of a trick to it. Carefully, slowly, I slice the onion through the middle to make a flat side and slip my thumb under the dry gold-brown peel, exposing the smooth whiteness underneath. I lay half the bare onion flat on the cutting board and use the tip of the knife to nip off the top and the root end. I curl my fingers underneath to keep them away from the blade. The recipe says "coarsely chopped," so I cut thick slices, then hold the sliced onion back together while I cut again in the other direction. I take my time. The knife snicks quietly against the cutting board. The sound relaxes me. There's a rhythm to this. Onion and garlic in the pot. Sizzle them in oil. Check the instructions again.

Gather and open cans. Drain the can of beans, rinse them. The recipe calls for canned tomatoes broken up by hand, so I hold each one over the pot and push through the soft flesh with my thumb, squirting juice out, before tearing the tomato into chunks. The juice in the can is cold from the cabinet. Ripping up the tomatoes makes my fingers feel grainy. Something, maybe the acid, irritates my skin. I rinse my hands and dry them on the white towel that hangs next to the sink.

Wash and dry the kale, slice out each rib, cut the leaves in thin ribbons. Drop. Stir. Square off cubes of bread from a peasant loaf, football shaped. Cubes from a curved loaf, there's a trick to that, but I do my best. Everything goes in. I thought I remembered cheese, but when I double-check the recipe, it's not there. Salt, pepper. I adjust the heat to bring the soup down from an energetic boil to a bare simmer. That's the last of the instructions. The spicy, creamy, comforting scent of ribollita drifts upward. I breathe it in.

I'm opening the silverware drawer for a spoon when I notice her.

On the step stool in the corner of the kitchen, next to the refrigerator, sits Nonna. She is wearing a bright yellow Shaker sweater and acid-washed jeans.

Nonna has been dead for twenty years.

Nonetheless, she's right there. Wearing what she wore and looking how she looked in 1991.

In my grief, I am hallucinating. I must be.

She says, "Hello, *uccellina*."

The name she had for me, Little Bird, from the mouth that spoke it. I am hallucinating the voice as well. Low, sharp, familiar. The first time I tasted espresso I thought, *This is what Nonna sounded like.* This is her. The whole Nonna, solid. Right here, sitting in the kitchen.

She can't be. Can't be, but is.

"You are surprise?" says Nonna. "But you bring me here."

Her rough English. Her salt-and-pepper hair, the pattern of it along the hairline, unchanged. Same sweater pushed up to her elbows, each row of yellow stitches tight and even like corn kernels on the cob. Same once-white Keds. She looks as she should. Except that she shouldn't, at all.

"Don't be afraid," she says, and I wasn't until she says it but then I am, and I would flee except that the only way out is through a crowd of strangers who want to put their swarming, sweating hands on me and given that, there is really no escape.

I back against the glass cabinets and say, "Nonna, what's going on? Why are you here?"

Nonna says, "You bring me with the smell of ribollita, and I bring the message. I come to tell you. Do no let her."

"Her? Who?"

The folding doors swing open. Cooler, fresher air pours in, bringing the murmuring sound of the invaders, which fades as the doors swing shut. I hear one shoe strike the squares of the kitchen tile, then another. I can't close my ears so I close my eyes.

"What smells so good?"

Silence.

"Ginny, what are you doing? Are you cooking something, what for? Are you okay?"

I open my eyes just a sliver. Nonna is gone. I see Auntie Connie's yeast-colored shoes. I smell her beerlike smell. Then too late I see her fingers, reaching.

Contact.

When someone touches me wrong it isn't a feeling. It isn't hate or fear or pain. It is just blackness and a chant in me: *get/out/get/out/get/out*.

I push past Connie, I can feel bone under the flesh of her shoulder like the shank end of a ham, and I nearly trip on the step down into the next room and everyone is there, not just shoes but knees and elbows and torsos and open mouths. I have to get out, but they're all in my way. I shove through. I feel oven-hot skin, clammy fish-flesh skin, damp chicken-liver skin, they're all around me. My heart beats faster, the chant matching, *get/out/get/out/get*. Out of the question to go all the way upstairs. Need whatever's right here.

I duck into the coat closet and pull the closet door shut fast fast fast and turn away from the sliver of light under the door. I reach for Dad's rain boots. They squeak against each other like cheese curds. I kneel down, pull them up into my lap, and shove my hands inside. Leather would be better but this particular old rubber-boot smell is still a Dad smell.

The onions, I need the idea of the onions, I soothe myself with it. Slowly growing golden. Giving off that scent, the last of the raw bite mixed with the hint of the sweetness to come. I press my forehead down against my knees, crushing the boots between my chest and thighs. My forehead is hot. My knees are hot. Thin, long strands shaved on a mandoline start as solid half-moons and melt away over time. More salt? No, just patience. Stir. Wait. Adjust the heat. Wait. Stir.

Light floods in. Real light.

"Oh, Ginny, please." It's Amanda's voice. She has a voice like orange juice, sweet but sharp. Right now it's watery and harsh with tears. I look down and see her shoes, glossy and black as trash bags. The pointed toes make triangles against the floor.

"I'm sorry," I whisper. I reach out to pull the door shut but with my booted hand I can't do it. The wide round toe of the boot thuds uselessly against the door.

She bends down to me, speaking softly. "You can do this," she says. "You were doing fine before. You were just fine."

I shake my head no, no, no. I wasn't fine. She can't tell that. She only sees the outside, which isn't how I feel at all.

She puts one hand on the toe of a boot. She says, "Can't you come out? It isn't for much longer, I promise."

I say, "No."

She puts her other hand on the other boot. But my hands are protected. I can't feel anything.

"It's hard enough without this," she says. "I'm barely holding it together, and I can't have you melting down on top of everything else right now. Don't you understand? Don't you realize how this looks?"

I open my mouth to apologize again when a high-pitched siren drowns everything out. Amanda's hands vanish first and then her toes. I hate noise but I know what this one is, and she can handle it. By twisting my wrist and using the heel of the boot to catch the edge I manage to pull the door shut again, and although I close my eyes against the light I can smell the smoke in my nose, a charred, acrid smell. Vegetal, not chemical. Angry voices. Amanda shouting, "Don't worry, it's just in the kitchen, everyone, it's okay."

Amanda always takes care of things, whatever happens. She's like Ma that way. Trusting her is like relaxing into a hot bath. Or, like it used to feel when I took baths. I don't anymore because steeping in hot water makes me feel like an ingredient. An egg, a noodle, a lobster. Now I take showers.

I press myself tight against the closet wall and take deep breaths. The siren stops and the only sound is chattering voices. I fade the noise away. I focus on the feeling of my hands in the rain boots, the warm closeness around me. The feeling of Dad nearby. A reassuring presence. But then when I think of Dad, I think of Nonna's ghost, in the kitchen with me. So real.

Her warning.

Do no let her.

I push my body against the back of the closet but there's nowhere further or darker to go. I stretch my fingers all the way down into the toes of Dad's boots. I close my eyes and think of onions, how over time they change in predictable and expected ways, if you handle them correctly. If you do it right, there are no surprises. Ma said *You can't get honey from an onion* but it turns out that, in a way, you can.

In my life I've had good days and bad days. Miserable days. Painful days. And no matter how bad the bad ones get, there's a mercy in them. Every single one of them ends.

This one, thank goodness, does too.

CHAPTER TWO

Shortbread

Grandma Damson's
Scottish Shortbread

2 cups flour
2 sticks butter
1/2 cup sugar

Mix ingredients and rub together with cold fingers until the mixture resembles coarse crumbs. Divide into 2 equal balls & roll out 1/2 inch thick in a circle, trimming edges as needed. Cut each circle in eight wedges. Use a fork to press the edges into a pattern like the rays of the sun. Prick dough with a fork to dock it. Bake at 350° for 25 minutes or until underside is lightly browned.

When I wake up, I move as if through water. My body is heavy, my brain is slow. My attic bedroom is a big room full of small corners. There are windows in some of its nooks, but not the one with the bed. I roll over and find the clock. Ten already. There is something heavy and warm on one of my feet. I squint. Midnight. I'm sure she's just as happy as I am to have yesterday over, to have the invaders gone. She doesn't like crowds either. She's not a people cat. I ease my foot out from under her long-haired white form, inch by inch. Although sleeping, she complains with a half-swallowed meow.

The image of Nonna in the kitchen comes back to me, and I wish it hadn't. There's already more than I can handle. Now do I have to worry about dead relatives ambushing me here and there? Grandpa Damson on the front porch, under the portico? Dad's second cousin Olivia, the rumored suicide, waiting for me when I step out of the shower? Ma in the hall in the middle of the night, scolding me back to bed? I can't worry about it. I have to assume Nonna was a hallucination. But her warning tickles the back of my brain, and I have to chase it out somehow.

Listening, I tune in to the faint noises. Scratching and swishing and knocks. The acoustics of this old house make it sound like even the sidewalk is only a few steps down the hall. So it takes a while to figure out whether or not these sounds are coming from inside the house. In the end, I think they are.

The stairs creak under my feet, but Gert is busy wiping down the mantel and doesn't look up at the sound. I watch her lean into the motion, pushing hard in long strokes to strip the dust off instead of just moving it around. Her long black ponytail sways. Gert has always had waist-length hair, the longest I've ever seen.

Gert has cleaned the house once a week ever since I can remember. Over the years I learned her story. Her parents, both Jewish, fled Romania for Cuba during the Holocaust. Then during the revolution it was her turn to flee. She changed her language but kept her religion, and brought us sweets from both traditions. Gert has a voice like the poppy seed filling of hamantaschen, inky and sweet, but it's her Cuban pastries I really remember. Even now, remembering, the taste of her coconut turnovers fills my mouth. Creamy, papery white filling. Rich yellow pastry falling apart in flakes.

Gert leans back and shakes the cloth out, whipping it hard from the corners so it snaps. She lifts the bucket of water from the tile of the fireplace and turns toward me.

"Ginny," she says. "Hope I did not wake you."

"No," I say.

She approaches me the only way I can stand, straight on, in plain sight. When I look down, she places the heel of her hand on my forehead and presses against it, like a blessing.

"I am sorry," she says.

"Thank you."

Gert has always been easy for me to get along with. Maybe I would get along with everyone if I only saw them for three hours once a week. My mother, my sister, they were always around too much. There were too many opportunities for me to screw things up. Dad I saw less, and he liked me more. There could be a connection.

"Your sister is in the kitchen," she says, gesturing, and I realize there are more sounds from that direction. A series of thuds, some metallic, some not. I go to see.

"Good morning, sleepyhead," says Amanda, from her high perch. She's standing on top of the step stool, pulling items from the kitchen cabinets and letting them fall into a large black plastic bag spread out on the floor.

"Why are you still here?" I ask.

"I said, good morning."

"Good morning," I echo.

"It didn't make sense to go all the way back out to New Jersey," she says. "The girls were so tired and it was so late. You just missed them, actually. Brennan took them out on a duck tour, you know, Liberty Bell, Penn's Landing, the whole nine yards."

When she says it I realize I overheard them talking about *duck* last night, after the house was dark and I took my hands out of Dad's rain boots and went upstairs to my room. It got me started thinking about what flavors go with duck: orange, cherry, star anise. They also talked about *home* and *safe* and *burgers*. The house carries sounds everywhere.

Amanda drops a box of cereal into the trash bag.

I ask, "What are you doing?"

"I can't stand it," she says. "Eating their food. What they left behind. I . . . I couldn't eat . . . knowing they . . ."

Some of that was my food, not theirs. She might know it, she might not. It doesn't matter. "Okay, but we're going to have to buy more."

"I'll figure it out," she says. "Remind me, I need to trim your bangs, they're completely out of control. How can you even see?"

"I can see fine."

"No, no, let's just go take care of this now while I'm thinking about it," she says, climbing down. Behind us in the dining room I can hear Gert lifting and setting down the picture frames, dusting in between.

I sit on the edge of the bathtub. Amanda holds the comb out toward me and I grab the other end. I let her closer than anyone else, but she knows my limits. While I'm combing out the tangles, she says, "I should take you shopping. How long have you had that sweater?"

"I don't know."

"You need some new clothes, Ginny."

"I don't *need* them."

"You could diversify, though. Wear something besides black."

"I wear things besides black." I hand the comb back to her and tug down the sleeve of my sweater, which doesn't quite cover my wrist. It shrank. My fault. I should have left it for Gert to wash.

"Besides navy and black and brown. Do you own anything red?"

"I don't know."

"Red would look gorgeous on you. Hold still. You ready?"

"Yes." I close my eyes tight and she starts to snip. I don't like the sound, but I know how to keep still around sharp things. I examine a single cornflake in my mind. Not its taste, just its shape, uneven and pockmarked. A mountainous landscape the size of a fingernail.

Amanda works for a while in silence, then says, "You're going to love this. Shorter bangs will frame your face better. We both have the same problem, wide face, tiny chin. If you don't break the line it's a giant triangle. When I was in Lorna's wedding she made us pull our hair back and the makeup gave me a monster breakout so I looked exactly like a freaking Dorito. Cool Ranch. Ah, I wish I had your skin."

I picture her slipping my skin off my skeleton and climbing into it like a jumpsuit, and say, "That's really gross."

"I meant you're lucky," she says, and just goes on snipping. "Pale skin with dark hair, the contrast thing is all the rage. I just look washed out if I don't tan, which was a lot easier when Brennan and I were in L.A. I'd love to show you what looks nice on you. Makeup too. Emphasize the blue eyes, maybe a nice red lip, like a little china doll. You could look so pretty if you tried. We should definitely go shopping this week."

"Okay," I say, because it's easier to agree, for now. I don't tell her what happened the last time Ma took me shopping, six months ago. Metal hangers shrieked against metal racks. The salesgirl wore a flesh-colored top with stitching down the middle that looked like sutures. When I tried on a light blue floaty dress it was so thin it didn't even feel like clothes and the salesgirl said *Oh this eight is too big but the length is good here let me show you if we nip it in at the waist like this.* She pinched me on both sides and I slapped at her hands but she thought I was joking or something and she pressed with both hands and I squirmed and twisted but couldn't twist away so I slapped harder and everything blurred and Ma said *Quiet, quiet,* but I didn't know I was being loud, and we left without buying anything. I don't tell Amanda any of that.

The silence between snips grows longer. Amanda says, "We'll need a break from packing at some point. Maybe we can go later in the week."

I say, "Packing?"

"All done." She sets the scissors down on the sink. I stand up and all the wisps of discarded hair fall on the floor. "There, don't you look so much better?"

"Thank you," I say, even though it wasn't exactly a compliment. "You said packing?"

"Yes. I figured we could work together on packing up Mom and Dad's stuff."

"Why?"

"Well," she says, "life is going to intrude at some point. You know how busy I am with the girls. We're lucky Brennan's around to help for a while, but at some point his firm is going to send him back out on the road, and then I'm not going to be as available. And it wouldn't make sense to have this place just sitting here empty."

"It's not sitting here empty," I say. "I'm living in it."

"Well, but that's going to change."

"Why?"

"Ginny, we can't keep the house. We'll sell it."

It's a horrible thing she's saying, but I don't want to jump to conclusions, like with the skin, so carefully I ask, "Are you joking?"

"No."

"Well, we're not selling it," I snap.

She exhales, forcefully, loudly. "I was afraid you were going to have a knee-jerk reaction."

"My knees aren't jerking anywhere."

"I meant you didn't even think about it."

"I thought about it. Just now. It's a terrible idea."

"Keep your voice down!" says Amanda.

"You keep your voice down!" I reply.

Amanda leans against the sink and crosses her arms. "It's too much house for one person. Besides, do you know how rare it is for a place like this to go on the market? A Portico Row four-bedroom, going on two hundred years old, with all the original detail? I was telling my friend Angelica about it, she's a real estate agent, she was practically drooling. Wash West was scary as hell thirty years ago, Mom and Dad picked it up for cheap. And it's totally paid for. We could make an amazing amount of money."

I cross my arms too. "We have enough money."

"Spoken like someone without her own checkbook," says Amanda. "It never hurts to have more."

"It's home. You're talking about selling our home." I stare at a spot on her shoulder, where a tuft of my cut-off hair has caught and settled.

"It's not really about the money," she says. "It's about you, to be honest. Do you think you'd really be okay here? By yourself?"

"Why wouldn't I?"

"You've never lived alone."

I say, "It's not fair to assume I can't do something just because I haven't."

"Well, you've never . . . you're so . . . okay. Yesterday you started a fire. What if we hadn't been here?"

"But you *were* here. And it was only almost a fire." I can't tell her the reason I left the pot on the stove and ran away. I can't tell her about seeing Nonna. I've never been institutionalized, but I know I wouldn't like it.

"And you ran and hid in a closet."

"And?" I crouch down and start picking up the little black clumps off the featureless white floor.

"Don't bother with that, come on, leave that for Gert," says Amanda. She crouches down beside me. "Ginny, baby, are you gonna be okay?"

"Yes. I already said that."

"No, really, I mean it. Look at me."

She knows I can't. She remembers, belatedly.

"Sorry, Ginny, sorry, that's what I tell the girls."

"I understand."

She stands up and puts away the scissors in the top right-hand drawer, which is not where they go, and then says, "Actually, there's something I've been meaning to talk to you about."

"It can wait, I bet."

"No time like the present," she says. "I want to talk about your problem."

I sit on the edge of the tub and look at the little crystal knobs on the vanity drawers. "I don't have a problem."

"You do."

"I have a personality. That's what I have."

"Ginny, Ginny, Ginny. Please don't push me away."

"Well, please don't be an asshole," I mumble at the floor.

She says, "This is exactly what I'm talking about. You have two speeds. Scared and angry. Don't you want to try being normal?"

I stare at the wisps of hair scattered across the floor. It looks like someone has shaved one of those rare black squirrels. I breathe a few times to calm down. She doesn't need to know about the Normal Book. So I say, "Normal doesn't just mean what you want it to mean."

"Okay," she says. "But, I mean, try to see where I'm coming from. You're my sister and I care about you. Things are different now. You've always had Mom and Dad to . . . rely on . . . and now they—" She stops, pulling the washcloth off the ring next to the sink and pressing it against one eye, then the other.

She's right, I'm used to having Ma and Dad around. This was the first time in years they'd gone away. When Dad turned sixty-five in September, he retired. Ma's present to Dad was a trip, just the two of them, visiting every state he hadn't been to yet. He wrote the name of each state on a card and shuffled them around on the floor, arranging and rearranging, taking into account weather, local festivals, highways, everything. They were supposed to come back in six weeks. In Maine, something went wrong with the heater in their cabin, and the room filled with carbon monoxide during the night. Of all the ways to go, it's one of the quietest. If they had to die, which we all do, I think they would have been okay with how they went.

The front door rattles and slams open. Amanda rubs the wash-cloth across her face and hangs it back up. I try to think of some-thing comforting to say but she has already squared her shoulders and turned her back to me. If she's going to pretend she hasn't been crying, I might as well follow her lead.

"We're back," calls Brennan's voice.

In the living room, Amanda sweeps Parker up into a hug. Parker is the younger sister, four years old, blonde like her mother and grand-mother. Amanda waggles the fingers of her free hand, threatening a tickle, and Parker giggles. "Did you have a good time?"

"Ducks are awesome!" says Parker. "Philly is awesome!"

"Shannon, did you have a good time?" asks Amanda.

Five-year-old Shannon is toying with the zipper on her jacket. She flips the plastic zipper pull, a flat pink rectangle, up and then down.

"Shannon?" Amanda repeats.

"Yes," Shannon says, flipping the zipper pull up and down again.

I hear Brennan whisper to Amanda, "I think we distracted her for a while." I'm not so sure. I know from experience you can be sad anywhere.

They've explained to both the girls that Grandma and Grandpa aren't coming back, but it may or may not have sunk in. It hasn't sunk in with me, really. This is my parents' house, full of their things, the same as it has always looked. I expect them back any minute.

Gert says, "Oh look, it is the girls!"

"Girls, this is Gert!" says Amanda. "We've known her for a long time. Probably since we were your size. Ginny, you think so?"

"Yes," I agree automatically. I'm watching Shannon, who is still toying with the zipper pull. She hasn't looked up once. I only see the top of her tiny dark head.

Amanda says, "It's funny, they're just like us, right? Two girls, a year and a month apart. I don't know how Mom and Dad did it. They're exhausting."

Parker shouts, "I'm exhausting!"

Brennan and Amanda and Gert laugh.

Gert says, "If you want, I can come back and do more cleaning tomorrow. I do not want to be in the way."

Brennan says, "Actually, Amanda, I was thinking we could take the girls home."

"I don't want to leave Ginny alone, though."

"Why not?" I ask.

She says, "I worry about you on your own."

"I'm socially awkward," I say. "I'm not retarded."

"I didn't say you were."

Parker says, "I'm not retarded!"

"Hush, honey, that's not a nice word. Aunt Ginny shouldn't have said it in the first place. You know, Ginny, you really need to watch what you say around these ones. Little pitchers have big ears."

I say, "Pitchers don't have ears."

Gert says, "I will come back tomorrow."

I add, "Retarded is a medical term. It has a specific meaning."

Amanda says, "Ginny, not now. Gert, it's okay. Maybe we should go home and rest up a bit. Ginny, you could come with us."

I say, "No, thank you."

Parker squirms out of Amanda's arms, sits down on the floor, and starts unzipping her jacket. Brennan walks over to her and starts zipping it up again. She makes little animal noises, grunts of protest.

Amanda says, "Fine. Gert, I'll just write you a check, okay?"

"Okay."

I think about speaking up but she is already writing the check, so I don't. I have a credit card for most things but we pay Gert in cash, and Ma made sure I was prepared. She left me twelve envelopes of cash, six for Gert and six for the person who delivers the groceries. Both happen once a week, and since Ma and Dad were supposed to be gone for six weeks, twelve envelopes should have been enough. Now they're too much. There are still eight envelopes upstairs in my nightstand drawer. Amanda hands the check to Gert.

"Shannon, you ready to go, sweetheart?" asks Amanda.

"Yes, Mommy."

"Ginny, I'll see you in the morning," says Amanda. "The girls will stay with Brennan and I'll come back to help you pack."

Gert says, "You are packing up your parents' things?"

"Yes."

"You are thinking of selling the house?" she asks.

At the same time, Amanda says, "Maybe," and I say, "No."

Gert says, "There will be plenty of time to decide these things."

"Yes," Amanda says.

As Amanda turns her back to me, and I see all their backs—Brennan's, Amanda's, Parker's, Shannon's—it comes in a flash. The smell of ribollita. Nonna's espresso voice. *Do no let her.*

I say, "Don't—"

Amanda says, "Don't what?"

But I don't know the answer.

So I just say, "Don't drive too fast," and she says, "Of course not," and Brennan says, "Take care, Ginny," and Parker says, "Bye, Aunt Ginny!" and Shannon says something, but too softly for me to hear.

When they are gone, Gert says, "I have another half hour to clean, that is okay?"

"Of course. Take whatever time you need. Oh, and don't be scared when you go in the downstairs bathroom and see all that hair on the floor. Amanda cut my bangs."

"I can see. You look nice."

"Thank you," I say.

She says, "I only have to take out garbage from kitchen, and I will be done there."

I remember Amanda up on the step stool, throwing soup and cereal and rice down into a plastic bag. "No, don't worry, I'll take care of that. Would you start on the bathroom instead?"

"Yes, of course. And do not forget the grocery list, okay?"

"Thank you." This is the rhythm we set up for the trip. Once a week, Gert comes to clean. She takes the grocery list with her. The next day the groceries are delivered. Someone from the store brings them, I think, but I don't lie in wait to see who, I just pick up the bags from the entryway and shelve everything. So much has changed, but we are still sticking to this part of the rhythm. I, for one, need it.

I go into the kitchen. The bag is still there, open, on the floor. The cupboards, nursery rhyme–style, are bare.

It doesn't make sense to throw out perfectly good food. If Amanda can't stand the thought of touching anything that belongs to our parents, how can she even stand to be in this house? It's theirs, it's all theirs.

I go through the bag. A container of oatmeal has burst and spilled out, but other than that, everything's intact. If I put things back in the cabinets right away, she won't be fooled. But if I wait until the new groceries are delivered, I can sneak things back in, and she won't even know. Luckily she didn't get as far as the refrigerator, with its orange juice and mustard and countless jars of jam.

Is this what I was supposed to stop Amanda from doing? Throwing out our parents' food? I don't know why Nonna would come from beyond just to tell me so, but I do a lot of things without really understanding why. Ma taught me a lot of rules and I follow them. In that context, there isn't that much difference between saying "Thank you" to a compliment you don't agree with, and obeying a dead person's warning. You assume there are reasons.

Since I don't have long before Gert leaves, I prioritize. Make the shopping list first, then hide the trash bag. I start with the usual basics, milk and eggs. Then I always get some fruits and vegetables, but this week I'm not sure what to do. Maybe I need to order more, or less. I don't like all this uncertainty. I scribble a few notes, adding oatmeal and butter to the list, and some other things I'm in the mood for: cider, oranges, breakfast sausage.

Gert comes to say good-bye and I hand her the list.

"Thank you, he will come tomorrow, probably in morning. There is— I wanted to say one other thing. Your parents," she says. "We will all miss them."

"Thank you."

"It is hard at first. I know yesterday, it was very difficult. I will not tell you it gets easier. But it changes."

I realize she must have been here, at the house, after the funeral. I didn't really see faces, only bodies, mostly arms and backs and feet. She would have known not to say anything then. She would have known I couldn't stand it.

Gert says now, "Do not let the grief drown you."

I think *Do no let her.*

I say, "I'll try."

When she leaves, I'm still remembering this house packed full of strangers yesterday, and it reminds me how alone I am now. No one left here but me.

I remember Great-aunt Connie's question at the funeral about whether I miss my parents, and of course the answer is yes. Yes, I miss them. Yes, I desperately want them here, to talk with, to trust, to lean my head against. This is the way I've always been. I think of the answer long after the person asking the question has lost interest and walked away.

So this is what distraught feels like. It feels like a stomachache. It feels like a firm hand wringing out the paltry juice from a Key lime, or a French press squeezing the flavor from coffee grounds. It feels like the air bladder that winemakers use to press the juice from the grapes, which they say is gentle but still presses, presses, presses until all the liquid has leaked out and pooled. I've read about that. It's easy to imagine.

I try to shake the feeling with action. I haul the bag of groceries upstairs and slide it into my closet, pushing it back as far as I can against some old cardboard boxes. But as soon as I'm still, the memory returns.

Nonna said, *You bring me with the smell of ribollita, and I bring the message.*

I go to the kitchen.

On the stove, cleaned and almost as good as new, is the empty pot I used to make the ribollita. It smelled wonderful. It would have been delicious. I lean down and put the pot back in the cabinet. I put the step stool back in its corner, but it is just a step stool right now.

She looked so real. One hundred percent. It doesn't make sense that I hallucinated her. I didn't even remember that sweater until I saw it. I only remember one sweater of hers, and it wasn't yellow. But I thought about her, made her food, and there she was.

Nonna believed in ghosts. Is that what she was? Not a hallucination, but a ghost?

I miss my parents, and I wish they were here. Dad especially. Can I bring him, by trying? Can I do something that reminds me of him and see his shape on that step stool, looking back at me? Could I say, *Dad, I miss you,* and hear him say, *I know*?

I look up at the elegant skylight and try to think of my dad. First, his voice, sharp and round at the same time like tomato juice. How he lifted his chin up every time he looked at himself in the mirror in scrubs, and how he jerked his chin down whenever he looked at himself in the mirror in a suit. I picture his cropped white hair, his small ears, his energetic walk. Nothing happens.

When I was eight I read a book about ESP. I decided to practice bending spoons with my mind every night. No one could know whether practicing would make it possible, if nobody had ever stuck with it long enough. I practiced every night for a couple of months, and then one night, I just didn't think of it. It was the most important thing and then it wasn't. Before ESP it was round things, and afterward it was Turkish rug patterns, then letters written by nuns. But along with those, and every day since, it's been food.

When I think of Dad, nothing happens. Maybe I need something beyond the memory, something physical, something his.

Ma kept the alcohol for company in the dining room china cabinet. All the sweet after-dinner liqueurs nestle there together. But there is one bottle she never knew about right here in the kitchen. I reach deep into the cabinets and remove Dad's hidden bottle of Lagavulin. I set a tumbler on the counter and pour him two fingers of scotch. *This is a tumbler, watch it tumble,* he said. The golden brown liquid, more gold than brown, somewhere between weak tea and apple juice. I stare at it. Nothing.

Out loud I say, "This is a tumbler, watch it tumble," an incantation or a toast or both, and drink it down.

It's like drinking a handful of matches. It burns and then smokes. I fight back a cough. There's a note of something deep and earthy, like beets or truffles, which then vanishes, leaving only a palate seared clean. Nothing lingers. I hope they didn't suffer. I don't think they did.

Yes, I miss them. The answer I've come up with, far too late for the question. Yes.

Still, no Dad.

This brings on a wringing, squeezing ache, because I desperately wish I could talk to Dad again. Ma, she was closer to Amanda. Amanda was a more standard daughter. Dad and I didn't waste time feeling. We just did things. Acted. Were. Not like the others, who talked, asked, wondered, dreamed.

I remember once hearing Dad refer to my sister, out of her hearing, as *Demand-a.* That was when I first realized there was a difference between how people act and what they think. No one had ever told me. Now I realize it's because they didn't think they needed to. Other kids my age had already figured it out.

I pour another shot of scotch for the smell, but I'm afraid to drink it. I'm already dizzy. More would be unwise. Ma never let me drink alcohol, along with the other things she never let me do: go on dates, get a job, move out, travel to other cities alone. It was part of the deal we made years ago. I could cook whenever and whatever I wanted, and she would buy me all the ingredients and utensils and pots and knives I asked for, and set aside half the shelves for my cookbooks. In return I would follow her rules. She always said we'd talk about it again when I finished college, only I still haven't, and now she's not around to talk about it anymore.

Do not let the grief drown you, said Gert.

Do no let her, said Nonna.

I'm complicating things that should be simple. I should do the simplest thing I can think of.

I make shortbread. The plainest of cookies, the best first kind. I know it by heart. Flour, butter, sugar. Two cups, two sticks, a half cup. Mixed and rubbed and blended until it clings together. Rolled out in a circle, not too thin. Cut in wedges. Pricked with a fork and pressed along the round edge with the flats of the tines.

The butter is a little too cold, and I warm it too much in my hands, so it sticks. I shouldn't rush. I make myself slow down. I roll the dough as best I can and cut a lopsided circle. I scrape the drooping wedges off the counter, arrange the survivors on a cookie sheet, and slide them into the oven. Rich, wet butter hisses against the metal. As it heats up, the oven releases vague traces of past dishes clinging to its walls.

It's Grandma Damson's recipe. We only met her a few times. She didn't think it was proper for Ma to go down to Macon without her husband, and Dad was always so busy at the hospital, so we only went sometimes for holidays. She made shortbread at Christmas, so many times over so many years she was like a machine. I'd watch her and nothing ever varied. Batch after batch, dozens on dozens.

I know the recipe is written down in Amanda's neat childhood print on a card in the cabinet. It was her first and last contribution to a recipe project she'd lost interest in immediately. But I don't need it. I've made countless variations on this recipe. Chai-infused shortbread diamonds. Rosewater shortbread squares. Cocoa shortbread sandwiches spliced with Nutella. But tonight, in honor of Grandma Damson, I make hers, from memory.

In a sense, I fail. No ghosts materialize in the kitchen, not Grandma Damson, not Nonna, not anyone.

But out of the mess I make a dozen ideal shortbread wedges, perfect in shape, size and flavor. Warm and delicate. With a glass of cold milk, they are delicious. When shortbread melts on your tongue, you feel the roundness of the butter and the kiss of the sugar and then they vanish. Then you eat another, to feel it again, to get at that moment of vanishing. I eat myself sick on them. Midnight watches me, waiting for a scrap to drop, but she waits in vain. She gives up eventually, stalking off with a twitching tail-tip and an arched back.

I tuck Dad's bottle of scotch back where it belongs, my stomach groaning. I stay crouched down staring into the cupboard for a while, looking at the pots and pans my parents left behind. What would I leave behind? Nothing. A small heap of black clothes. A cat, lovely and indifferent. These are negative thoughts, so I try to shake them off. What does it matter what I leave behind? I won't be here to feel sad about it anyway.

I can't always put the right word to a feeling, but right now, I can. I feel ill and unhappy. Thinking of food doesn't exactly help. In these situations there's only one thing I can do. To calm myself, I read the Normal Book.

The Normal Book is soothing in a different way than food. Not an escape, but an affirmation. Which is a word I learned from advice columns, so it's fitting that the whole thing is made up of advice columns. When I need to, like now, I scan the fractured lines.

it may seem normal to your friend, but you need to tell someone about his	considers her perfectionist behavior normal, and you need to decide how
normal to have good days and bad days at first after any major change	hero-worship of one parent over another is normal but can still be destructive
used to be a stigma but medication is now considered normal, or at least	can't let the desire to be "normal" override every other thing, Annie
it's normal for a child of that age to ask questions that his parents don't want to	got a normal haircut and good clothes like she wanted, so why won't she take

The Normal Book has been with me as long as I can remember. My parents knew about it, but no one else. I feel calmer now. It clears my head.

Now that I think about it, if Grandma Damson's ghost had come, what would I even have said to her? I doubt she would have known about Nonna's message. Then again, maybe ghosts know everything there is to know. They're sure to have more answers than I do, in any case. I'm not even sure I know the questions.

Hours later, as I try to fall asleep, I can smell the soft, buttery scent of the shortbread. The air currents have brought it up into the farthest corner of the house. It will take all night to fade. Even though the shortbread itself is gone, I smell it as if it were right here on a platter on the nightstand. It smells warm.

CHAPTER THREE

The Georgia Peach

The Georgia
Peach

2 parts ginger ale or tonic water
2 parts peach schnapps
1 part amaretto
1 part orange juice

Combine fizz, schnapps, amaretto, and
juice. Pour over a single ice cube in
a martini glass. Serves one as written,
depending on the parts.

When my phone rings, I can't tell if it wakes me up because I'm not sure I've been asleep. It never rang much before, so I fumble with the unfamiliar buttons and somehow end up on speakerphone with the unknown caller saying "Hello? Hello? Ginny?"

"Yes, this is she."

"Hey, it's me."

"Me?" I figure out how to switch off the speaker and put the phone to my ear.

"Me. Amanda. Your sister." The orange juice voice comes through.

"Hi."

"Everything okay? You sound weird."

"You sound weird," I reply, even though she sounds like she always does.

"I do not. Well, maybe. I'm pretty stressed. Okay. Great. So." She takes a deep breath. This means she's going to start talking about something I don't want her to talk about. Or she's smoking. But Amanda doesn't smoke. As I once heard Ma say of something deeply unlikely, it would be like the Pope drunk on Manischewitz.

She says, "I wanted to have this conversation in person, but I just can't get out of the house."

"Is something wrong?"

"It's just life," she says. "The girls are kind of a handful today."

"Take your time," I say.

"Well, but we need to start packing things up."

"Why?"

Another deep breath, blown air. "We talked about this. I have time now, I may not have time later."

"But why even later?" I ask. "Why can't we just leave things where they are?"

"We just can't. Oh, and I meant to tell you, I don't think she's going to come today, but I didn't want you to be worried if she does. If she shows up and I'm not there. Just let her in. Show her around."

I'm completely lost. "Who?"

"Angelica. My friend from high school, the real estate agent. She knows the Center City market like the back of her hand. She's going to check out the house and make some recommendations, maybe show it to some people."

"Why?"

"So maybe someone will buy it."

"But we're not going to sell it."

"Well, we'll see how it goes."

"You're not listening to me," I say. "I don't want to sell it. That doesn't mean maybe. That means no."

"Seriously, Ginny? I don't see how you get a veto in this situation. It's not like you need all that space."

"You want to kick me out of my house?"

"No, I just, no! Parker! Get back here! Listen, sis, I gotta go, just keep an eye out for Angelica, she's a real sweetheart. Start pulling together some of the stuff for charity."

"Charity?"

She says, "I could have sworn I told you this. Didn't I? We need to pack up their clothes for donation regardless. That's in the will. That's what they wanted."

"You've seen the will?"

"We'll talk about that later. Start packing up the clothes in their bedroom, okay? Make yourself useful. I'll be there when I can."

"Okay," I say, and hang up. She can't know the effect she has on me. Otherwise she'd behave differently. She couldn't know that if she tells me to do something, I don't want to do it, and as soon as she tells me not to do something, it makes me want to. With Ma it wasn't this bad. With Amanda, I feel much more contrary.

I try to see things from Amanda's point of view. This is an exercise the advice columnists generally advocate. They have different ways of saying it. *Take a new angle. Pivot ninety degrees. Remember that the villain is the hero of his own story. Put yourself in her shoes.* I've tried putting myself in Amanda's shoes before but it doesn't work. I'm too literal. I can't stop picturing her shoes, and how uncomfortable they must feel, and I never get to the emotional stuff.

Maybe I should just do what I would do if this were an ordinary day. Of course if it were ordinary Ma would be here. In the spring or summer I'd go with her to the community garden first thing in the morning, before anyone else got there, but now it's winter. If I didn't have anything in particular I wanted to cook for breakfast, I'd stay in bed and open my laptop. I'd visit thirty-seven food blogs to check for updates, then five daily advice columns, and then nine cooking sites, and finally Kitcherati, which is my favorite. I like eGullet and Serious Eats but they both spend a lot of time talking about restaurants, and I only care about the cooking and not the eating, so Kitcherati is the best place for me.

They say you learn by doing, but you don't have to. If you learn only from your own experience, you're limited. By reading the Internet you can find out more. What grows in what season. The best way to strip an artichoke. What type of onions work best in French onion soup. Endless detail on any topic. You can learn from people who are experimenting with Swiss buttercream, or perfecting their gluten-free pumpernickel crackers, or taste-testing everything from caviar to frozen pizza to ginger ale. All of their failures keep you from having to fail in the same way.

I reach for my laptop, but then change my mind. Maybe I should do what Amanda suggests after all. If I'm organized when she gets here, maybe she'll stop worrying about me. Then again, if she's made up her mind to worry, there's probably not much I can do to stop her.

The house is quiet but not silent. I get up out of bed and walk downstairs. The stairs creak just like I expect them to. A car goes by in the street with a soft whoosh like I expect it to. The morning light beams in through the skylight at the front of the stairs just like I expect it to. I stand on the second-floor landing and hug myself around the waist. It's a big house. Everything feels large, and empty, and permanent, the same way it has forever.

I had just gotten used to living here in Ma and Dad's absence, and now I need to get used to the idea that they're not coming back. I can't, not yet. I can't even believe that they're gone. Maybe this means I am in denial, as the advice columns say. Maybe it just means they haven't even been dead a week and they were plenty alive last time I saw them.

The night before they left I heard them talking. Ma said, *It's not too late to stay.* Dad said, *I don't want to stay. I want to go.* Ma said, *I worry about her.* Dad said, *Well, stop.* They went. Now they're dead. I can't believe that, but I also can't process it. *Process* is a very popular advice column word. So is *issues.*

Most of what I know about how to act and what constitutes psychological disaster, I've learned from advice columns. On some level I know this is absurd. It's troubling to know I study the emotional range of humans as if I'm not one. But after a while you see patterns. Patterns help you figure things out. The columnist almost never says, *Do this.* Or, *That's not normal.* Or, *Leave him.* She says, *Think about it.* She says, *Be clear about what you want.* Or she says, *There is no normal. There's only what's right for you, and being honest.*

I like *There is no normal.* It appears several times in the Normal Book. But whether I am normal or not, whether my life is a good one or not, I know it isn't my perception that matters. Ma's did. Dad's did. Amanda's does. Really, my perception seems to matter less than everyone else's, if it even matters at all.

Thinking of the Normal Book reminds me that Amanda's coming over. If I'm unlucky, this Angelica person will too. There are a number of things I want to hide from my sister—the envelopes of cash, the food she threw out that I reclaimed—but above all I don't want her to see the book.

I find the Normal Book on the floor of my room. I must have dropped it when I fell asleep. I look for a place Amanda won't find it. Under my bed is too obvious. There are many nooks and crannies in my attic space, but there must be somewhere else more secret. I head downstairs to the library.

Midnight is curled up on Dad's leather chair. I shoo her off. She sniffs a few things, investigates a few corners, and yawns ostentatiously. *Ostentatious* is one of my favorite words. I learned a lot of words when I was young by the same method. When I read a word I didn't know, I looked it up in the dictionary. Then I learned whatever was on that page. When I first read the word *osteopath* in one of Dad's medical books, I opened the dictionary to *osteopath,* and from that same page I learned *ostentatious,* and also *osso buco.* This worked well except for once. When I was ten, my mother slapped me for the first and only time, because I told her she was niggardly. It was on the same page with *Nietzsche* and *night-blindness.*

The dictionaries are here, nestled among all the other hundreds of books in the floor-to-ceiling bookcases. This is where Dad spent most of this time when he wasn't at the hospital. His leather chair is here, and his desk, with another chair behind it. The desk is a broad, flat slab of wood, with legs but no drawers, therefore no hiding places. I look at the walls of books instead. The Normal Book would be at home here, but thinking ahead, I can't chance it. Amanda didn't finish what she was saying about the will. Maybe Ma and Dad wanted their books to go to charity too. It won't work.

I walk out into the hall and remember when Ma chose the paint. Mountain Sage out here, Irish Oatmeal in their bedroom, the master bathroom in Ice Blue Gloss. She gave me the samples from the paint store and I cut them out in little identical squares, playing the game of remembering which was which, knowing every color by its name.

The carpets on the second floor are soft under my bare feet. The next room down is Amanda's, a pale buttery yellow called Chardonnay on the walls, boxes of shoes still under the bed. Then my old room, now a spare, painted in the same color. Another bathroom, its cabinets full of towels and medicines and soaps. When I graduated high school I moved upstairs to the attic. Ma didn't want me to at first because she thought it got too cold up there. But I insisted, and since there wasn't a rule against it, she let me go ahead. My rebellions have always been small ones.

I descend the stairs. On the ground floor there is the living room in front, then the dining room, both floored with long bare planks of hardwood, both with the swirling patterns lining the ceilings. In the living room is a fireplace, which works, though I have never built a fire in it. Behind me on the right is the bathroom, behind me on the left the kitchen.

Under the stairs, there is the coat closet. Two days ago—was it only two days?—I hid there and put my hands in Dad's rain boots. What I really wanted was the closet in their bedroom. I walk upstairs to look at it. I rub my cheek against the rough wool of a winter suit Dad hadn't worn in years. He hated suits. I don't know what Amanda put on him and on Ma, after. I didn't see.

I look down. On the floor of the closet are Dad's dress shoes, probably the only wearable thing he hated more than suits. They smell of leather. Next to them are Ma's bedroom slippers, the ones that always made her laugh. Years ago she told Dad she wanted marabou slippers for her birthday, so he took her wool slippers and sewed a strip of marabou across the toe. The slippers are gray-green cable-knit and the marabou is a frilly hot pink. A few feathers have been shed on the floor of the closet. When I touch the soft marabou I hear Ma laughing, even now. Ma's laugh sounded exactly like spearmint bubble gum. Her voice was like regular spearmint, clean and cool, but the laugh was a gum bubble popping.

I don't know if there's anywhere in here to hide the book. I look around. Their suitcases sit next to the bed. Amanda must have gotten them back somehow. No, I don't want to think about that. Think about the window seat, the fireplace, the closet, the bureau. This fireplace doesn't work and I don't know if it ever has. Ma keeps a rectangular pot of bright red geraniums there instead. Watering them is part of my routine on Mondays and Thursdays.

If I have to leave, what will my routine be then? I can't even imagine.

Amanda wants to sell this house with me still in it. I've never lived anywhere else, and can't imagine any other home.

Do no let her.

Don't let Amanda sell the house? That could be what the warning means. The warning won't help me stop her—*Amanda, we can't sell the house because our dead grandmother said so*—but it would still be nice to know what and who it is I'm supposed to be stopping.

Need to stay focused. Hide the Normal Book.

I tap my fingers on the mantel of the fireplace while I'm thinking. Thumb to pinky and back. One two three four five four three two one. I look down at the fireplace. It might work. I get down, move the geraniums aside, and peer up into the darkness. I can't imagine Amanda will go digging around in here. I crouch inside the chimney and fill my lungs with air in case I need it, and reach my hand up.

Three-quarters of the way around, my fingers find a loose brick. Excellent. I wiggle it loose and tease it out, setting it down gently on the red glazed tile around the base of the fireplace. Reddish dust the color of smoked paprika sprinkles down and settles on my shoulders and hair. Hold in the sneeze. I reach my fingers into the gap where the brick used to be. I need to know if the space is large enough for the Normal Book.

It is, but—there's something in there already.

Holding myself steady with one hand, stretching and reaching up with the other, I stick two fingers into the space and draw out what's there. An envelope. Not addressed, not sealed. Inside, a letter. There are no names but I know the handwriting. Scrawled, messy, almost unreadable.

I need you to forgive me. You always tell me I have a great mind but sometimes it's not so great. ~~She~~ ~~Her~~ It's my fault and I can't pretend it's not. You say it's okay but I don't know. I can't tell. Maybe if I tell you I'm sorry, if I take responsibility, you'll truly forgive me. I love you too much not to say something.

There isn't a date on it, but there's a yellowish tint to the paper, and the letter almost falls apart at the crease when I unfold it. It's old, maybe ten or twenty or even thirty years. When did Dad need Ma to forgive him for something? And what was it? Who is the *she,* the *her,* crossed out? Another *her.* I don't know who they are, and I don't know how to find out.

Then, it occurs to me, maybe I do.

I saw Nonna. She told me I brought her. How did I do it? Thinking about the person clearly isn't enough. Neither is food or drink. Dad's scotch didn't bring Dad, and Grandma Damson's shortbread didn't bring Grandma Damson. There's something else to it. There has to be. If I could figure out what brings them, I could find out if they have the answers I want.

Maybe they only come if they have a message. Nonna wanted to tell me not to let someone do something. Don't let—who? Amanda? She seems most likely. But how am I supposed to stop her from doing whatever she wants to do? Am I too late, has it already happened?

Panic, panic, can't panic. Think of food. Think of sugar. I am a sugar cube in cold water. I won't dissolve. Precise edges. Made up of tiny, regular, secure parts. If the water were hotter I would worry, but it's cold. I stay together. Precise. Clean. Surrounded, but whole.

Okay. I need to cook. It'll calm me down.

I fold the letter and put it back in its envelope, and slip the envelope inside the front cover of the Normal Book. Then I tuck the book into the gap inside the chimney and slide the brick back into place. More paprika-colored dust falls on my shoulders. The pot of geraniums goes back too, making a perfect rectangle within a rectangle, settling into the spot where it belongs.

Everything in its place, I head down to the kitchen and pull the step stool into position.

On Ma's side of the cabinet, all the way on the top shelf, is a box. I bring it down. It's a small Japanese tea box, covered neatly in red-and-gold chrysanthemum paper, worn gray-black at the corners over time.

These are Ma's recipes, the ones she made for company, neatly copied in an identical hand. I think she had penmanship lessons. They do things like that in Georgia. The box is filled with identical cards, lined up like Confederate soldiers. When she taught me to cook, sometimes we used these cards, and sometimes cookbooks, and sometimes just things she knew from memory. I've taught myself a lot about cooking over the years, but Ma's lessons were where it all started.

Food has a power. Nonna knew that. Ma did too. I know it now. And though it can't save me, it might help me, in some way. All I have besides food is grief. I close the glass doors over the cookbooks, protecting them from the heat and grease of kitchen air.

There are two cards in the box in a handwriting that isn't Ma's. One is the recipe for Grandma Damson's shortbread that Amanda wrote down, years ago. So neat and even. Dad always joked about that. He said I had the handwriting of a doctor, that I take after him. Took. Our family had two matched sets. Ma and Amanda with crisp, regal penmanship, Dad and me with illegible scrawls. The other card, clearly older, is labeled THE GEORGIA PEACH at the top. I read through the brief instructions. On the back of the card is only a name: Mrs. John Hammersmith.

I get started.

The martini glasses are not hard to find. I set one out. Next I go out to the dining room and open the china cabinet, tugging out each bottle to read its label, clinking them together until I find the right ones. Schnapps, amaretto. Along with the bottles I find a shot glass and bring it all back to the kitchen. I take the ginger ale and orange juice out of the fridge, and I'm ready.

First, a cube of ice in the martini glass. I look at the recipe and decide I need to combine the liquids separately, so I measure a shot of ginger ale and pour it into a Pyrex measuring cup. I add an equal amount of the schnapps, then a half glass of amaretto and another half of juice. I stir with a spoon and pour it over the ice cube, which makes a single cracking noise as the temperature around it changes.

There's too much liquid. It almost overflows the glass. Maybe the person who wrote the recipe owns larger martini glasses, or makes smaller ice cubes. It's so full I can't lift the glass without spilling. I bend over to put my lips to the rim of the glass. The strong smell of alcohol hits my nose, wafting up, and the closer I get the sharper it smells.

I brace myself to drink at least a little. I decide to count to three first. So I'm awkwardly hunched when the woman's voice behind me says, "That doesn't look entirely dignified, but I admire your spirit."

I turn. The woman behind me is lovely, her full-skirted navy dress covered in tiny white polka dots. Her brown hair is neatly rolled into curls above her shoulders. Her lipstick is a perfect, precise red, and she wears wrist-length white gloves.

I say, "Mrs. John Hammersmith?"

"Oh, call me Necie, please," she says. "This isn't the Junior League."

"My mother was in the Junior League," I say. I know this because she had their cookbook. We made recipes from it. City chicken. Pimento cheese. Ambrosia.

"Who is your mother? Might be I know her."

"Caroline Selvaggio. Damson, originally."

"Caro!" she says cheerfully. "And how is dear Caro?"

"Dead," I say, before thinking it through, and once I realize my mistake, I wish I could take it back.

Necie Hammersmith laughs. "Oh, sugar, your face," she says. "It's okay. I'm sad to hear she's dead, of course, but you must understand it doesn't sound like such a tragedy. I'm dead too. A long time now."

"Ma just died a few days ago."

"I'm sorry to hear that," she says. "I would have thought longer, by the way you're acting. You don't seem all that sad."

"I am. I'm very sad."

"Well, you don't look it. And your father, how's he?"

This time I break the news slowly. "As it happens, he and my mother were killed in the same accident."

"They made it this long, though? Good for them. We didn't . . . I mean, I don't want to speak out of turn, but it didn't make a lick of sense. They went together like whipped cream and sardines. That and the speed of it. You weren't an eight-month baby, by any chance?"

I answer slowly, "I believe I took the same amount of time as other babies."

"Strange," says Necie, straightening her gloves. "They just seemed in such a rush. Though I suppose his fellowship was ending and she wanted to move with him to . . . where did they move?"

"Philadelphia."

"City of brotherly love," she says, "how delightful."

"So you were my mother's friend?"

"One of her best. Which is why I supported her, hosted the shower, all that. Of course I had my doubts, we all did. He wasn't exactly a charmer, your dad. But I'm glad to hear it all worked out so well for them. Lovely daughter. Long lives. Well, it's just wonderful, that's what it is."

I try to put together a question, but I notice the light starting to peek through Necie's dress and then her hair and her skin, as she begins to fade.

44

"Lovely speaking with you," she says, her voice softer on every word, until the "you" is barely audible. Then she's gone.

On one hand, Necie's told me nothing at all. That my parents had dissimilar personalities, which I already know, and that they got married in a hurry, which doesn't much matter.

But on the other hand, I'm so excited I want to run around the kitchen in circles. I've learned something very important.

She's helped me discover the key to bringing the ghosts: their own recipes, in their own writing. If I can bring any ghost whose handwritten recipe I have in my possession, who else can I see? What else can I learn?

I dump the rest of the cocktail down the sink. I turn to the cookbook shelves, full of recipes.

People use it as an expression, to mean something else, but it's also a statement that's literally true: there's no time like the present.

CHAPTER FOUR

Midnight Cry Brownies

Midnight Cry Brownies

1 stick butter
½ cup cocoa
1 Tbsp espresso powder
    3 eggs
    1 cup raw sugar

1 tsp vanilla
½ cup flour
    ½ tsp coarse salt

Preheat oven to 350°. Melt butter & stir in cocoa & espresso powder thoroughly. Let cool slightly. In a larger bowl, beat eggs until pale yellow, then add sugar & continue to beat. Add butter mixture to bowl. Stir in vanilla & flour until just combined. Pour into 8x8" glass pan lined with lightly oiled foil. Sprinkle salt on top. Bake 30 to 35 minutes, until toothpick in center comes out clean.

I begin pulling cookbooks out of the cabinets one at a time. Flipping through the pages. I collect a pile of the things that fall out. Recipes cut from magazines, torn from newspapers. Train tickets with no dates. A boarding pass with Dad's name on it. Once, a popsicle stick, stained orange.

I stack up all the handwritten cards, and at first, the options seem vast. So many cards. So many possibilities. Sweet or savory, quick or complicated, luscious or sharp. Some are written in cursive, with large loops, and some in a tighter block print. But the more I go through, the more I realize there aren't as many options as I thought. Nearly every recipe is classic Tuscan. Polenta, bistecca fiorentina, a beef ragu. Three different recipes for osso buco. But though her handwriting changed over the years, these are all Nonna's. I wonder who she wrote them for. Her daughter-in-law? Her only granddaughters, Amanda and me? Herself?

The last card in the stack is pale blue. Different from the others. This handwriting is unfamiliar. I've never made the recipe before.

Midnight Cry Brownies, it says. Written in a tilted, light, feminine hand. The ink is a little hard to read. Maybe she wasn't pressing hard enough. If I work at it, I can make out every word. I could follow the recipe.

Who wrote it? The name makes me think it was someone sad, crying at night, in the darkness. What did she have to be sad about? As much as I do?

My choices are limited. I can try to bring Nonna again, I can try to bring Ma, or I can make these brownies. Brownies it is.

I analyze the recipe, comparing it to more familiar versions. I pull down *The Joy of Cooking* from Ma's side of the cabinet, and it falls open with little prodding to Brownies Cockaigne. Amanda's favorite. I cross-reference. A smaller pan, smaller amounts of ingredients. Espresso powder, interesting. Twice as much sugar as flour, a reasonable ratio. Raw sugar, which I do have, although the taste should be about the same as half white sugar and half brown, if I needed a substitution. No chocolate, only cocoa. Probably a slightly cakey brownie, instead of dense and fudgy. The salt is an obvious difference. Counterpoint. I'm not sure whether it will remain atop the brownies or sink under the surface as they bake.

The only way to find out is to try.

Even though these steps are fraught with import and complexity and the potential for invoking strangers' ghosts, the process is still calming. I let myself relax into the pattern of the recipe. I line an eight-by-eight-inch pan with foil and spread oil into it with my fingers, careful to follow each step, in order. The calm is in the rhythm. Start the oven preheating, with a click and a faint whoosh of blue flame. Melt the butter, stir the cocoa and espresso powder in. The chocolate slurry cools briefly while I get the rest of my ingredients together. Crack the eggs into a large bowl. Whisk them by hand, cramming air into the spaces between the molecules. Golden sugar raining down into the froth, then more beating, the new mixture dragging against the whisk like quicksand. Just a few more steps. Add the slurry, then flour and vanilla, stirring as little as I possibly can. The light touch is essential. Overmixing would flatten the whole batter right out.

The thick brown batter pours in a glistening ribbon into the foil-lined pan. Rich and heavy, collapsing under its own weight. I scatter coarse salt over the top, then slide it into the oven immediately so the batter doesn't lose any more air. The wooden spoon doesn't clean the bowl well, but I have at least thirty minutes while the brownies cook. The rich, dark batter coats the inside of my mouth. The dark bitterness of the espresso cuts the sweetness. I scrape a metal spoon against the wooden spoon to get all the batter off. I can't lick wooden spoons. I hate how they feel on my tongue. Too much texture. I lick the metal spoon instead. I am thorough.

In the allotted time, they swell, crust, settle, just like brownies should. I test at thirty minutes, then wait three more. On the second test a toothpick comes out clean, barely tinted with chocolate. They're done.

"Well there," says a voice.

It's an ugly voice, even just two words in. A wracked low howl of a voice. Unfamiliar. "What's all this?"

I'm afraid to look at her, but I do. No hair at all. Not even eyebrows. Slender, frighteningly so, her arms like toothpicks. Her cheeks gaunt. Her eyes look too big for her head. A hospital gown hangs loose on her skeletal frame. She reeks of cigarette smoke, years of it, a stale, deep, overwhelming smell. Who is she?

She's standing right next to me. It isn't right. I don't know what to do. I can't think. I introduce myself. "I'm Ginny."

"I don't care," she says. "What in the hell is going on?"

I didn't expect her and I don't know who she is but I force myself to ask a question. "Do you have a message for me?"

Long pause.

"How could I—"

A longer pause.

She says, "Well, even if I did, damn if I'd tell you. You're the one with the answers."

"What answers?"

"Tell me where Doc is!" she shouts. Her voice, louder, is even more unpleasant. "Tell me what's going on!"

"I don't know, I don't know. Tell me who you are first."

"Evangeline Matamoros." The name means nothing. She's un-crossing her toothpick arms, reaching out to touch the walls. I can't see whether she succeeds. I'm too busy shrinking back from her.

She cries, "Who the fuck are you?"

"Ginny," I say. "I told you."

"You haven't told me a fucking thing. Where am I? That's what I want to know."

"You're in my kitchen," I say.

"I'm supposed to be in the hospital. I ate dinner. They poked me with needles. I fell asleep. Then this! What the hell did you do to me? Am I kidnapped?"

Her voice gets louder and louder. "Answer me. Answer me! Come on!" The strain of yelling sends her into a fit of choking, loud coughs. I wish she would cough until I thought of something clever to say. Something to make her go away. If she weren't standing in front of the door I'd be gone already.

She looks so real, with skin and eyes and fingers just like a person, as real as I am, or more. In a blank moment between coughs I shout, "Ghost! You're a ghost!"

"That's stupid," she croaks. "I'm not dead."

"Well, you're not in the hospital either, are you?"

She coughs more, and laces her fingers over her naked head. Her shoulders and elbows look outsized because there is so little meat between them. She sniffs the air so loud I can hear it.

"Brownies. Fucking brownies?"

"Midnight Cry Brownies," I say.

She says, "How did you get that?"

"What?"

"My recipe," she hisses.

I'm stunned. "It's yours?"

"Brownies and ghosts. This is insane. Let me out of here."

"I'm not stopping you," I say.

Instead of heading out the doorway, she stands in its frame, crossing those fragile, pencil-thin arms again. I can't get around her. How can I get her to go away?

"This is some kind of fucking mind game, isn't it?" says the ghost. "Doc's idea, I bet? You never know, I was so in love with him, but he turned out to be a real vengeful motherfucker."

Dad was a doctor. But no. That couldn't be who she means when she says Doc. I can't ask her if he is because I don't want her to say yes. Right now I don't want to learn anything or know any secrets or settle any questions. I just want her to leave me alone. I back up some more.

"No. Please just go away."

"Mind game, mind game, that's what this is. Kidnap me and tell me I'm free. I don't think so."

"Please just go away," I repeat, shaking.

"Oh. Oh! Look at you. You're scared of me! That's . . . interesting."

Her tobacco stink is nearly choking me.

The ghost of Evangeline says, "It's like you really do think I'm a ghost."

She's close, too close. I can see the frayed edges of the ribbon sewn against the gown at the neck. I don't want to find out what happens if a ghost touches me. Before, I assumed it wasn't possible. Now, I'm terrified it might be. Evangeline is quiet. I assume she's looking at me. I won't look at her. I can't.

"BOO!" she shouts.

No choice. I dive through her out the doorway to the next room. Tripping on the door ledge, flying, falling, slamming into the ground before I know I've fallen, smacking the side of my head, hard. The world swims.

Evangeline howls with laughter.

"That'll give you something to cry about!" she shouts.

I twist. Look back. Hope in vain.

She crosses the threshold of the kitchen and follows me. Stands over me.

"A ghost. Huh. Maybe I am. Maybe I'm spoooooooky. Maybe I can do things ghosts can do," she taunts.

I think, *No.*

In that ruined voice, she says, "Yes."

There are more words but I don't hear them, pressing my hands over my ears to seal her out. She is still talking, still laughing. The sound is wretched but at least I can't hear the words.

To get up I need to get my hands under me. So I don't get up.

I do what I can, which is crawl. Crawl to the other side of the room, shoving myself forward with elbows and knees, like a lizard, like a soldier. Think of other foods, other meals. The most complicated menu planning I can think of, my truly desperate resort. The imaginary dinner party I've always wanted to throw, the seven-course "Continental Cuisine" menu, with a dish for each continent. One, the amuse-bouche, ceviche of scallops and shrimp, with the leche de tigre served alongside in a tall shot glass, to wake the appetite. Two, a Moroccan soup, lentils, rich with cardamom and cumin and pepper. Three, the fish course, miso-glazed cod. Four, a white, barely lemon-tinted sorbet, representing Antarctica, because who cooks penguin? Five, Australian lamb, from Paula Wolfert's seven-hour-lamb recipe, so tender it melts in the mouth like butter instead of meat. Six, a small triangle of classically American apple pie, the crust enriched with white cheddar from Vermont. Seven, three European cheeses: tangy Manchego with membrillo, creamy ashed Morbier with red pepper honey, sweet Gorgonzola Dolce on—

Right next to my ear, Evangeline hisses, "Sounds delicious."

Lightning flash, inspiration: If it were possible for her to kill me she would have done it already.

The cigarette stink hovers in my nose. Sorbets and cheeses and cod drain away. She's not gone. I can't just hide. I have to do something. The smell of brownies, the smell of cigarettes, the smell of my own cold sweat. I wonder.

When I pull my hands away from my ears she says, "Why don't you just die? Death is fantastic. So far I'm just *loving* it."

Crawl toward the wall, press myself against it, rise up to my knees, with effort. I heave the window open. And as the scent of Midnight Cry Brownies starts to swirl away in the air currents, Evangeline croaks out, "God, you're no fun," and finally, finally, she begins to fade away.

Alone again. I take stock. My neck aches from twisting. I feel bruised, all over, and on the inside.

I open more windows and wave a newspaper madly to fan the breeze, even though it's got to be close to freezing outside. It's the only way to make sure all the smells are gone. Even if they're mostly in my head anyway. My head is a dangerous place.

I smack the upside-down Pyrex dish against the lip of the garbage can until the brownies fall in. It's going to be a long time before I can stand this smell again.

Garbage day is three days off so I twist the neck of the bag and haul it outside. I go around the corner onto Ninth and into the block-long alley separating our block of houses from the ones on Cypress. Five houses down, I heave the bag into someone else's Dumpster. On the way there my body heats itself with adrenaline but on the way back the chill sets in. I forgot to put a jacket on. I was in a hurry. Whatever black shirt I'm wearing doesn't warm me. The cold bites into my bare arms like teeth.

Still, I stare at the front door instead of going back in. All the houses on my side of the street are nearly identical. Each with a marble portico, a flat brick front, three stories up. We are all Portico Row, built together as one block. Only the doors and the house numbers are different. Our house has soaring wooden doors that go all the way up, without a glass window above it, like some of the houses have. I stand on the marble porch and lay my hand on the cold iron scrollwork of the stair railing.

This is home, it's the only place I want to be, but at the same time everything familiar feels strange. It's the same as it ever was except without the people who most belong here, my parents, which makes all the difference. I'm the only one here, and I'm alone. Lonely. I've never been alone like this, against my will. The more I think about it the worse it gets. I get colder and colder and I still don't go inside. Stepping across the threshold again seems somehow impossible.

I don't know how long I stand at the top of the stairs. I'm only aware of the cold and nothing else. Unlike yogurt, yeast can live through being frozen. Maybe, today, for the first time, I know what it's like to be yeast.

Behind me a low voice says, "Forget your keys?"

Startled, I begin to fall off the stairs, and grab wildly at the railing. I catch it and for a moment I'm back in balance but then gravity is too much and I tear free again. I grab and miss the top rail and my right hand gets caught in the lower scrollwork and the flat rusted edge of the iron scrapes clear across my palm.

Behind me there is a solid slab to rest on, and I think I've fallen all the way down the steps onto the sidewalk until I realize that I'm still vertical and the slab is breathing. I wrench myself so far forward I hit my chest on the rail, but at least that part of the rail isn't sharp. Still, it strikes hard on my sternum, and it takes all my breath.

"Whoa!" yells the voice. "I am so sorry. You okay?"

I pull myself forward and sit down hard on the stairs sideways and press my forehead against the cold marble post between the iron rails. First Evangeline and now this and I'm a drop of water on a griddle. I'm completely out of control, and I can hear the beginnings of the chant, *get/out/,* but now that I'm not being touched maybe I can master it and I shut the world out: separating an orange into skinless sections.

Peel it, but not with your fingers. Level off the top and bottom. Set it on the board. Remove the peel in strips with a paring knife, pushing down from top to bottom with slow, curved strokes. Nick off all the white parts. Cup the cool, wet skinless fruit in your hand. Take care. Don't rush. Press the blade into the flesh of the orange, sink it down, a segment at a time, along the left side of the skin and then the right. Left and right. Left and right. As close as you can to the membrane. Press to the center with your knife, level and easy. If you cut right, the segment will fall out onto the board, triangular, gleaming. Left and right. Left and right. If you rush you'll cut yourself. Take care with it. Cut right along the seam, right where the sweet fruit meets the tough membrane. Left and right. Left and right. As close as you can.

I inhale and exhale. Lift my head from the comfort of the cold stone. Look up.

His skin is the color most people would call olive. But olives come in many colors, black and purple and sour green. Kalamata. Gaeta. Castelvetrano. If it had to be an olive his skin would be a cured Arbequina. I don't know how old he is. Older than me, not as old as my parents. His hair sticks up all over but still looks soft.

"You okay?" he asks, in a low voice with a quality I can't quite place.

"Yes," I say, because it's easiest. "I don't know you."

"I'm David," he says, and reaches out a hand.

"Don't touch me."

"Okay."

I cradle my injured hand in my uninjured one. "Just don't, don't even come close."

"Okay," he says. "I'm really sorry. Give me a sec, I mean, I'll give you a sec. Gotta see what's not in pieces."

That voice, it's odd, I can't figure out what it reminds me of. He hops down the stairs and I see the paper grocery bags now, their contents spilling out and strewn on the sidewalk. The oatmeal, the butter, the oranges. I watch a runaway apple roll across the uneven street and come to its final rest in a storm drain. He gathers everything else up quickly and brings the bags back up the stairs.

"Everything but the eggs looks okay," he says. "Those are a total loss. I didn't mean to startle you."

His voice is muddy, that's what it is. Dark and brown and muddy. A note to it like coffee left too long on the burner. And unsweetened, bitter chocolate. But there's dirt in it too, deep, dark dirt, like the garden in October.

"Okay, thanks, I'm going to go inside now," I say.

"Are you sure you're okay? You don't need to go to the hospital or anything?"

"If I did I could just walk there," I say, pointing. From here we can both see the PENNSYLVANIA HOSPITAL sign, blue and white, EMERGENCY DEPARTMENT specified in bright white lettering on cherry red underneath.

"Okay. I understand. I'll just set these up on the porch?"

I stand up and step back toward the door as he approaches, and as I open it to go inside, the lingering brownie smell hits me and I remember why I was standing out here in the cold instead of going in in the first place, and I let it fall shut again.

I press my back against the solid, reassuring bulk of the door and say, "I'm just going to stay out here a minute." His feet are on the porch part of the stairs, the wide, flat part, with mine. If he doesn't come any closer, I'll be all right.

"Are you crazy? It's freezing!"

"I'm not crazy," I say. I watch his feet.

"Well, you need to wash your hand out," he says. "There's rust in there."

His hand on my hand is a maddening feathery irritation and I jerk it back.

"No!"

"Okay."

He walks down the stairs and stops at a bike that's chained to the No Parking sign. There's a basket across the back so he must have used it to bring the groceries. He reaches into the basket and pulls out a bottle of water. To my surprise, he comes back up the stairs with it.

"Hold your hand out," he says. I don't move.

He says, "Rust. You don't want it infected."

My father's daughter, I know he's right. So I force myself to stay still, and open my palm. He pours water across it and it spills over the side of my hand and runs out between my fingers and spatters on the porch. I watch the spattering drops hit David's shoes since that's easier than looking at the raw scrape across my hand, which is beginning to ache.

"Well, it's not bleeding a lot, but it looks pretty bad."

"That's mostly scar," I say. "This whole part here? That's from years ago."

"But didn't your dad fix things like that? For a living?"

"Yeah! He was incredible." I know this story, I tell this story. "People got in accidents, lost one finger, two, three, my dad could sew them back on. But there are just some things you can't do, after a certain amount of time has passed. Your body doesn't want you to bleed to death, so it seals things up, and that's what happened to me. Dad couldn't do anything about it. In surgery, time is the enemy. If time's on your side, you can do amazing things. You can shear someone's finger clear off and then reattach it. If they got to the hospital fast enough, and they brought the finger with them."

He puts his right hand out and says, "Believe me, I know."

At the top of David's right palm, where it meets his fingers, there is a deep bone-white line, pink and slightly shiny on both sides like a raw pork tenderloin. It goes from the pinky to the middle finger, then hooks in the middle of the palm like the letter J.

"These were off," he says, running his left index finger along the scar, indicating all three fingers.

"How did—"

"I was in a car accident," he says. "So I don't know exactly. I wasn't conscious. There's a lot of metal in a torn-up car, and it's sharp."

"Move your fingers," I say.

He obeys, tipping each one down in rapid succession from pinky to thumb and back again. They move perfectly.

"So you got fixed."

"Your dad fixed me," he says. "I mean, I never even met him, because I was out, and they had some other doctor come and talk to me afterward."

"Dr. Shaw," I say. Dad talked about him.

"Yeah. But Dr. Selvaggio, he was the one who put me back together again." David points toward the hospital, toward the sign. "Right next door."

"That's great! Good as new!"

"I was fine," he says, looking down at the iron railing. "But there were two of us. And she, my wife, Elena, she wasn't fine."

"She was injured?"

"She died," he says.

"I'm sorry," I say, because that's what you say when people die.

"It's been about a year now."

I say, "Someone told me not to let grief drown me."

"That's what my mom says too, but I don't buy it."

"You think I should let it drown me?"

He says, in his muddy, dark voice, "I think it doesn't matter whether you let it or not, it will."

"Are you still drowned?"

"Some days," he says. "Some days, definitely."

"She said it would change."

"Who?"

"The woman who told me not to let grief drown me. Gert. She said it might not get better, but it would change."

He nods and nods. "Well, all her grief is pretty far back. She's dealt with it already. My dad's been dead a long time."

"What?" Suddenly he's talking nonsense, and I feel like the ghosts in my life are making more sense than the people, which I think is not a good thing.

David says, "You look really confused."

"I am really confused, that's why."

"It's been, probably, fifteen years since Dad died? Sixteen? Not that she had an easy life before that, either, but that was the last time she lost someone. So what I'm saying is, it's not like she doesn't know what grief is like, because she absolutely does. More than most. I'm just saying, maybe she doesn't remember just how hard it can be on a daily basis, when everything's still fresh, not to jump in the river and just check out. Okay, you still don't look any less confused."

"You think Gert knew your dad?"

He says, "Yes, Gert knew my dad. Very well. Gert is my mom, you know."

This sounds ridiculous but, now, obvious. "I didn't know!"

"Well, no wonder you were confused." His laugh is short and soft. It's so different from his muddy voice that at first I don't realize the noise is coming from him, and it takes me a moment to process. "That's why I bring the groceries to your house. Because she asked me to. I'm not a real grocery store delivery service. I'm just a guy with a bike. It gets me out of the house, I think that's why she does it."

"You're always the one who brings them?"

"Yep, it's me."

"Well, thank you," I say.

"I'll be back again," he says. "Next week. You sure you're okay?"

"Yes."

"Get that hand wrapped up. You know how?"

"I know how."

"Of course. By the way, Mom told me? About your parents? I'm really sorry."

"Thank you. I'm sorry too."

He says, "I won't tell you it gets better. I don't think it's fair to tell someone how to grieve. Because some people, it takes them a long time to get over it."

"What about the others?" I ask.

"What?"

"You said some people take a long time to get over it. What about the other people? Do they get over it faster?"

"No," he says. "No, some people get over it slowly, and the rest of us, well, maybe we never do."

CHAPTER FIVE

Omelet

I carry the groceries inside. David is right. The eggs are all broken, bashed right in, the inside of the carton swimming in golden-yellow yolk. I drop the whole carton in a new trash bag. I put everything else away in the refrigerator and the cabinets. While I'm in the kitchen I'm just fine, focused on the task, but when I get up to my bedroom, I start to feel a distant tickling of fear again. The smell of brownies has wafted up to the corner and settled in. Even faint, it's too strong to stand. I can't even stay in there for more than a minute. So instead I walk to the top of the stairs and put my hand on the top of the banister there, where the finial is formed into a pineapple shape. I cup my hand over it because it's familiar.

That Evangeline ghost, that horrifying vision. She said it was her recipe. I cooked, she came, and when the smell of the food went, she did too. Is that the answer? The smell of their food brings them? In any case, I know what to avoid. No cooking from their recipes, no ghosts. I can't risk it. Who can tell. Maybe Nonna was a fluke, her message not even meant for me.

I'll stop. I don't want to, because I still feel like ghosts are my best hope for answers, but another ghost like this one and I'll wear my heart right out. Better not to risk it.

I take all the handwritten recipe cards I've found and tuck them into Ma's chrysanthemum tea box for safekeeping. I put the box back

JAEL McHENRY

on the highest shelf, behind glass. No more. Even if I'd found something to invoke Dad with, maybe it would be a disaster. Maybe he'd come back angry. Maybe he didn't love me as much as I think he did. As long as I don't see him face-to-face I'll never know, and that might be a good thing. And I think of David with his Arbequina skin and his voice like mud and his overwhelming grief. Dad fixed his hand, but the rest of him is still broken.

Things can always be worse. How has that stopped occurring to me?

In my mind, I shove away the lingering brownie smell with a strong dissimilar scent: roasted garlic, soft and golden, all its bite rendered away under a glistening slick of olive oil. Carefully separating it from the papery, sticky skins. Pressing a yielding clove against my tongue and feeling the warmth of it along with the sweet salt taste. Not sweet like sugar is sweet, but in a more complex, magical way. Transformed by heat into something it previously wasn't. Not better, not worse, just different.

I dress my wound exactly as Dad taught me. Hydrogen peroxide first, to eat away all the dirt and rust and anything else that isn't healthy skin. It foams like baking soda in vinegar. Slather it with Neosporin and keep it under bandages so the skin doesn't stretch too much. Skin heals best in a moist environment. That way it's less likely to scar. I remember him telling me exactly how healing works, how the skin cells knit themselves back together after trauma. I didn't understand it all because I was five years old. But I always loved the sound of his tomato juice voice.

I think about lying down on the spare bed, but I'm not tired, not now. Instead I go into the library. Here I won't be haunted. I know what's here. Tall bookcases packed with books, from ceiling to floor. Like the cookbook cabinet downstairs, these shelves are divided. On the wall to the right of the door are Ma's books, and one shelf of cooking DVDs, all of which I've seen several times. All the other shelves are filled with Dad's books except the bottom shelf on the left-hand side, which is stacked with three black storage boxes I don't think I've ever looked in. The books are plenty to intrigue me. It's easy to separate his books from hers. Hers are the paperbacks.

Ma belonged to a ladies' book group with a southern theme. Like the community garden, she organized it, and ran it like an empire. She was an organizer. But she wasn't a reader. She probably spent less time with the book than she spent deciding what cake to take to the meeting. She made really good cake.

For a moment I can almost smell the cinnamon, hear her whisk clicking in a melamine bowl, but then it's gone.

Once upon a time Amanda loved this room as much as I did. We have so little in common, but we were both avid readers growing up. I read almost nonstop when I was little, and it saved me in school. I hated classes, hated teachers. They always wanted me to do things I didn't want to do. But because I was a reader, they knew I wasn't stupid, just different. They cut me slack. It got me through.

Reading couldn't help me make friends, though. I never got the hang of it. I would talk to kids, and over the years a handful of them even seemed to like me enough to ask to come over, but after that first visit to the house they never lasted. Ma told me what I did wrong but I could never manage to do it right. *Act interested in what they say,* she said, but they never said anything interesting. *Don't talk too much,* she said, but it never seemed like too much to me. So it wasn't like people threw tomatoes at me, or dipped my pigtails in inkwells, or stood up to move their desks away from mine, but I never really managed to make friends that I could keep.

And I got used to it. I got used to a lot of things. Writing extra papers to make up for falling short in class participation. Volunteering to do the planning and the typing up whenever we had group work assigned, because I knew I could never really work right with a group. And the coping always worked. Up until three years into college, where despite Ma's repeated demands to try harder, I stalled. Every semester since, I was always still trying to finish that last Oral Communications class, which I had repeatedly failed. This semester I only made it six weeks in before it became obvious I wouldn't pass. I think maybe we'd both finally given up.

I pick a book at random from Ma's shelf. Instead of sitting down in Dad's leather chair, I walk into my parents' bedroom so I can sit down on her window seat to read. It seems fitting. The book is one of Ma's southern romances, about a belle on an iron balcony with a disapproving family. There's a young man, an upstart, forbidden by society but entranced by beauty and emboldened by love. It's the usual, but I keep turning the pages to find out what happens next. It's not hard to see why Ma was such a fan. There is something intriguing about knowing how things are going to turn out, but being constantly surprised by how they'll get there.

I'm still reading when I hear the door open downstairs, and Amanda calls out, "I'm finally here!"

By the time I get downstairs she's in the kitchen, setting a canvas grocery bag on the counter. "I brought some cereal, and milk, and a few other things. Don't want to go hungry." Then she opens the refrigerator and sees that it's not empty. "Oh. What's all this?"

"I ordered the week's groceries," I say. "That's what I do every week. How did you think I was eating while Ma and Dad were gone?"

"Honestly, I didn't give much thought to it. I've had a lot else to think about, you know. Well, now we've got way too much stuff."

"It'll get eaten."

"True. It's so cold in here. Is that window open?"

I reach over and close it. "Sorry."

"Ginny, what happened?"

"What?"

"Your hand!"

"Oh. I caught it on the railing out front."

Amanda says, "You caught it on the railing? Does it hurt a lot? What does Dad—" She stops short. "You should get it looked at."

"It's okay."

"Do you usually hurt yourself this much?"

"It doesn't hurt much."

"This often, I mean."

"Once isn't that often."

"Fine. Okay."

"Okay," I echo.

Amanda asks, "So did Angelica come by this morning?"

"Not yet." I realize how disastrous it would have been if she'd stumbled upon me interrogating or being interrogated by a ghost. I was lucky David didn't come in at a worse time either. Although maybe he would have just dropped the bags off and rung the bell as usual, so then I could have controlled the interaction. That's how I get through. Control the interaction. When control is lost, everything is lost.

Amanda says, "Well, she'll probably be by later today, then." She grabs a scrap of paper out of the junk drawer and starts writing. "I'll put her number up here on the fridge in case you need to get in touch with her, but now that I'm here, she'll probably call me about most things."

"I really don't want to sell the house."

"Let's not open that can of worms again right now, please."

I take a different approach. "What does the will say?"

"About the house? That it belongs to both of us."

"Half and half?"

"Half and half. Can we get started, please?"

"Okay."

I bring the roll of trash bags from under the sink and Amanda gets the empty boxes from her car.

We pack up our parents' clothes for charity. I start with the bureau, but my mind isn't on the task. There is too much swirling in my brain, and I can't discuss any of it with Amanda, not a bit. The ghosts. The secrets. When I pack my dad's clothes into boxes I try not to think about the letter he wrote, and when I pack Ma's clothes I try not to think about her receiving it. She must have forgiven him for whatever he did. I try not to think of Necie's ghost saying *It didn't make a lick of sense. They went together like whipped cream and sardines.* She loved him. They loved each other.

My abraded hand itches underneath the bandage, so I make myself not scratch it. I hear the clinking of jars from the master bathroom, where Amanda is working, and then for a while I don't hear anything.

I call out to her, "Amanda?"

She says, "I'm here," but softly, and her voice is squashed down somehow. I get up to see what's happening.

She is sitting cross-legged on the floor, a perfume bottle in her hand. A ridged white cylinder with a bird on top. L'Air du Temps. Ma's.

"You remember?" she says. "She used to let us wear a little on special occasions. Here and here." She turns her wrist upward and taps it in the center, then tips her head and places her finger on the side of her neck.

"Yes."

"It doesn't smell right. I've been sitting here smelling it and smelling it. But it just isn't the same as when she wore it."

"It's chemistry," I say. "The warmth of a person's body and the oils in their skin react with the perfume. So it's different on everyone."

"Oh, Ginny," she says. "It'll never . . . she never . . . she's gone."

"I know," I say. Then I realize she's not telling me. She's telling herself.

"They're gone," she says, and curls in on herself, bringing all her limbs toward her stomach.

She's wedged on the floor between the vanity and the wall and there is no good way for me to get down there. Instead I put my hand on top of her head and stroke her hair. I always find that reassuring when I'm sad. She pulls her knees up to her chest. Her crying is soft and steady like the technique for drizzling oil into homemade mayonnaise, never much but never stopping.

I say, "I miss them too."

She says, through tears, "I know you do, sweetheart. It's easy to think you're not feeling anything because you're not showing it, but I know you loved them. I know it's hard."

"It's hard," I echo.

Amanda wipes at her cheeks with her fingers and says, "This is not what I thought would happen."

"To Ma and Dad?"

"Well, no, or yes, because I certainly didn't expect . . . okay, no, I've got to stop crying, you started me up again. No, I thought I'd be able to handle this."

"You are handling it."

"Without tears. Okay, so that's how I'll do it from now on, without tears. I'll be like you, right? I'll just do something else. There's plenty to do. I'm just going to make a list of what furniture we have in what rooms. I'll start downstairs." She stands up and wipes her cheeks again, this time with force.

"Okay," I say.

I go back to the bureau and keep moving things out of drawers and into boxes. The lingerie I put directly into a black garbage bag, since no matter what we do with our parents' other belongings there is no question of saving my mother's underthings. I don't always know what's appropriate, but I know that.

Once the top drawer is empty of clothes there are just two more things in it to deal with. One is a small cedar box. I think this is where she kept her good jewelry. It's locked and I don't see a key in the drawer. Amanda may know where it is. I set the box up on top of the dresser so we'll both see it.

The other thing at the back of the drawer is Ma's Bible. It has a worn black cover of very soft leather. I fan the pages out with my fingers. No marks, other than the family tree written inside the front cover, which makes sense. Ma was never the type to write in books. She taught us not to. Dad's medical textbooks are marked up from front to back, in pen and pencil and three colors of highlighter, but Ma's books are all factory ink.

I am just trying to remember the last time Ma snuck us into church when I hear the doorbell ring. Amanda can deal with it, so I don't really need to rush. But I need her to see that I'm capable, that I don't need to be coddled, so I set the Bible down next to the jewelry box and head for the stairs.

As I walk I can hear the high-pitched sounds of women greeting each other, but they are trilling nonsensical syllables, like "Duh!" and "Cuh!" Then they chirp with laughter.

Inside near the front door there's a man in a suit, and two women with incredibly shiny blonde hair that's exactly the right length to touch their shoulders. One is Amanda. The other might as well be. The pointed chin, the shiny shoes, a neatly fitted dark suit that reminds me of the one Amanda wore to the funeral. I wonder if they shop together.

She says, "Hi! I'm Angelica! Nice to see you, Ginny."

As if I weren't disoriented enough. She sounds like Amanda too. That orange juice voice, comforting and biting at the same time.

I know I'm supposed to shake her hand, so I steel myself and do it. Angelica's hand feels like hanger steak cooked too far past medium, tense and constricted.

"Listen, I'm so sorry!" she says. "I meant to call, but we were just around the corner unexpectedly, and I told Warren about this place and he thought it might be up his alley, so we thought we'd swing by!"

Warren is a flan-colored man in a suit, with one of those shirts that has a collar that's a different color than the rest of the shirt. He reaches for my hand, but he's too far away to actually reach, which is okay with me. So I give kind of a nod and wave to acknowledge him. He bares his teeth and says, "Sorry. You look flustered."

Fluster is on a dictionary page with *flush* and *flux* and *fluvial*. I say, "Yes."

Amanda says, "Well, yeah, we weren't expecting anyone yet, so the place is really, it's not, you know, not cleaned up or anything."

Angelica says to Warren, "I told you, didn't I?"

"I just wanna get a sense, we'll be two shakes," says Warren.

I hang back. This is not a situation I can control, so my best course of action is to keep quiet and stay out of the way. I look up and get transfixed by the slowly rotating ceiling fan. Even as I'm looking up I realize I should be looking away, but can't. There's something about the pattern.

Hypnotic.

It's been forever since this happened to me. It did all the time when I was little. If I don't break the pattern I'll stand here drooling for half an hour.

So I force my eyes closed, and remember a Korean restaurant Dad took me to for my fifteenth birthday. Ma was out of town and Amanda wasn't invited. We cooked wet, slippery beef over grills set into our table but most of all I loved the panchan. Countless tiny dishes of exotic things, which Dad explained to me one by one. Kimchee, sour, hot. Spicy radish, a yellow so bright it glowed. Green beans dotted with wheels of jalapeño. A clear, trembling walnut jelly. I remember each panchan, savor its imagined taste again.

Now that I've leveled out I open my eyes. I'm back in the world. I gather my strength. The first thing I hear is Warren saying, "It's really cold in here! Doesn't the heat work?"

"The heat works fine," Angelica reassures him.

"We like it cold," Amanda volunteers.

"As long as the heat works," he says.

"It works."

Warren says, "Rock and roll." I don't see what music has to do with it.

Angelica points out a few features, the working fireplace, the high ceiling with its ornate and imposing molding, the long hardwood planks throughout the whole first floor. Warren cranes his neck wherever she says to. Amanda trails them into the kitchen. I am invisible.

I don't follow, but Warren's voice is sharp and loud, so I can hear him saying, "You know, I was really hoping for an upgraded kitchen, with stainless steel. The Sub-Zero, the granite. High-end."

Angelica says, "Do you do a lot of cooking?"

"No," he says. "But I want something less . . . retro."

"Okeydoke!"

I go upstairs while they finish touring around the ground floor. I guess correctly they will not be coming up to the bedrooms. I watch the street from my parents' window. Warren and Angelica shake hands good-bye on the porch. He walks away. Then Angelica pauses, and turns, and rings the doorbell again. Amanda lets her in.

As I come down I hear Angelica saying, "Hey, I'm sorry about that, truly. I should have come by first to take a look at the place. I guess it wasn't really what he wanted. But he kept wanting to see more and more places. I had to do something, so I took a chance."

Amanda says, "He seems like a guy who's hard to say no to."

"You can say that again," says Angelica. "Oh, hey, Ginny."

I need something to say, so I try, "It's nice to meet you."

"Actually, we've met," says Angelica. "But it's been ages. In high school I used to come over here and study."

"Study." Amanda laughs. "She used to come over here and read *Seventeen*."

"My parents wouldn't let me subscribe. Strict household. You guys were lucky."

"Yes," I say, "we know."

"I came for Thanksgiving once too. I still remember it. All that food. Your mom was an amazing cook."

"She was," I say, because it's true, though I must have cooked half of that meal, and Angelica didn't even notice. She probably never looked in the kitchen. Then again, if I don't remember her, should I expect her to remember me?

Amanda says, "Well, that talent skipped a generation in my case."

I say, "Anyone can learn."

"By the way," says Angelica, "I couldn't say it while Warren was here, but I'm sorry about your parents."

"Thank you," Amanda and I say in unison.

Then we're all silent.

Angelica says, "I'd forgotten just how awesome this place is. I mean, I remember the molding, of course, and the high ceilings and the giant doors—it always seemed so big—but these details are great too, like there, the tile around the fireplace. You guys are going to make a killing on this place."

I think Amanda can tell I'm about to say something because she quickly says, "Well, nothing is final, we don't even know if someone's going to make an offer we like. We're a long way from a final sale."

"Oh, of course," says Angelica. "The only certainty is uncertainty."

She runs her fingers along the edge of the mantel. I hope she's not looking for dust, because knowing Gert, she's not going to find any.

"You must have missed it when you were in L.A.," Angelica says to Amanda.

"L.A.'s just so different," says Amanda. "The house wasn't what I missed."

Angelica turns to me and says, "You've lived here all your life?"

"Yeah."

"It'll be a big change for you to leave."

"It would be, yes," I say.

Amanda says, "Since you're here, Cuh, you want to tour around a bit?"

"I would, but I'm starving."

"Well, then why don't we go to lunch first?"

"Fabulous!"

Amanda says, "Okay, Ginny, we'll see you after lunch, then. You okay here?"

"Of course."

She says to Angelica, "I just need to wash my hands, meet you at the front door," and she's gone.

I look over at Angelica's shape in the doorframe and think of Nonna's warning, *Do no let her.* Is she the one I'm supposed to stop? How can I? If I could find the right ghost to ask, maybe I could find out. But fear still holds me back.

"Amanda says you like to cook," says Angelica.

"I do."

"You should get in the habit of making something every morning while we're showing the place," she says, looking up at the branching pattern of the molding and down at the long boards of hardwood. "Baking, especially. Cakes, cookies, breads. Makes people like the house more. Makes them think it's a home."

"It is a home," I say.

"*Their* home," she clarifies.

Amanda's orange juice voice calls from the hallway, "Get a move on, Cuh!" and both of them chirp and chatter their way out the door. I'm left alone.

I walk up the stairs, they squeak under my feet, I walk into my parents' closet, pull the door tight shut, and sit down with my hands in Dad's shoes. I need the dark. I need the comfort. I look for a food memory to calm me and I settle on ceviche. A tart bite, a clean, fresh wave of flavor. Think of the process. Raw fish is translucent, but when you drip the lime juice onto it, it becomes something else. Cubes of white-fleshed fish begin to flake. Shrimp turn pink. Texture becomes color. Visible streaks, almost stripes, show the grain.

The shoes haven't always been part of my self-soothing, but the small dark space has. Ma used to call it recharging my batteries. She knew the strain of interacting with people wore me out. So after school, or other activities that took me out of the house, she'd give me permission to recharge my batteries for one hour. Never longer. When I sit down on the floor of the closet I set a mental clock. Even though she's not here to tell me what to do, I'm doing what she'd tell me if she were here.

Whether this is a good sign or a bad sign, I have no idea.

The hour isn't up yet when the doorbell rings. I want to ignore it. I am comfortably settled in the far corner of the closet, where no light can reach. But what if it's Amanda and she's forgotten her keys? She'll have a fit.

I settle Dad's shoes back in place, right on the right and left on the left, and go down to open the door.

"Hey, remember me?" he says. "David?"

"Yes, of course." His voice sounds a little less muddy than before, a little more like very strong coffee. His brown hair still sticks up all over.

"How's your hand?"

I hold up the gauzed mitt. "Just fine, thank you."

"I brought you something."

He hands me a carton of eggs, flipping the top open to show their round, smooth white tops. "Voilà. One dozen, intact."

"Oh, my sister bought some too, so we have more than we need already."

"I just thought I'd replace the ones I broke. I feel bad about that."

I realize I've been rude. Ma would be appalled. "Sorry, no, we can always use eggs, right? Come on in. I'll put them in the fridge."

I head for the kitchen and he follows me at a distance. He gives me plenty of space. I like that. It makes me comfortable, which right now is the thing I most need.

"Wow, this is a great kitchen!" he says. "Huge! The stove's so vintage. Love it."

"You like to cook?"

"I'm not very good at it."

"It's not hard."

David says, "People who are naturally good at things always think they're easy."

"No, you just have to learn, is all."

"And you have to get all the right ingredients, and plan ahead, and it takes so much time . . . it just doesn't seem worth the effort. I don't have the energy."

I say, "You're overthinking it. Are you hungry?"

"Well, actually, yes. I haven't had lunch."

"Hand me the eggs."

He does. I pause to think. All the ghosts have come when I cooked from recipes. Handwritten recipes. I can do this without worry.

"Here," I say. "I'll show you how easy it is to make an omelet. It's so fast, you won't believe it."

"You really don't need to," David says.

"I know. But this'll be so quick." I like being the expert for a change, and focus immediately on the task. Butter and eggs are all I need for my mise. A fork, a bowl, a plate. A knife for the butter. The pan's already waiting on the stove. Silently, I crack and beat the egg, heat the pan, drop in the butter, pour the egg in, swirl and swirl and fold and flip it out onto the plate. The whole business takes less than two minutes.

"That's amazing!" says David, taking the plate from me. "You make it look so easy."

"I love it," I say. "So I learned it." It's an explanation that leaves a lot out. But I learned a long time ago that people don't really want explanations. Ma taught me almost everything I know about cooking, but the omelet, I learned from Julia Child.

He leans against the kitchen wall to eat. He wolfs down the fragile envelope of egg.

When the plate is clean, he says, "Thank you. That hit the spot."

"Do you want another?"

"I've abused your hospitality enough."

"It's not abuse!"

"I didn't mean it literally," says David. "But thank you. You don't need to."

"Just so you can see it again," I say, and make him another. Heat the pan, drop the butter, shake. Swirl. Flip.

He says, "That's amazing, how fast you are. I could never do that."

"Of course you could. You just have to learn."

He eats the second omelet more slowly. His eyes are on the plate and not my face, so I tell him everything. How to whisk the egg. How to heat the pan. How much butter to drop in and when. Most important, how to shake the pan to cook the egg nearly all the way through to the point of almost-doneness, without going too far. How to tip and roll so the omelet comes out curled just right on the plate. Julia makes them in about twenty seconds on the DVD, but that's because she already has the eggs cracked and whisked and ready to go. There's always a trick like that.

The front door bangs and Amanda's voice calls, "Hey, what smells so good?"

"Omelet," I yell. To David I say, "Do you know my sister?"

"No," he says through a mouthful.

"Hey, Amanda, I'd like—" I'm saying as she walks in, and she stops short in the doorway with her hand on the sill.

"Excuse me, who are you?" she says, her voice sharp with acid.

"I think Ginny was about to introduce me," he says. "I'm David. I'm—"

She interrupts him and doesn't reach for his hand. "What are you doing in my kitchen? With my sister?"

"It's not your kitchen, I made him an omelet, he was saying he doesn't cook, he brought eggs," I try to explain, but she's not even looking at me.

"Back up, back up," David says, and I almost do, but that's not how he means it. "I'm Gert's son, David."

I say, "He delivers the groceries. The eggs got broken, so he brought new eggs."

He says, "I'm really not sketchy. I swear."

Amanda drops her hand from the doorframe and says, "I'm sorry. Let's start over. I'm Amanda, Ginny's sister."

"Do you live here too?"

"Yes," she says.

"No, you don't," I say.

"It's a lovely home," says David.

"Thank you," says Amanda. "Do you and your wife live in the area?"

Nobody says anything.

She says, "Your ring. I assumed."

David says, "There was an accident. Last year." I hear the unsweetened chocolate again in his voice now, drying, bitter.

"I am so sorry," says Amanda. "I didn't know. I was living in California. Mom kept me up on some of the news, but—I am so sorry."

David says, "You couldn't know." There's more silence.

"Amanda, do you want an omelet?"

"No, thank you."

Then I remember she just came back from lunch, so it was a dumb thing to say, but at least it was something. Ma said, *Nature abhors a vacuum, and that goes double for conversation.*

David says, "My mom sure does love your family. You know she won't let anyone else clean this place?"

"Who else would?" I ask.

"She's got a whole business," he says. "Four employees. This is the only house she still cleans herself."

"I didn't know," says Amanda. "Do you work for her too?"

"No. I do this as a favor. I'm not a full-time delivery boy."

"Oh, what do you do?"

"Well, actually, I guess I'm between things right now. Right now I'm just a guy with a bike."

We all trail off into silence again and this time I can't think of a single thing to break it.

Eventually, David turns to me and says, "It was nice to see you. Thanks for the cooking lesson. Enjoy the eggs."

"Thank you," I say.

We all sort of shuffle toward the front door.

"Have a nice night," he says.

"You too," my sister and I say in unison.

Amanda opens the door and lets him out, like a fly.

Immediately after the door falls shut, she turns to me and says, "I can't believe I am such a tool."

"You're not a tool." I don't know how she means it. A hammer? A saw?

"An idiot. That thing about his wife, and then, the job thing, geez. Sometimes I can't say anything right."

"Now you know how I feel."

She doesn't say anything so I sneak a look at her face, but she's looking at me intently and I can't make myself hold her gaze.

She goes on, "Well, it's no fun. Anyway, I was all thrown. I come back home and you're standing in the kitchen with a complete stranger. What was I supposed to think? You have no instinct about people at all. You'd let an axe murderer in and make him fettuccini alfredo."

"That's not true."

"It practically is. I worry about you."

"Stop worrying."

She hisses, "I can't."

"Well, stop talking about it, at least."

"Okay."

She goes upstairs to pack some more. I rinse the pan out in the sink and swipe it with a towel. I rub away a few stubborn droplets and lean down to put the pan back. Then I rinse the spatula, dry it, and put it away in a drawer full of long-handled things. Everything in its place.

Amanda is wrong. I do have an instinct about people, and it tells me David is just fine. I wonder if he doesn't cook because his wife did all the cooking until she died. I wonder what she was like. Like Ma, maybe, capable and in charge, always repeating rules and being protective. I felt smothered sometimes but I know Ma always tried to do what was right for me. One of her unsuccessful lessons in how to make and keep friends was *Be a little mysterious.* Of course I could never find the right level of mystery. If I asserted myself, she said, *Don't be too insistent,* and if I hung back too much, it was *Don't be such a little wallflower.* I preferred to think of myself as a cat. If I think of my behavior as cat behavior instead of people behavior, it pretty much always makes sense. Maybe that's part of why I love Midnight. Maybe she reminds me of me.

Maybe it's like David said. People who are naturally good at something think it's easy. Ma was born charming so she couldn't explain to me how to be that way. Amanda can't explain people to me either. When we were kids we were each other's best friend, but the older she got, the more she pulled away. I'm not good with Amanda, not anymore. I used to be. That was when we were little and she looked up to me. Now she thinks she knows better than I do. About everything. I wonder if Parker and Shannon are like us, the older sister teaching the younger sister what she knows. I wonder if things will change for them, like they've changed for us, over time.

When it's time to go to sleep she makes up the bed in her old room. I hear her call her family to say good night. She still has an orange juice voice no matter who she's talking to, but sometimes when she talks to the girls, it's a lighter, softer voice, like orange juice cut with club soda.

I wait until it's very late, and then go back to Ma and Dad's room. It's risky. Amanda might wake up. But I need this reassurance, and there's only one way to get it.

I slip the Normal Book out of its hiding place in the chimney and make sure none of the paprika dust has gotten on my clothes, then sit down on the window seat to read. I wish it were day outside. I'd prefer more light, but I don't want to turn on a lamp. That might attract attention.

Cross-legged on the window seat, Midnight curled up in the doorway like a fat, useless security guard, I thumb through the book. Some of the cutouts are newspaper. Some are printouts. The earliest clippings are yellowed with age. I've been gathering them a long time. I cut them neatly in squares, and paste them in double columns down each page.

Dear Abby: I don't normally ask for help, but I'm really worried about my

He will miss his mother when she goes to work, and may cry. This is normal

to some, but then again, normal to some makes Caligula look like kindergarten

raised in a home where it was normal to get beaten if you didn't behave, so now

paralyzed, depressed, angry. Is this just normal grief? A typical reaction of the

normal to blow off steam over a drink or two after work. But my boss heard

nausea is normal in the first trimester. If you resent your body right now, know

So, Aberrant in Aberdeen, quit wondering if you're "normal"! That's

There are so many flavors of normal, it doesn't matter which one I am. That's what the Normal Book tells me. There really is no normal. After all the upheaval of the last week, after the funeral and the ghosts and my unreasonable sister and everything, it's worth reminding myself. As strange as my life gets, it's just my life. I'm still in it. Whatever happens, I'm going to have to find a way to get by. Hopefully, on my own. Because I don't like the other options.

CHAPTER SIX

Mulled Cider

MULLED CIDER

Cider

Orange

Peppercorn

Cinnamon

Cloves

Gently heat cider over low flame. Add whole spices. Cook for two hours, or until flavors meld. To serve, slice oranges and float in cookpot or individual mugs.

Amanda and I work in silence most of the next day. Since it won't do me any good to refuse to cooperate, I come up with a new plan. I delay. I pack as slowly as I can. I think about each move before I make it and afterward I think about the move I just made. I fold everything neatly, much more neatly than I need to, folding and refolding to get everything absolutely right. I check every pocket, turning them inside out, slipping my fingers down into each corner to feel for anything left behind.

After my parents' bureaus are empty, I try to start on the closet, but it feels different. The clothes in the drawers were just clothes.

The clothes on hangers remind me of their bodies, as if my parents are still inside their clothes and I just can't see their faces or hands. It's very unsettling. So I soothe myself. *It's okay, it's okay.* Think of red velvet cake, as Ma made it. White flour sifting down like unmeltable snow, the basis for everything that follows. Blending, tinting, leavening. The soft, liquid batter firms as it bakes in the oven. Growing ever more solid. Rising, thickening, settling. Staying improbably red. Finish the cake with a thick sweet cream cheese frosting, so it all looks pure white again until you press the knife into it, exposing its red heart.

"Ginny," says Amanda. "Are you listening?"

I say, "Yes," because I am now.

She says, "Can you handle this?"

I stare at a lace collar that once lay against my mother's neck and say, "Not right now."

"Okay," she says. "It's all right. Tell you what, why don't you go look through the boxes in my old room?"

"Okay."

I turn away from the closet and go to Amanda's old room. I pull the boxes out from under the bed into plain sight. A few old pairs of shoes, a box of T-shirts from camp, a small collection of stuffed animals. They are already sorted and just need to be labeled.

In her closet there is another unlabeled box, and I tug it out to start going through it. There are layers of construction paper and notebooks and homemade book covers with no books inside. Children's drawings. Amanda's drawings. Rainbows, unicorns, flowers. I lose interest halfway through. I write AMANDA KIDHOOD on the side and put it with the stack of boxes against the far wall. These are all things Amanda can take away with her. Whether we sell the house or not, these things don't need to be here.

I should tell her again that I don't want to sell the house. She didn't want to talk about it yesterday, but at some point, we'll have to. I have to confront her, and I have to figure out Nonna's warning, and I have to make myself realize that Ma and Dad are not coming home. Any one of these things alone is enough to give me a stomachache. All together it's more like a stomachache after a birthday party. Yellow cake and chocolate frosting and too many cups of sickly sweet punch. I never had my own birthday parties but I went to Amanda's.

The Normal Book is hidden, the letter I found in the fireplace is hidden, is there anything else I need to hide? I go up to my room and count the envelopes of cash that Ma left for me. I realize I forgot to pay David for the groceries he brought. But he'll come back in a few days and I can leave him extra money then. I tuck the envelopes in between the mattress and the box spring in the meantime. If Amanda finds them I can say I just wanted to keep them safe. And lecture her about respecting people's privacy.

I walk down the stairs, slowly. As I near our parents' room I don't see or hear any sign of my sister. I look at their closet. It's empty. She's packed everything away. I take two steps back. Near the door she has a box of shoes. On top are Dad's dress shoes and Ma's slippers. I listen for Amanda to figure out where she is. A glass clinks, far off, and then I hear a soft thud like the refrigerator door closing. She must be in the kitchen. I take both pairs of shoes and put them back on the closet floor where they belong. Then I close the door.

Amanda is sitting at the dining room table, eating a peanut-butter-and-jelly sandwich and drinking a glass of milk.

"Hey," she says, looking up.

"Hey."

"I guess I should have asked if you wanted to eat too."

"No, I'm not hungry," I say.

"You're not dressed yet."

"I'm dressed."

"Pajamas are not dressed. Angelica's coming later. No one's going to buy the place with you lurking around in black pajamas like a ninja."

I say, "Well, maybe that's okay if no one wants to buy it, since I don't want to sell it."

"Not again," she mumbles, almost to herself, but she wants me to hear her.

"It's half mine," I say. "I get a vote."

"Let's please just not do this right now. I don't want to get in a big argument. Here's a great question to get in the habit of asking yourself. It's how I always make sure everything gets done. Whenever I have a free moment, I ask myself, could I be doing something useful?"

I think of Angelica, and remember what she said. "Yes, I could."

First I go upstairs and change out of my pajamas as Amanda suggested. Then I go to work in the kitchen.

I don't really need a recipe, but I pull down one of my favorite cookbooks anyway. It's an awkwardly large, heavy old tome called *Drinkonomicon,* and as Dad used to say, anything not listed on its 738 pages isn't worth drinking. I run my finger down the list of mulled cider ingredients and set to it.

The pot, the jug, the cutting board, first. Break the seal of the hard red plastic cap. I pour the cider into a tall pot and turn the burner up high. I hone the knife before slicing the orange into whisper-thin, windowpane slices. I pinch the spices out of their small glass jars. Whole cloves, stars of star anise. A cinnamon stick. A few black peppercorns. Lay the orange slices on top. Turn the heat down to a bare simmer, until the bubbles are only a suggestion around the edge of the pot.

Since I'm in here anyway looking at the spice shelf, I go through the jars to determine what I need the next time I place an order online. Cinnamon, definitely. Bay leaves. Some of the more interesting powdered chilies. Ancho, aleppo, chipotle. People think chilies are just chilies but they each have a completely distinctive heat. The sweet sear of habanero, the smoky burn of chipotle, the tart green vegetal bite of jalapeño.

"Making yourself some cider?" Amanda says, looking down over the top of the pot.

"It's for the smell. Angelica said the place should smell like cooking. Have some if you want." I hold the ladle out to her.

"Don't mind if I do," she says, helping herself to a mugful. "It's really sweet that you would do this. I'm so glad you took Angelica's suggestion. Thanks."

The doorbell rings.

When I see who comes in, I wish for the relatively inoffensive custard-skinned Warren. I look back, almost fondly, on his stupid suit.

Besides Angelica, there are two adults, and two kids, little boys whose age I can't possibly estimate. They are older than Amanda's girls and younger than teenagers. I take several steps back as soon as I see them. One is very loud. The other, even louder. They dash around the ground floor and I stand on the stairs in the hopes my body will block them from charging up to the second floor as well. Their parents don't seem to make any effort to keep them in check. Confining them would be like confining race cars, weasels, tornadoes.

Angelica claps her hands and says, "Okay, everyone? Let me show you this gorgeous parlor to start with! This way!" Most of the family tracks her, but the mother comes my way.

"You grew up here, right?" says the mom. I back up to keep a decent distance between us. The heavy carved banister of the stairs works as a natural barrier. I grip its solid bulk with both hands. I should always talk to people with a stair banister between us. I might lead a happier life.

I answer her. "Yes."

"Was it a great place to grow up?"

"Sure," I say. "I broke my leg falling down the stairs, but it was just the one time."

"Oh." She asks, "But the neighborhood's safe, right?"

"Yes. There aren't nearly as many muggings as there used to be."

Suddenly there's a clatter and a howl, and it turns out that one of the children has burned himself reaching into the pot of hot cider, and the other one turned the heat up instead of down, making the situation worse, and everything's high-pitched howling wails and chatter and shouting, so I just stay out of the way at my perch on the stairs, and everyone retreats quickly, and I'm left alone, thank goodness. I walk into the quiet kitchen. And after all that no one even turned the stove off. I extinguish the flame and ladle myself a mug of cider, then leave the rest to cool so I can put it in the fridge for later.

Amanda comes back in and stomps around a bit, but doesn't talk to me. She probably blames me for the accident with the kids. So the same thing that got me praise half an hour ago is now evidence of my incompetence. I decide if I can't do anything right, I might as well not do anything I don't want to do.

Instead, I go into my parents' library. The desk, the leather chair, the floor-to-ceiling books. I'd rather be reading anyway. I run my fingers over the spines, title after title after title. Three-quarters of the way around the room I find the title *How to Be Good*. Curious, I open it up. I'm disappointed to find it's fiction.

I scan the shelf for something to read. Romances. Science books. Dictionaries. A few histories. In the end it comes down to the two books with the most interesting titles: *The Oldest Living Confederate Widow Tells All,* and *An Anthropologist on Mars.*

I think about widows and I think about Mars, and I decide Mars sounds more pleasant. I listen for Amanda. She's down the hall in the room that used to be hers, going through the boxes I set aside. Every once in a while I hear a soft, pleased squeal. She sounds happy to be rediscovering things she thought lost.

Reading in Ma's window seat, comfortable on those yellow cushions, would make me happiest, but I don't want Amanda to find me in there. I push the library door mostly shut and drop my body into Dad's big leather chair.

An Anthropologist on Mars turns out to be nonfiction, and about science. A series of essays. The people in the book are all damaged in some way, and it's a good thing for me to read, because it reinforces the message of the Normal Book: there is no normal. People are people, and that means a broad spectrum. Loose wires, crossed signals. The brain can take hairpin turns, at birth or after. I'm not the most unusual, by far.

One essay in the book is about a woman who has built herself a hugging machine. It makes me somewhat jealous. A thing you can crawl into and feel loved. People frighten me but physical reassurance is something I crave. My family hugs me, but my family's getting smaller. I wiggle around in the chair, with its wide, heavy arms, and try to get it to hug me, but it doesn't feel right. A machine would be perfect.

After a while I can see that the line of sunlight under the door has shifted. It's getting later.

I hear Amanda's voice calling, "Ginny, where are you?"

"Library!" I shout as loudly as I can, to make sure she hears me. I stand up from the chair and close the book, then look around to see what I could be doing that would make it look like I haven't just been sitting here reading for the last two hours.

The chair is in front of those black boxes of Dad's, the only things on the shelves that aren't books. I haven't looked in them yet. I pull one off the shelf and take the lid off to start looking through.

Amanda doesn't come in, though, and if she calls out again I don't hear it. I quickly lose myself in the contents of the box.

Photographs. That's unexpected. Dad always took a lot of pictures but I assumed they were neatly arranged in photo albums. Dad loved order and so did Ma. But all the photos in this box are shuffled together from all times and places, with no logic or order to them at all.

Pictures of him and Ma, long ago. She looks at the camera. He doesn't. Pictures of his mom, Nonna, looking much younger in a place I don't recognize. A blurry shot I think is Grandma Damson. I open up the next box and it's the same thing, countless photographs all shuffled randomly together. Third box, same thing. There must be hundreds of pictures here.

I sort them out onto the floor in piles. There are hills and beaches and bricks and trees, people from close up and far away. Everyone looks at least a little familiar, except one person, and I sort her into her own pile.

When I'm done I count her up. There are twenty-nine black-and-white pictures that look like identical copies of each other. A woman in front of a gray sky. I line all the pictures up in a row. Why so many of the same? Who is she? The photos have no marks on the backs, all the lines are clean, and I can't tell how old they are. It could be five years ago or it could be twenty. Faded color is a giveaway but there's no color here. All I can see of her clothes is a trim white collar. No clues in the background, no buildings or trees. I look at her face. In some pictures she is looking directly into the camera. In others she is looking down and to the side. I wonder if there's something she's looking at, something out of frame.

More than anything else I wonder why my father had twenty-nine pictures of someone who was not his wife.

I don't know why these pictures are here. I don't know who she is. She could be anyone. But in a sense, she helps me make up my mind what I need to do next. This is a question I can't answer, but there's another question, one even more important, that I've been hiding from.

Who did Nonna mean when she said *Do no let her?*

I was terrified of the ghost Evangeline, but terror's no excuse. There must be a reason I can bring ghosts with the smell of their cooking, and it must have something to do with her warning. Evangeline was a mistake. I can bring a family member instead. Family is safe. Nonna, or Ma. I may not always get along with my mother, but I know she loves me. That counts for a lot.

It's time to cook the food of the dead, and see what happens.

UNFORTUNATELY, JUST MAKING the decision isn't enough. I need the opportunity. Amanda doesn't budge. She packs up valuables, sometimes efficiently and sometimes inefficiently, but she spends all day working in the house and she sleeps in her old room at night. Sometimes when Angelica comes by she'll take a break and go out for lunch, always reminding me first that Angelica's phone number is on the fridge if there's an emergency, but I never know how long she'll be gone. One time it's three hours, another only fifteen minutes, and she comes in explaining that Angelica got a call to show a house so plans changed. I can't be sure she'll stay away long enough for me to cook a ghost's recipe, and if I can't be sure, then it isn't safe. I hide the pictures of the black-and-white woman one day when she's out getting coffee, tucking them under a loose bit of carpet on the floor of my closet, but there isn't time enough for anything else. I have to be vigilant.

After the cider I don't cook anything to encourage other people to think of my home as their home. I put all the pots away and leave a spotless, empty stove. One time I'm downstairs when Angelica brings an artsy-looking redhead in, and when Angelica sniffs the air and says "What smells so good?" I can honestly say, "Nothing."

During Angelica's visits I try to keep an eye on people, and I reward myself with time on the computer afterward. The Internet is magic to me. It provides all the advantages of dealing with people, without the drawbacks. If it had been around when I was little, I probably would have burned my eyes out staring at it, digging deep into obscure and useless archives. Or Ma would have had to put rules on how much I could use it. But now I know how to manage it, how to focus.

First I place an online order for spices, the cinnamon and bay leaves and ancho chili powder I've been wanting. Then I read Kitcherati, specifically a thread called "The Fear of Bread." It turns out to be about how people are nervous to make bread at home. I can see why. Ma said it was easy: *Yeast into warm liquid, enough flour to absorb the moisture, knead until it feels right.* But I couldn't watch when she did it. It always made me sick to think of yeast being a live creature. It's funny. Gizzards and livers and unborn chicken embryos don't bother me, but I can't handle eating yogurt and I never make any recipe that calls for yeast. The one thing I insist on my food being is dead.

I don't have anything to say on this thread, but I post on Kitcherati nearly every day. Without the person in person, I actually like questions. With plenty of time to think, I can put together intelligent points. The Internet term for someone who watches without contributing is a lurker. But on the Internet I'm not a lurker. I guess I'm a lurker in life.

Three days go by. Amanda packs, Angelica shows the house, I spend my days at a simmer. The invaders come mostly in pairs. They ooh and aah over every aspect of the house—the skylight over the stairs, the fleur-de-lis wallpaper in the back upstairs bathroom, even the finished attic I use as my bedroom—but they always find some flaw, something to complain about. On one hand, I don't like being here, but on the other, me not being here doesn't mean they won't come. All told I suppose it's better I be here to warn them off, in my own way. Even if it's torture, and I've given myself more one-hour battery-recharging rests than I can count.

That's ridiculous. I can always count. There have been five.

Because of the ghosts I'm afraid to cook, but I can't do without it completely. It's too much of my life, my routine. I watch cooking programs instead. Ma had a whole set she loved. Some used to be on videotape but Dad got them all put onto DVDs for her. She cried. I put one into my laptop and watch it, and then another one, then another one. Julia Child making omelet after omelet. The Two Fat Ladies lining a terrine mold with streaky bacon. Jacques Pépin deboning a chicken.

I watch them cook. I know that if I needed to, I could replay the sequence of events in my head and cook what they're cooking. I have scores of conversations in my head I can play back when I want. Because cooking matters to me I could do the same with these videos. So I watch, and I file them away. I watch Julia Child make crepes, and goose, and suckling pig, and monkfish. She puts flowers in the suckling pig's eyes and I find it kind of creepy. Still, it's better than watching the people who want to buy our house stomping across the carpets. It's at least less creepy than that.

Once a day I unwrap and rewrap my hand, hearing Dad's tomato juice voice instructing me. *Remove the previous dressing and discard. Apply antiseptic ointment directly to the wound for proper hydration and to prevent infection. Wrap thoroughly and affix the bandage firmly.* By the third day the scrape marks are pretty much gone. I leave the dressings on for one more day because the gauze makes me think of Dad, but eventually the wound is healed, and I have to open it to the air.

When Thursday comes again at least I have one bright spot to look forward to. Gert will come and clean, and take away the grocery list.

I write out the grocery list in advance so I'll have it ready when she comes. I add dried pineapple and chicken breasts and string cheese to the usual supplies.

Gert arrives midmorning. Amanda greets her with a drawn-out "Hiii!" when she comes in, and hands her a check immediately, then disappears upstairs again. I should be trying to slow her down more actively, but it takes too much out of me. Whatever is being packed can be unpacked.

Gert presses the heel of her hand against my forehead and says to me, "I have a small something for you."

She hands me an index card. It's her recipe for those coconut turnovers I remember so well. I can taste them just reading the words. All handwritten, copied in a careful hand in deep black ink. I can tell she presses hard. The shape of the letters pushes through the reverse side of each card. It's raised under my fingertips like Braille.

"Thank you," I say.

She says, "It is always good to bring something new into our lives. This is an old thing to me, but I thought it could be a new thing to you."

"You brought us some, years ago."

"But you have never made them. And I think you would like to."

"Yes, I think I would like to."

"You are a very good cook," she says. "Better than I am. Better even than your mother."

"No one's better than Ma," I say.

Gert says, "You are better at cooking. Time for me to start," and heads toward the back bathroom first.

I follow her in and ask, "Can I help?"

"It is my job, Ginny. You do not need to help."

"Okay."

So I watch from the doorway, as I've done many times before, while she goes through the routine. She has an order, a structure. She runs a small amount of water in the tub and wipes it out. She pours bleach in the toilet and leaves it to sit. Then she does the vanity, down to the small crystal knob on each drawer. Once the vanity is done, she cleans the sink, then sprays the mirror. Then she returns to the toilet and scrubs that. And wipes down the wet mirror, until our reflections appear again, blemish-free. Cleaning has its own rhythm.

I follow Gert into the kitchen, where she speaks for the first time in half an hour. "This is a wonderful kitchen. I love the sunlight."

"Yes," I say, and we fall into silence again. She scrubs out the sink with white powder, wipes it out, rinses it. Her ponytail sways back and forth, lashing at the cabinets. She places the sponge back in its carrier. She fills a bucket with water, dips the mop in it, and begins to mop the floor in long, wide strokes. The mop glides over all the squares, a shapeless thing over the shapes.

We're quiet again for a while.

I'm trying to relax and just let myself enjoy the fresh, sharp smell of clean things. But seeing Gert makes me think of David, and I remember something he said the other day.

"David said ours is the only house you still clean," I say.

"When did he say that?"

"Last week. I met him when he brought the groceries."

"I am glad you met him," she says.

"Well, I'm glad you still clean our house."

"Your mother, she helped me when I needed help, a very long time ago. I owe her more than this, but this is in my power."

I don't know why I didn't think of this before. Maybe ghosts aren't the only ones with answers. I say, "How long have you known my parents? Twenty years?"

"More."

I say, "Gert, do you know anything my father did that my mother had to forgive him for?"

The mop is still then. She says, "Ginny, why would I know this?"

"I don't know if you do. I found a letter he wrote to her. And he asked her to forgive him. But I don't know what for."

"Maybe you do not need to know," she says.

"I'm curious."

She squints up at the ceiling. It looks like she's examining the skylight but she may just be giving herself time to think. She says, "You have heard of the proverb 'Curiosity killed the cat'?"

I say, "I'm not very good with proverbs." I interpret them too literally. Rules are better than proverbs for me. The Normal Book says, *It's normal to lean on proverbs and platitudes.* But she's right. Maybe I don't need to know.

The mop snakes across the squares of the floor, dripping when it's lifted, and then snakes across again.

"I do not know the answer to your question. But you know what your mother would say," Gert says, and goes back to moving the mop in a regular pattern, with no breaks in between.

I know what she means, but Ma said a lot of things. She said *I don't know whether to be glad or not that you're pretty. If you were ugly they'd leave you alone.* She also said *Sometimes you have to cut toward your thumb.* She said *Everyone has a worst sin and yours is to be gullible.* She said *Stop that* and *Don't touch* and *Be more careful, Ginny,* and *That's just like your father* and *No, you can't* and *Because Amanda's different, that's why* and *Back to your books now* and *Don't you pay them any mind* and *Meet you back here at four sharp* and *You know how much we love you.*

I take the kitchen towel down from its hook next to the sink and toss it into Gert's basket. It needs a wash. I replace it with another from the cupboard. When the kitchen floor is almost completely wet and the water in Gert's bucket is brown and soapy, I back out of the kitchen to let her finish up the corner without my feet getting in the way. The kitchen smells bright and clean now, like a cilantro stem, or a freshly unwrapped bar of soap.

As soon as the last tile has been wiped and rinsed, Gert leans the mop against the wall, looks at me, and says, "You met David."

"He seems nice." Ma taught me that whether or not this is true, it is always worth saying.

"He is nice. But very troubled."

"Since the accident?"

"Some before that too, but since the accident, it is the worst."

"Since his wife died."

"His grief," she says, shaking her head. "Such grief."

"Worse than mine?"

"No one grief is worse than another. They are all terrible. They all destroy. But you need to find the way to use yours. I put mine in this bucket and toss it out at the end of every day. Maybe you put yours in your cooking. Amanda, maybe she uses hers to put things in order, or to draw a wall around her family to protect them. I don't know. She is your sister, you know her better."

"Maybe."

"There are ways to use grief," she says. "We all have to find our own. David, he has not found his yet."

"Is there any way to help?"

"I have tried what I know. To bring him out of his home, out of himself. But so far, nothing."

She reaches up and tugs the clean towel to anchor it in place. She says, "He has some trouble, but he is my son, a good son. Like you are good daughter."

I am such a good daughter, I am afraid to invoke my mother's ghost for fear we'll do nothing but argue and she'll tell me she's glad she's dead. Which is a whole set of revelations Gert doesn't know about. I'm not going to explain it to her, either. Instead I say, "I don't know if I'm that good."

"You are good," she says. "Your heart is good."

"Thank you."

She beckons and I follow her upstairs to the washer. She starts the water, measures the bleach, waits, then drops in the white towels, one by one. The darker towels she sets aside for the next load. She keeps things separate. In cooking, everything is about combination. Bringing flavors together. In cleaning, it is all about taking something with dirt on it and removing the dirt. Keeping these things, the dirty and the clean, apart.

We all have our own patterns, I guess. Gert has hers. I have mine. And whether we like it or not, they persist.

CHAPTER SEVEN

Biscuits and Gravy

Biscuits and Sausage
Gravy

2 cups flour
2 t B.P.
1/3 C shortening

2 t sugar
1 t salt
2/3 milk with 1 T vinegar

Cut shortening into dry ingredients. Stir in milk — may take more — dough should be soft and puffy. Knead lightly 20 times. Roll or pat out 1 inch thick. Cut in circles. Bake at 450 for 10 to 12 minutes.

3/4 lb sausage
1/4 C flour
1 to 2 C milk

Crumble and brown sausage in large pan. When brown, add flour and stir to coat. Return to heat and add enough milk to cover sausage. Cook 10 minutes, stirring frequently, as gravy thickens. Adjust with add'l milk for desired consistency. Grind on black pepper. Serve.

On Thursday afternoon I hear Amanda on the phone, which is nothing new, because Amanda is frequently on the phone. But afterward she calls out to me, and I find her staring into a box of Christmas ornaments and slapping her phone against her open palm.

Ma used to pound certain cuts of meat flat with a wooden rolling pin. It made that same sound.

"There you are. Listen," she says. "Brennan got called away, damn, this is such bad timing. He has to go back to the L.A. office. Could be a few days, maybe longer, we don't know."

"Okay."

"They won't let him extend his bereavement, their policy, it's just draconian."

Draconian is on a page with *drab* and *dragée* and *dragnet.* "Okay."

She goes on, "So he can't watch the girls anymore. So I'll have to bring them here."

"Okay."

"It's not okay, not really," she says, bowing her head down and tying her pale hair back in a ponytail. "You're not responsible for other people, you don't understand what it's like."

"You're right, I don't."

"Well, at least you know it. So. I need to go home now. Why don't you come?"

"Now?"

"Yes, like I said, now."

"To do what?"

"What does it matter, Ginny, geez!" She slaps the phone against her hand again. "Brennan's flight leaves in three hours. It's a half hour drive. And the girls are freaking out. Probably we should stay there overnight, we can come back here in the morning. We'll have to bring over something to keep them occupied or they'll be breaking all the knickknacks. The right book will take care of Shannon for hours but Parker won't sit still for that, not that Parker sits still for anything, that girl, I swear."

"There's no rush," I say. "Stay home as long as you want, then come back when it's convenient."

"If I wait for things to be convenient nothing will ever get done."

She makes a sweeping gesture toward the staircase. "Run upstairs and get a change of clothes and let's go."

"Okay."

I tuck a pair of jeans and a navy polo into a backpack. I think about taking the Normal Book but it's too risky. I pack the laptop, and my wallet, and a pair of underwear.

"Come on," yells Amanda.

I've got my foot on the first stair and my hand on the pineapple finial when I remember what Nonna said.

Do no let her.

My senses are flooded with oregano and tomatoes and long-simmered beef. I try to swallow past a sudden knot. Maybe I'm not supposed to leave the house. Maybe that's what I'm not supposed to let Amanda do: convince me to leave. Take me away.

She stands at the base of the stairs with her face toward the door. I look at the spot where her ponytail sprouts out of the back of her head.

I say, "No, I'll stay here."

The ponytail whips the air. "You said you'd go!"

"I changed my mind."

Amanda points her chin up the stairs at me. "I swear, Ginny, you are so frustrating."

"I don't want to leave Midnight here alone." This is the truth, though not all of it. "I need to stay here and take care of her."

"The cat will deal."

"I'm not going." I tighten my grip.

"Fine. Stay. We're going to have to figure this out when you move in . . . long-haired cats make such a mess. You probably don't notice because Gert takes care of it."

"Move in? I never agreed to that."

"Oh, great," says Amanda, "you're gonna pick now to start an argument?"

I swallow my anger. Instead I say, "You should go."

"Yes, I should. Love you. Be good."

And she's gone.

One thing at a time.

I listen for the car door closing, the rev of the engine, the tires hissing down the snowy street. Once I'm sure she's gone I spring into action. I've been guessing and I have to stop guessing. I have to find out.

I have to ask Nonna what she meant.

With the ribollita recipe out on the counter I start cooking. I try to get through each step as quickly as I can without rushing. If I cut myself and have to stop, that could throw everything off. I go through the whole recipe. Onion and garlic, slicing and chopping. The beans, the tomatoes, the kale. The bread. Stirring it all in the pot, checking back to make sure everything's correct.

But nothing happens.

I taste a bit of the ribollita, and go back over the directions. It isn't that. I didn't screw up. There just isn't anything there anymore. No magic. Did it get used up?

There is a whole stack of cards here I could use. Nonna's other specialties. Ragu di carne or bistecca fiorentina, for example. I'd have to go out and pick up some ingredients but I can do that in an emergency. I can go to the Korean grocery on the corner and put the credit card down on the counter and sign the slip. I can do it if I have to.

I want to be brave. Maybe if I just go ahead and do what I'm afraid of, I'll find the bravery. Maybe that's how normal people do it. Not normal, don't think normal, I tell myself. Average people. Other people. Bravery means forging ahead instead of asking questions. *Act first, ask questions later* never made sense to me. Act first, sure, that makes sense. The second part, not as much. Once you've succeeded, there are no more questions. Or at least the questions are different ones. And if you fail, questions won't help.

I remember Amanda saying, *You only have two speeds, scared and angry.* Maybe I could try something in the middle.

But this is much more than just walking down to the corner. There's something even scarier I can, and should, do.

Not Nonna this time. I need to talk to Ma.

I'm scared but it can't wait. I don't know when I'll be alone again. This might be my only chance. I go upstairs and fetch the pictures and the letter from their hiding places. I look at both things and make a decision. I bring the pictures into the kitchen and place them on the butcher block.

I get up on the step stool and take the chrysanthemum-patterned tea box down from the top shelf. The greasy, translucent stain on this note card is Ma's. The fingerprint on the hand mirror in the top drawer of the vanity in the back bathroom is Ma's. Knowing she's dead isn't what makes me miss her. It's the little things. They take me by surprise. Then I get stomachaches and I have to distract myself and disappear inside a dark small space or a process so deep it swallows me. I miss her because she's not here. If I invoke her ghost, she'll be here, and I won't have to miss her then. With Dad, I don't have a choice. Ma is different.

If I don't do this, I will always wonder what would have happened if I did.

I shuffle the cards. I take a deep breath. I shuffle them again, and then make myself open my eyes to read what's on top.

Okay. Biscuits and gravy it is.

No shopping to do. I have everything I need for this. Simple enough I could do it without looking at the recipe, if the recipe weren't the whole point.

Will it even work? Only one way to know.

More deep breaths. Lots of deep breaths. Shortening cut into flour, pinching it with dry fingertips into clumps the texture of oatmeal.

Dusting the counter with a thin layer of flour, holding half a cup aside in case the dough needs more. Kneading the dough exactly the right number of times, keeping track, eighteen nineteen twenty. Rolling the dough out exactly an inch thick. Punching through circles with the biscuit cutter. Not twisting the cutter, very important. That can seal the edge and keep the biscuits from rising right. Gathering and re-rolling the scraps, working them as little as possible, also to preserve the rise. Biscuits go in the oven, timer set.

The gravy is even easier. Brown the sausage. Sprinkle on a table-spoon of flour. Stir and cook. Watch the powder absorb the fat from the sausage, blunting the shine. Judge by the smell and color to know the raw taste of the flour is gone. Add milk, stirring as you go, until the milk covers the sausage. White swirled with a sandy tan color, until the barrier between the two breaks down. Low heat and lots of stirring. It all thickens up. A veil of gravy clings to the spoon. Almost done.

The last step on the card. Lots of black pepper, ground directly in.

A little translucent at first, she resolves into a solid-looking body on the stool. Her hair is longer than I remember, but otherwise, she looks about right. White cotton pajamas, a matched set. A navy blue sleep mask, narrow in the middle like a peanut shell, dangles loose from a cord on her neck. Flushed cheeks. There is a coin-sized stain on the right knee of her pajama pants, the color of chocolate or old blood, which I'm sure she's not happy about.

"Hi, Ma," I say.

"Oh . . . oh, Ginny. My God. I can't believe I'm here." She gestures around at the living world.

"You're a ghost, Ma," I say.

She says, "I never believed in ghosts."

This makes me laugh uncontrollably for at least half a minute. Truly uncontrollably, I can't control it, the laughter coughs out of me. As I start to calm down I can kind of hear her laughing too.

I look up and see her make a familiar gesture. Ma pushes the hair out of her eyes. Usually I only catch a glimpse of this but this time I am watching closely as she moves. Her hand, her hair, her face. This hurts my heart more than anything else. I have to hold one hand in the other hand, nails biting the skin, to keep from reaching out to her. I push until it hurts and keep pushing.

"Is Amanda here?" she asks. This hurts most of all.

"No, Ma, she's not here right now."

"Is everything okay?"

"Of course."

"Where is she?"

I say, "At home. She's coming back later. I'm the one who brought you, Ma. You're here because I made one of your recipes."

"Biscuits and gravy," she says. "I smelled it."

This reminds me the biscuits are still in the oven, so I hasten over to remove them.

Ma says, "Those smell a little burnt."

"I'm sure they're okay." They're not. On the bottom they are as brown as the soles of Dad's shoes. I should have taken them out earlier.

"So is it anything you cook? Can you see anyone?" she asks.

"I don't know."

"Have you talked to Julia Child?"

"Why would I bother Julia Child, Ma?"

"That's what I'd do. If I . . ." She pauses a long time. Finally she adds, ". . . could."

"We're different."

"I know."

Seeing her here, I'm overwhelmed. I want to be logical and grown-up and intelligent. I also want to curl up and put my head in her lap and sleep for decades. More than anything I want her to tell me she misses me as much as I miss her.

"We miss you," I say. "Amanda and the girls and me. Gert. Everyone."

"When is she coming back?"

"Gert?"

"Amanda."

"Talk to me," I say, louder. "I'm the one who brought you."

"Here I am. And we're talking."

"Yeah, kind of."

"Don't be difficult."

"You always say that! I'm not being difficult. I'm being me."

Ma says, "Then maybe difficult is what you are."

My fear has become anger now and my control is going fast. More than anything else I want to chuck one of these biscuits right at Ma's head. But that would prove her point. Only difficult people chuck warm biscuits at their dead mothers. I assume.

Breathe in, breathe out. To calm myself I pretend I have a green grape on my tongue and am pressing it gently against the roof of my mouth. I want to spend more time being calm, but I don't know how long Ma will stay. "Difficult," she called me. The imaginary grape drops out of my mouth and rolls away across the floor and I snap, "I can take care of myself."

"Oh, can you?"

"Ma!"

She says, "I'm just asking."

"No, you're not!"

"I just want you to be honest with yourself."

"You didn't care about honest. You cared about easy."

"That isn't true."

"You liked Amanda better because she always did what you said."

"That isn't true," she repeats. Repeating yourself is a sign of lying, and she's the one who taught me that.

"You never liked me."

"Ginny," she says, "please. Do you really think now is the time for all this?"

It's a very reasonable question and it makes me want to chuck a biscuit at her head again. Instead I say, "You're right. Let's focus. Tell me who this is."

I pick one of the pictures and hold it toward her. The black-and-white picture of the woman against the gray sky. Looking up at the camera or the person behind the camera, my father.

Ma looks down. This feels so strange to me because I have never met her eyes and had her be the one to look down. I was always the one. Things are different now.

She says, "I'm not going to talk to you about that."

"Why not?"

"It's for your dad to tell you. Not me."

"But is she— Who is she?"

"She's not anyone, Ginny."

This is infuriating. "Of course she's someone."

"She exists, yes. But—you don't understand, Ginny. She's not important."

"Tell me who she was anyway."

"Okay," Ma says. She sighs. "She was a nurse at the hospital with your dad."

"What was her name?"

"Ginny, how could that possibly matter?"

"I want to know." I shake the picture at her again, so she knows I'm serious.

"Okay, fine, her name was Evangeline."

"That can't be right!" Evangeline, the ghost. Skinny, hairless, terrifying. She cried out against Doc, her love for Doc, her hate for Doc. If she was a nurse at the hospital—if Dad had all these pictures of her—

Ma says, "Why do you look so scared? Sweetheart, what's wrong?" She reaches out a hand toward me, but stops, so it hangs there outstretched in the space between us.

"Was she . . . were they . . ."

"Sweetheart, slow down, be calm. Tell me what you want to say."

"Is she . . . did they . . . is this what you had to forgive Dad for?"

She pushes the hair away from her face again, shaking her head, looking up at me. "Your father never needed my forgiveness for— What are you asking, Ginny?"

"I just said it. Is this what you had to forgive Dad for?" I brandish the picture.

"You don't understand at all, Ginny," she says.

"Then help me understand!" I want to fling the picture down but I don't want to damage it. I want to throw something, hard. I can feel my arms tingling, my throat closing. I slap my free hand down on the butcher block so hard it stings. I focus on that feeling so I don't crumble.

"I can't," she says. "Your dad has to be the one to help you."

"But I can't talk to him! I can only talk to you!"

With her frustratingly cool, gentle spearmint voice, Ma responds, "Ginny, your dad never wanted to talk about this with you and I respected that. I still respect that."

I shout, "But you're both dead! I'm still alive! Don't you think what I want is more important?"

She looks me in the eye and says, "No."

This time I look down. I put the imaginary grape in my mouth again. I set the photo down safely, pick up the spoon, stir the gravy. I can still smell it, and as long as I can, we can keep going. I have to make myself be calm, so I do. I make myself speak slowly. I say, "There was a letter from Dad asking for your forgiveness . . ."

"What letter?"

"Up in the chimney. In the bedroom fireplace."

"I never— Oh." The tension in her shoulders shifts. "I guess I did put a letter up there. And forgot about it. If I'd remembered I would've gotten rid of it. That was . . . that was a long time ago."

"But I found it. I have it. It asks your forgiveness, and all I want to know is, was an affair with Evangeline the thing he wanted your forgiveness for?"

The spearmint voice again. "Sweetheart, that's none of your business."

"Of course it's my business! You're my parents."

"No, that doesn't make it your business, not at all."

I'm confused. "But you said Dad could talk to me about it?"

"That's different. That's totally different."

"You don't make any sense."

Ma says, "Sweetheart, I love you so much, but you just don't understand and there's no way I can explain any of this to you."

"You know I'm not stupid," I say, still clutching the spoon, unable to let go.

"Of course you're not!"

"Why don't you think I'll understand?"

Ma says, "Just trust me."

I say, "No."

The smell is getting faint. Stirring doesn't help.

"Ginny. We don't have time for this. I'm trying to tell you. About Amanda."

"Always Amanda!" I shout.

"No, you don't understand. Listen to me. Are you listening?"

I look straight at her, and listen.

She says, "It's very important that you not let Amanda," and her mouth is moving but I can't hear what she's saying and too late I notice her edges are translucent like an aspic and she's gone.

I sit down hard on the kitchen floor, reeling, exhausted. I spent too much time asking all the wrong things.

When she's gone I want her here. When she's here I want her gone. She's right, I'm difficult, and in many ways. It's all too overwhelming. I lean against the wall next to the shelves of cookbooks and stare at the door of the oven. The light inside is still on. The oven door is so clean I can see the outline of the bulb. I wonder what the oven door at Amanda's looks like. I wonder if Amanda has ever even used her oven. At her wedding shower she opened up a box with a big pot in it and said, *But the only thing I know how to make is reservations!* Everyone laughed, except Ma, and me.

I could have asked Ma anything. She was right here. But I fell into the old habits, the old patterns, right away. To be fair, so did she. I don't want to blame her because there shouldn't be any blame. But it makes me sad, and it makes me resigned. There's not much point in trying to change, it seems. I really thought there might be.

Getting up from the floor, I reach for the stove. I turn up the heat under the gravy, stirring, hoping. The smell is faint but unmistakable, rich and porky and smelling like home. It doesn't bring her back. Nothing brings her back. The gravy cools into a thick sludge. When I was a kid I ate it fast. First I had to be sure there were an equal number of sausage lumps on each piece of biscuit, but then I didn't pause until it was gone. Today I eat three helpings of it over biscuits, sitting on the floor of the kitchen, hoping in vain with each bite.

Midnight comes in to nudge against my bare feet, and I let her lick the last of the gravy from my fingers. Stroking her long, soft fur helps me push away the thoughts that are boiling in my head. I can't be at a boil right now. I just can't. Amanda is coming back in just a few hours and I have no answers, only questions.

Ma was on that step stool, in this kitchen, close enough to touch. As long as I can still bring her here, she isn't gone. I guess this is a good thing and a bad thing. It still feels like they're about to come back. Maybe they will. That's impossible, but ghosts are impossible. Lots of things are impossible. And yet they happen.

Have I succeeded, or failed? I didn't bring Nonna, but I brought Ma, and her message is almost the same. I know a little more than I did before. Another piece of the puzzle.

Amanda. Stop Amanda. I don't know what I'm supposed to stop her from doing, but I know where to start.

The house. Right now, Angelica doesn't scare me. Right now nothing does. Right now nothing could hurt more than having my mother's ghost appear in our kitchen, immediately size up the situation, and ask how my sister is doing. So now is the time for me to do things that would normally make me run, desperate for the solace of the closet floor.

Angelica's number is still on the refrigerator, right where Amanda stuck it with a magnet a week ago. I dial it. She doesn't pick up. I don't leave a message. I decide this isn't a problem. She'll probably come by with more unwelcome visitors soon, and I can tell her then.

In the meantime, I perform a thorough search of the kitchen cabinets. Physically crawling inside a cabinet at twenty-six is not like crawling inside a cabinet when you're five. For one thing, when you're five, it's awesome. For another, when you're five, you actually fit.

But Dad tucked his scotch bottle back here to hide it. It's not out of the question that other things might be hiding. So I kneel down and empty the cabinets of their All-Clad and their Le Creuset and of Grandma Damson's long-neglected, well-seasoned cast-iron pan. And I thrust my head in, working my shoulders through the narrow gap, to see for myself what's all the way in the back. I reach an arm and trail my fingers along the seam where the back wall and bottom shelf of the cabinet meet.

The most interesting thing I find is the crank for the pasta press.

Which is good, because now I can make pasta. The happy thought distracts me. I love to make pasta, and it's been ages. I think there's some semolina from Talluto's in the back of the cupboard. I picture the soft, stretchy dough becoming relaxed and slick. Absorbing flour. Long, translucent sheets become piled-up ribbons of tagliatelle. My stomach gurgles. In the tight space the sound is magnified.

Even from deep inside the wooden box, I can hear the front door open. There are voices, besides. At first I think about staying down. Hiding. But this is unreasonable. I may feel invisible sometimes, but with half of me sticking out in plain sight, I'm not.

I inch out of the cabinet, back pockets first, careful not to hit my head. By the time I get up and smooth my hair down, they're in the living room already. Angelica and two women. I watch them from the doorway to the kitchen. They haven't seen me yet. The taller woman wears a gray suit like Angelica's navy one, and shoes so tight I can see her flesh swelling along every seam. The other woman wears all black and waves her hands around. Her fingernails are red and gleaming, perfect long ovals, like Hot Tamales. Amanda's look like that sometimes. It's a manicure. I've never had one. I wouldn't want someone's hands on my hands like that. Picking and scratching and rubbing while I squirm. It couldn't end well.

Angelica says, "You can see how high the ceilings are in here, aren't they great? It just lights up on sunny days."

"Lovely," says the one in tight shoes.

Angelica points up and shows them the scrollwork along the ceiling, which makes them ooh and aah. It's enough. More than enough.

"Excuse me," I say to the three women.

"Hi, Ginny," says Angelica. "Sorry, I thought you were out. We'll be here just a few minutes."

"No," I say.

The woman in the suit says, "No?"

"No?" asks the woman with the red fingernails.

"No," I say again.

No one responds.

After a moment Angelica says, "This is one of the current owners, ladies." She sounds so completely like Amanda, down to the way she takes a breath.

I say, "I'm sorry, this house is not for sale."

The one in the suit says, "Did someone beat us to it? Let us make a counteroffer, at least."

"It's not for sale."

She says, "Then why did we trek all the way over here?"

"I'm sorry," I say again.

Angelica says, "No, no, don't worry, Jen. It's just a small misunderstanding."

"I'm sorry you came all this way for nothing," I say.

"Ginny!" says Angelica, her orange juice voice pitching higher, into the grapefruit range. "We can have this conversation later. Just let me finish showing Jennifer and Holly around."

"No. Please leave now."

The one in the suit says, "Okay, this is too weird. Hol, let's go."

"You have a beautiful home," says the other one, waving her hand over everything as she follows her friend toward the door.

Angelica says, "I'll call you later! So sorry! We'll clear this up!"

The door closes and I hear heels clicking against the sidewalk.

I know I've been rude. Knowing it doesn't change anything. I can't take this anymore, and some things are more important than being polite. There used to be a rule, but now it doesn't apply.

Angelica says, "Ginny, that wasn't very nice."

I mumble all my words out in a rush. "I know. I just want you to stop, okay? No more people. We're not going to sell. I'm staying."

Angelica says, "That's not what I discussed with Amanda. I was given to understand the two of you wanted to sell, and you'd be moving in with her."

"No."

She says, "That was the plan."

Trying not to sound agitated, I tell her, "The plan has changed."

"I'm not sure you can do that," she says. She is taking care to pause before and after everything. So am I.

"It's half my house too," I say. From the legal perspective, ignoring all others, that's true.

Angelica says, "I'm going to have to speak with your sister about this."

"I understand."

"Why don't we call her right now?"

"She's busy at home. Brennan has to go back to L.A. Tonight."

"I could still—"

"Don't bother her," I say, and with some effort, I raise my eyes to Angelica's face and stare directly at her eyes. They are brown, and narrow, and not like Amanda's at all. One one thousand. Two one thousand.

She looks down.

"Well. Okay. Anyway. I'll talk to Amanda."

"Okay."

I close the door behind her.

Was I successful? I don't know. My hands are tingling a little. My stomach feels empty and hollow. At least I'm not in a panic. I can walk from room to room without diving into the closet or losing myself in new iterations of the Continental Cuisine dinner party menu. (If the dessert were ANZAC biscuits or a pavlova, the meat course could be a beef daube, or a carbonnade flamande . . . there are so many possibilities.)

Shouldn't use the word *normal*. There's no such thing, I remind myself. A line from the Normal Book: *Normal is a setting on the dishwasher.* But still, for once, I wonder if that's how I'm feeling, right now. Not happy, not sad. Just . . . normal?

I put the black-and-white pictures of Evangeline under the carpet in my closet again. I can't think about her right now. I can't make sense of what Ma told me. The only thing I can do is look for a recipe Dad wrote so that I can see him and ask him these questions. I pull book after book from the shelves of the library, leafing through them, sliding them back in place. Nothing else turns up. Not a single thing.

I go back to the kitchen, but I think I've finally looked everywhere. Nothing else behind the glass doors of the cookbook cabinets. Nothing among the pots and pans. Nothing in the junk drawer. An unbent wire hanger swept from side to side reveals nothing lodged under the fridge. My father has never written anything resembling a recipe on anything resembling a piece of paper. It's torture to know that whatever this is, a gift or a curse or both, his is the ghost I will never be able to see.

Dinner is a bowl of cereal, under milk just beginning to go sour. It's the last of a carton and I don't feel like opening a new one.

I'm not surprised when my phone rings. I'm only surprised it took so long.

"Ginny," says Amanda. "Come on."

"I tried to tell you," I say, bracing myself against the back of the chair, setting my spoon down in what's left of the milk.

"Regardless, that was really mean of you. Angelica was all worked up."

"I wasn't trying to be mean."

"Well, being mean is something that we sometimes do without trying. That's what I tell the girls."

"Did Brennan make his plane?"

"Yes, we got him out of here on time, barely. He's still in the air, he'll call when he lands. Don't try to change the subject. I'm angry with you."

"Be angry, that's fine," I say. "As long as you're listening to me."

She's silent for a minute, then she says, "Okay, Ginny, I'm listening."

"I don't want to sell the house. I told you that."

"And you don't see why we need to?"

"We don't need to."

"Okay, I need to. And maybe you think that's selfish. But I can't take care of two houses. And you don't know the first thing about it."

"I can learn."

"We don't know for sure. It would be so much easier—" She breaks off. There's a howl in the background. Her voice shouting "Is everything all right?" is so loud I take the phone away from my ear.

She says, "This is actually the worst possible time to talk about this. I have to go."

"Okay. Let's not talk about it. But while we're not talking about it, don't let Angelica show the house."

She says sharply, "Look, I don't have time to fight with you right now."

"I'm not fighting. I'm just saying." I feel strong. I make my points clearly. "Let's just simplify. You're right. There's too much going on. Let's just let that one thing go, for now. Okay?"

She says, "Well."

"Just for a week," I say. "You can just put it on pause for a week."

She says, "Okay."

I say, "I'll see the three of you in the morning then, right?"

"Right."

"Good night, Amanda," I say, and that's that.

That night, on my way to bed, I stop and look out my parents' window. While my attention was elsewhere, it snowed. The world stands blanketed outside, so thoroughly snowed over that the streetlight's glare bounces off the snow and back up through the window. I sit on the window seat, lean back against the yellow cushions, and look out at the world.

Even with the shades the light is unusual. Not as bright as full day. Like it's perpetually the undisturbed half hour before sunrise. Only because the light is never-changing, it's hard to tell if the sun will ever come up.

CHAPTER EIGHT

Butternut Squash Soup

I wake up on the window seat, sunrise shining right into my eyes. I haven't fallen asleep here before. For a moment I worry Ma will yell at me but then it all comes back into my head. All the truth. So I reposition my sore neck on a better pillow, and I try to make sense of everything.

What happened in the past. Dad wanted Ma to forgive him. Dad took twenty-nine pictures of Evangeline. Evangeline loved and lost someone named Doc. But Ma thinks none of this is important, or if it is important, only Dad can talk to me about it. But I can't get him, because he didn't leave me any recipes. Dead end.

Then, what's happening now. I'm not supposed to let Amanda do something. Both Ma and Nonna say so. Is it the house, or something else? I've stalled her on the house at least. That's something. Maybe during the week's reprieve I will figure something else out. I don't know how, but it's possible.

I HAVE TIME to shower and put different clothes on before the doorbell rings. I go down to answer it, thinking Amanda probably has her hands full. But then I see the grocery bags, and I realize it wasn't Amanda who rang the doorbell, it was David.

I open the door, and he is unhooking his bike from the No Parking sign. Last night's snow is beginning to melt, so there is slush on the ground and his shoes look wet and muddy. He already has his helmet on his head. It is white and webbed and reminds me of tripe.

I come out onto the marble stairs under the portico and call down, "Thank you."

"Oh, sure, you're welcome!" he calls back. Then he turns his attention back to his bike again, turns the key in the lock.

He is rushing to get away. I think about why that might be. "She's not here," I say.

He turns the key back the other way, leans the bike against the signpost again, and takes the steps in three long strides. "So what is the deal with your sister?" he says, his muddy voice stretching out all the low vowels. "When she came into the kitchen and saw me there? I thought she was going to punch me in the throat."

"She's protective."

"I'll say."

"My mother was too."

"But . . . you're a full-grown adult. Aren't you?"

"Yeah. But—" I try to find the right way to express it. I settle on, "I've never been out on my own."

"It's overrated," says David, waving his hand as if a fly were bothering him. "I live on my own now. In a basement. It sucks."

"But you lived with your wife first."

"Yes, I did."

"That didn't suck."

He says, "Well, some days it did, but most of that was just surface stuff. You know, fights about who left dishes in the sink, or arguing over money. Stupid things. Somebody came home later than they should have and didn't call. Misunderstandings, suspicions, things we argued about that we didn't need to, if we'd tried to stop ourselves. Nothing that seems important now. Nothing that mattered."

He thrusts a wallet at me, open to a picture of a woman who's beautiful in a way I've never seen. Her face isn't a feminine face. It's all strength and angles, no give, no curves.

"We met in Peru," he says. "Mountain biking. Traversing the Cordillera Blanca. It was like we'd known each other forever, from the day we met. Something about her."

"Love at first sight?" I've always wondered about that.

"Something like that, I guess," he says, his voice all black coffee and baking chocolate now, dark but pleasing. "We just fell so hard so fast, and I stayed there longer than I was supposed to, and I spent all my days and nights convincing her that when I came back to the States, she had to come with me."

The end of the story is obvious. I know how it turned out. It still sounds romantic. "And she did."

"And she did. And it was wonderful, it was everything I wanted. Even on the days when I was furious with her, or she was furious with me. I couldn't imagine living without her. Then one day I had to."

I close his wallet and hold it out for him to take. His hand brushes mine and I flinch away, hard.

"About that," he says.

"About what?"

"You," says David. "I told you something very personal about me. Now I think it's only fair you tell me something about you. What's with that? Not wanting to be touched? Or is it just me, you're scared of me?"

"No," I say. "It's not just you. I . . . I don't like to be touched."

"At all?"

"Well, no, I guess. Some touch is okay."

"Like what?"

"Like my parents hugging me, or Amanda, if it's family, people I trust, it's different. And your mom does this thing." I demonstrate, reaching out, pressing my palm against his forehead. "That's okay."

"So just strangers? Touching you?"

"Well, that, and some other things." I count them off on my fingers for him. "I don't like loud noises, like sirens, they make me jump. Textures can bug me too. I've cut the tags out of all my clothes since I was a kid, because I could always feel them and I couldn't think about anything else if I was always thinking about how my tags itched." Even thinking about it makes me twitch a little, feeling an unpleasant itch on my neck, even though I know there's no tag there.

I go on, "And I say what I think, and people don't like that either."

"No, they usually don't."

"So Ma always gave me rules, that's how she dealt with it, and when I follow those rules I'm fine."

"Which is why your sister freaks out about a stranger in the kitchen. Because there isn't a rule for that. And you don't get out much."

"I get out fine," I say. "I mean, when Ma was alive, I didn't go out much for things like groceries, because she could always do that. If I did go out, it was almost always uneventful."

"Almost always?"

"One time out of ten, maybe, there was a problem. Like if I went down to the Korean deli. Someone at a parking meter would touch my arm to ask if I had change. Inside the store someone would squeeze past me to get to the ice chest in back. Things like that. Something would set me off. So most times it was nothing, but when it was something, it was awful. So she would go out instead, because it was easier, for both of us."

"That sounds tough."

"It wasn't, really. I worked around it. We worked around it. I went to school and everything. Elementary, high school, college."

"You graduated?"

"Almost. One more class. Oral comm. I could get through everything else. I'm very smart. I write very good papers."

"I believe it."

"But giving speeches is not my strength."

"I believe that too. You don't even look at me."

"It's not you," I say.

"I know," David says. "So what do you have?"

"Have?"

"Like a complex? A phobia? A disorder?"

"A personality," I say.

He laughs at that, a soft laugh, a sound that ripples.

David says, "A personality. I like that. Listen, I gotta go, I'm start-ing a new job and I don't want to make a bad impression." He hooks his thumb toward the street, indicating his waiting bike.

"What job?"

"Bike messenger," he says. "I used to do it before the accident, and Mom's been hinting strongly that I should get back into it. And then after what your sister said yesterday, I realized, I really can't just be between things for the rest of my life. I like biking, so, why not? And I'll like the paycheck. Which reminds me, you forgot to pay me last week."

"I did."

He says, "And from the look on your face, you were about to forget to pay me this week too."

"I did forget."

"Well, if you don't have it, you don't have it," he says, strapping his helmet back on. "No big."

"No big?"

"No big deal. I mean, don't make a habit of it or anything."

"Okay."

"Let's do this," he says. "With the new job I'm not sure I'll be back next week, so I can't just say I'll get it then. Can you write me a check?"

"No, I don't have a checkbook." I realize I could go upstairs and get the cash and pay him with that, but he's already asked the question and I've already answered it, so it seems wrong to change the terms now.

"Can your sister write me a check?"

"Yes."

"Okay. Then why don't you send it to me? Here's my address."

He bends down and tears the corner off one of the paper grocery bags, then scribbles a few words on it with a pen from his pants pocket. He sets it on the railing for me to take, and I tuck it into my jeans.

"Thank you," I say.

David says, "Wish me luck."

"Luck."

Because I stand on the porch and watch his bike disappear in the distance, headed toward Broad, I am still standing there when Amanda's car pulls up, with Amanda and the girls inside. She parks, and I beckon them up the stairs. I'm about to offer to carry their things in when I realize I need to carry the groceries in first. So I do that, and take a moment to put David's address in a kitchen drawer so I don't accidentally wash it.

By the time I get back to the front door Shannon is quietly hauling two little pink suitcases up the steps. One is covered with rainbows, the other with cartoon cats. They thump in near-unison each time she climbs a step. Amanda has hoisted Parker up on one hip and says, "Good morning, Aunt Ginny."

Both girls echo, "Good morning, Aunt Ginny!"

"Good morning," I say. "Shannon, let me take one of those suitcases, okay?"

She shakes her head, the dark hair whipping back and forth across her little face. "No, I'm balanced," she says. "It's not so hard."

"I'll hold the door open for you then, okay?"

"Okay."

Once we're all inside the house, Amanda sets Parker down, and the little blonde dashes to the back of the house, then back up to the front.

"Yes, please, do that, wear yourself out," says Amanda, not too loudly.

Shannon sets the suitcases down at the foot of the stairs and says, "Is this okay?"

"Yes, sweetheart," says Amanda.

Parker barrels at me and flings her arms around my legs and I realize, belatedly, I'm being hugged.

"Hi, Aunt Ginny!" she says.

"Hi, Parker."

Then she runs off again.

Shannon says, "Parker loves you, Aunt Ginny. I love you too." Then, like her sister, she hugs my legs. This time I'm prepared and can analyze it. The leg hug doesn't bother me. It's firm and decisive. And they're so much smaller than me, they're no kind of threat.

Amanda says, "Aunt Ginny loves you too, Shan. Why don't you take your jacket off and put it with your suitcase, please?" Shannon nods and unzips her pink coat.

Amanda whispers to me, "It confuses them if you don't say it back."

Before I can answer, tiny running footsteps approach. Parker stops in front of us and says, "It's Grandma's house! Where's Grandpa? Where's Grandma?"

In the act of hanging her jacket on the coatrack next to the door, Amanda freezes. I see her go from a normal woman in motion to a block of ice in less than a second.

Shannon is the one who answers. "Remember they told us that Grandma and Grandpa went away. They're not here anymore. There was an accident and they died."

Parker says, "But I wanted to tell Grandma and Grandpa what I want for Christmas!"

"You can tell me," I say.

"I want a puppy!" says Parker.

"No puppies," says Amanda, coming to life again. "Not until you're older. You girls are too young to take care of a dog."

Shannon says, "I don't like dogs. I like cats. I have them on my suitcase. Aunt Ginny, you have a very pretty cat. Where is your cat?"

"She's probably upstairs," I tell her. "Midnight is very shy."

"So is Shannon," says Amanda. "They should get along fine."

"Shannon, are you shy?" I ask her.

She shrugs and says, "Long-haired cats are the prettiest. There are also short-haired cats and they sometimes call them domestic short-hairs. There are also cats without any hair at all."

"They're called Sphynx, right?"

"Sphynx, yes, that's right. But most cats have soft fur and that's why I like them. Hairless cats aren't pretty."

Amanda says, "She has very strong opinions about cats. And not just the domestic kind. You should hear her talk about the fishing cat we saw at the zoo."

"It comes from Asia. It's not white like your cat, Aunt Ginny. It's gray with black stripes. And bigger."

Amanda suggests, "Maybe you should draw Aunt Ginny a picture of a fishing cat later. Then she could see what it looks like. Maybe you girls could both sit in the dining room and color with crayons, how does that sound?"

The girls agree it sounds fun. The dining room table is broad and solid, and we need to place books on the chairs so the girls aren't sitting with their chins at table level. Amanda sets out a coloring book for Parker and a few sheets of blank paper for Shannon.

"You girls stay put, and if you need anything, you just shout for me, okay?"

"Okay," they say in chorus.

To me, Amanda says, "I'm going to get started on the library."

"Okay." I join her. When she reaches for the boxes of photographs, I have a moment of panic, but then remember I've hidden away the pictures of Evangeline. No, they're not here. They're safely under the carpet in my closet.

She sets a box up on Dad's desk and starts going through the photographs. "Why aren't these in albums? They're gorgeous."

"I know."

She turns a photo over, holds it up in my direction. "Is this one Nonna?"

"Yes."

"Gorgeous, gorgeous," she says, shaking her head. "We're lucky they're not damaged, just all tossed around like this. You think they're all Dad's?"

"I think so."

"He was . . . amazing. We can just put these in their own box for now, but I'm probably going to want these. I can scan you copies."

I'm only half listening, because I notice the picture in her hand is different from the others. It's black-and-white. The wall, the collar, the face. Evangeline.

In this one she is looking straight at the camera, and it feels like her eyes are boring into mine, which I don't like. I have to look away, even though she isn't real. As if I didn't want to look away, thinking of her ghost in my kitchen, howling in a ruined voice, crying out to understand something I couldn't explain to her: why people can be cruel.

I hid them, but I missed one.

Amanda looks at it and says, "Who's this?"

I realize it doesn't mean to her what it means to me. Of course it doesn't. So maybe this is a good thing. Her memory isn't as good as mine in general, but she's better at faces.

"I don't know. She doesn't look familiar to you?"

"Not at all. Was it just this one? She's not in any others?" Amanda begins pawing through the box.

"No," I say, which is technically the truth. None of the other photos in the box is of Evangeline. The other twenty-eight upstairs are her, but down here, it's just the one.

"Well, I don't recognize her. There's not a lot to go on. They're a little grainy, so maybe ten years old? Fifteen? Dad always had a great camera, so they could be older. Definitely not digital. Definitely film. It's so hard to tell with black-and-white. She doesn't look familiar to you either?"

"No, not at all. I mean, maybe. I thought maybe she could have been a nurse at the hospital?" The lie comes easily. I have information I shouldn't have, so I find a way to pretend I came by it honestly.

"Yeah, I don't know," she says, handing it back to me. "Dad never took me to the hospital, so I didn't get to know anyone there."

She pulls a picture of the four of us out of the box. Ma then her then me then Dad. The whole family, together.

In a soft voice, Amanda says, "I don't think he liked me very much."

I say firmly, "That's ridiculous."

"Is it? I always felt like I came in second." She covers up the half of the photo with her and Ma in it, leaving just Dad and his other daughter, me.

I've never heard her say this before. I tell her, "Don't feel like that."

"You should know as well as anyone, you can tell someone how to feel, but it doesn't make them feel that way." She drops both photos back in the box, puts the lid on, and pushes down gently on each corner in turn.

"You're right."

"Anyway. No, I don't know who that woman is, or why we have a picture of her. Dad probably didn't even take it. It was probably just mixed in with our stuff, like the developer was doing ours and someone else's and put this one in the wrong pile."

It amazes me how logical she sounds. I know what she says isn't right, but it sounds so much like it could be. Maybe Ma was right, at least about one thing. Maybe my cross is that I'm gullible. *Gullible* is on a page with *gull,* of course, and *guidance,* and *gyre.*

"Anything else?" asks Amanda, setting the black box of photographs on Dad's desk, not back where it belongs, but not in the pile of things taken care of. "We should get back to work."

"Oh. Yes. Can you write a check for groceries?"

"For next week?"

"No, this is for the ones that already came."

"What would you do without me?" She sees my mouth opening and hastens to add, "Don't answer that. Just write it yourself and bring it to me to sign. My checkbook's in my purse, in the kitchen. See how the girls are doing while you're down there."

Shannon and Parker are coloring quietly, and don't even look up as I go by. When I bring Amanda the checkbook I tell her so.

"Thank heaven for little girls," she says. "If they were boys I'd be a basket case. My friend Lily has two boys. They're always falling off things or spitting in her hair or peeing out windows. It's crazy."

"That does sound crazy!"

"But what can you do," she says, leaning over Dad's desk to sign the check. "Kids are kids. They have their own personalities. Like Shannon and Parker. They're so different. They have the same genes, but they're night and day. Shannon's so quiet, and Parker's just so outgoing. Thank goodness I don't have two like Parker, I guess. Two Shannons, okay, but two Parkers, no thanks. But I'm happiest with exactly what I've got, of course. Listen to me babble, I'm sorry. Believe me, you wouldn't want kids. They make you a fool."

"I want kids," I say.

"Don't go getting any ideas," she says. "That's the last thing I need right now, you getting yourself pregnant."

"That's not what I meant," I tell my sister. "I'd get married first."

"You're not seeing anyone, are you?"

"No." I don't remind her it's a stupid expression. Who don't we see?

"Have anyone in mind?"

"No." I've always wanted a husband and kids, but haven't really visualized the steps between here and there. It always seemed like there was plenty of time.

"Well, you know, I shouldn't laugh. My friend Lorna, she came to my wedding with one guy, and she asked me to be in her wedding six months later, and it was a totally different guy she was marrying. And Angelica, she got proposed to by a guy while they were both jumping out of a plane, you know, skydiving? On their second date! People do weird stuff. Not that I think you should do that."

"I'm not going to."

"Marriage isn't a cakewalk. And kids are no picnic," she says, tearing the check off and setting it on the corner of the desk for me to take. "Don't fool yourself."

I slip it into my pocket. "I don't fool myself."

"No, I guess you don't. I'm sorry I get freaked out. I just don't want anything to happen to you. Mom was so worried that something would."

"And nothing has," I say.

"Not yet," she says. "But how will we make sure that nothing does?"

I ask her, "Has anything bad ever happened to you?"

"Lots of times."

"Then how can you expect to keep me safe? Bad things happen to everybody."

Amanda says, "That doesn't help me feel better, you know."

I'm at a loss.

She says, "Listen, before the girls get sick of coloring I want to get this whole shelf packed up." Her gesture covers the entire west wall, rows of textbooks and reference books and histories stretching up toward the ceiling. "You can help me, or you can go through the stuff in your room instead."

"My room?"

"Your old room," she says. "I went through a bunch of stuff in my old room, and there was plenty of it, so maybe you should go through yours too."

If I go through my room, she won't, so I'm happy to go along with her suggestion.

Before I go upstairs I take a look in my parents' room, to make sure Amanda hasn't been poking around the fireplace. The red geraniums in the rectangular pot are exactly where I left them, undisturbed. When I look in the closet, I notice the shoes are gone, so I find the box labeled *SHOES* in the stack against the wall. The two pairs of shoes I care about are on top. I put them back in their places again. Maybe this time she won't notice. If I need to crawl into this closet, which I hope I don't, but if I really need to, I want the shoes to be there.

Down the hall, staring into a different closet, I pull out an unlabeled, plain brown cardboard box. Old dried tape fails to stick it together at the edges. It reminds me of the one I found in Amanda's room and labeled *AMANDA KIDHOOD*. And when I open it, it's my own childhood that's inside.

I sit down, leaning against a wall painted Chardonnay, and start pulling things out, putting them in piles. Pictures and notebooks, report cards and folders. Years and years of school. Years and years of Ginny.

I work down through the successive layers: second grade, third grade, fourth. Pictures of my tiny self, years ago, mixed in with my creations. Second grade, heavy bangs and a round face, an unreasonable shirt of red and white and navy stripes. Third grade, the year I wore nothing but black and white and gray, in various combinations.

I brace myself and reach for one of the notebooks. It's just like I remember.

I sketched in the margins, but nothing like what Amanda had in her notebooks. No cartoons of the teacher, no hearts or last names. Even if I didn't know from the squared-off Magic Markered number 2 on the cover that this is my second-grade notebook, the doodles clearly tell me exactly where I was.

"Aunt Ginny," says a small voice, "is your cat up here with you?"

I look up. Shannon.

"I'm not sure exactly where she is," I tell her.

"Is she okay, though?"

"I'm sure she's okay."

"What's that?" She points at the notebook, which I've opened. The pages are covered with patterns. Clear evidence I was in my Turkish rug phase.

"Just some drawings I did, a long time ago."

"Shannon!" calls Amanda's voice. "Where are you?"

"I'm here with Aunt Ginny!"

"Come down!"

"I'll watch her," I shout back, and gesture to Shannon to come over and sit next to me. Maybe because she's so small, I don't mind having her in my personal space. She wiggles in next to me and lifts her tiny chin up to see over the page.

"What's that one?" asks Shannon, and points.

The patterns don't pull me in the way they once did. But the knowledge is still there. Deep down. "These are motifs that Turkish weavers use in their rugs. They each have a meaning."

"Like a code?"

"Exactly."

"I like codes. I learned the whole hobo code from a book, like where a cat means the lady of the house is friendly and the curve shape means it's the house of a bad man."

"Same thing," I say. "This one that looks like an hourglass? It's called the hair-band."

"My hair-bands don't look like that."

"Well, Turkish hair-bands were different, I guess. Anyway, the hair-band meant that the woman who wove the rug was unmarried."

"Like you."

"Like me, but Turkish, and I don't know how to weave. But yes. Unmarried."

She points again. "This one?"

"The phoenix. They were wishing for rain."

"I don't like rain."

"I don't either, but the farmers need it."

"That's what Mom says when it rains."

"Your mom and I both learned it from the same person."

"From Grandma Selvaggio."

"Yes." I get ready in case she wants to talk about death again, but instead she points to the evil eye and says, "What's that?"

"The evil eye."

"Why does someone want evil in their rug?"

"It's not really evil. The symbol means they're glad that God is watching over them. They're thanking God for keeping an eye on them."

"But if it's God who's watching them, why is the eye evil?"

"You know, that's a good question. I don't know the answer to that."

Shannon starts turning the pages herself, looking over the symbols. I look down at them too. If I close my eyes I can still see an entire rug, the color and pattern and size, as if it's in the room with me. But it's a dead thing. Like the idea of ESP, and the letters written by nuns, the rug patterns are only artifacts. They're nothing special. Anymore.

Midnight comes in and leaps up on the bed, and with a happy cry Shannon leaps up after her. While the five-year-old strokes the cat's fur and sings her an endless, tuneless song, I empty the rest of the box. Once I've set everything in piles by what year it's from, I pull the piles apart and change them. This time I reorder everything by type. The pictures with the pictures, the notebooks with the notebooks. The story is still clear. The early report cards say things like *Let's get Ginny to come out of her shell!* and *Quite the little reader!* The later ones say things like *Unusually quiet in class* and *Fails to participate.* However you read it, they say I'm not quite right.

I take the piles upstairs to my own room and set them out neatly on the floor. Midnight probably won't mess with them, and if she does, I don't know what they're good for anyway. Just for reminding me how screwed up I am.

I need reassurance, but I make myself wait until Amanda and the girls go to sleep. We have peanut-butter-and-jelly sandwiches for dinner, and Shannon draws me a picture of a fishing cat, and the day passes into night.

While I'm waiting, I reach into the cupboard for dried pineapple. I added them to the grocery order because I find them reassuring, but they have to be the right kind. Ma started buying the fancy natural low-sulfur version from Trader Joe's in the past few years. Those are fibrous and taste good for you. These are the ones from my childhood, which just taste good. They are as yellow as lemons, crusted all around with sugar. The inside is as thick and wet as a gumdrop. When I was six I lived on these for weeks. That was during the obsession with round things.

Once it is fully dark and everyone is fully asleep, I go into my parents' room. I almost convince myself I don't need it, but I do. I go to the Normal Book one more time. Everything in the box tells me I'm not normal. Everything in the Normal Book tells me I am. Evidence on one side, evidence on the other.

can tell you your situation is unusual, but can't say it's not normal to wonder

normally I wouldn't even care what she does, but as a bridesmaid I'm finding

father alleycatting around his nursing home? Is that *normal*? And what should

thinks it's normal to be friends with his ex-girlfriends and I just can't help

tells me monogamy isn't normal for men and so I owe it to him to make

my normal weight is down around 130 but my wife thinks that's too thin, so I

not normal to go thousands of dollars into debt for clothes that don't even fit

to settle down like a normal guy but what they don't know is my roommate

Amanda's voice whispers, "What are you doing up?"

She's standing in the middle of the room, maybe five feet away. Startled, I echo, "What are you doing up?"

I'm sitting on the window seat to catch the light from the lamp-post outside. From my perch I can see clearly the fireplace, with the geraniums out of their usual spot, and I hope Amanda won't notice.

She says, "I thought I heard a noise."

"Just me."

"This house is a noisy house," she says. "That's how I thought all houses were until I moved in with Brennan. Our place in L.A. was new construction and all you ever heard was the highway."

"It's not how all houses are?"

"You'll love our place," she says. "Silent at night like you're in deep space or something."

"I don't think I'd love that."

"You'll get used to it."

"But I don't want to get used to it," I say. "Are you sure you want me to move in with you?"

"Well, I don't really see a better option," she says, walking over to me. I fold the book closed and place it on my lap, hoping the black of the book will blend in with the black of my pajamas, and go unnoticed in the dim light.

"But I want to stay here."

"I don't see how that could work." When she whispers, her voice reminds me even more of orange juice. "You're alone here. You shouldn't be alone."

"I'm fine alone."

"We've talked about this. I don't think it's safe."

"And I think you're wrong."

"Oh, Ginny. We're all the family you have left, you know."

"I want my own family," I say. "Not yours."

"My family is your family," she says. "Mom and Dad. That family. And we should be sticking together. Don't you think that's what they'd want?"

"What about what I want?"

"I don't think you've thought it through. This is what I meant before. There's more to it than you think. Do you want to pay the utilities? Shovel the snow? Change the lightbulbs? What if the hot water heater broke? You wouldn't even know what to do. Forget the everyday stuff, even. What if someone broke in and you were by yourself?"

I must have some kind of stricken look on my face because she says, "Okay, okay. Listen. The middle of the night is a lousy time to make a decision about anything major. Just think about it. Okay?"

"But . . ." I begin. I don't want to go. I don't want to live in her house with her family. If I had my own house and my own family I'd prefer that, but lacking my own life, I'd at least like to not intrude on hers. She says she wants me there, but I can't quite believe that. If I were her, I wouldn't.

"But what?"

And it comes to me. But . . . nothing.

There's no real reason to stay here, is there? The house is just a house. The people who matter most aren't in it. I can't keep the house anyway if Amanda won't cooperate. I tell myself I'm fine on my own, but am I? No friends to fall back on, no relationships, no support. Left to my own devices, I have no devices.

"Good night, Amanda," is all I can say, and she wishes me good night and leaves, and I'm hit so hard by the knowledge that I could be wrong, I almost forget to be relieved that she didn't ask me about the book.

I put the Normal Book, with the letter still inside its cover, back up inside the chimney, and slide the red geraniums back into place. I have enough presence of mind to do that. But as soon as it's done I let the strain hit me, and then I crawl into the closet and tuck my hands into Ma's bedroom slippers, gently stroking my cheeks with the marabou tops, letting the world recede away and feeling nothing but the soft feathers against my cheeks and the walls of the closet supporting my back. Dark. Support. Feathers. My world gets very small and comfortable, and I savor it, knowing it will have to open up tomorrow to be large and bright and uncomfortable again.

IN THE MORNING we pack and sort, sort and pack, with me dragging my metaphorical feet every step of the way. We work on the books in the library, and it goes very slowly, because the girls help. They pull books out from the lowest shelves and try to read the titles to us, which is a comedy. Shannon can get most of them right. Parker's about fifty-fifty. On the medical textbooks even Amanda is lost, with words in their titles like *hematoma* and *esophageal,* and I'm the one with a slight edge from listening to Dad's bedtime stories over the years. Dad's bedtime stories included words like *phalange. Phalange* was on a page with *pharmaceutical* and *pharmacology*, but the page was in one of these medical dictionaries, not the regular one. I spot

Parker tugging on a wide, heavy book that may actually be the same book I learned it from. She tugs and tugs, and when it comes free from the shelf, she tips right over. Luckily her sister breaks her fall, and everything is laughter instead of tears. I'm starting to think life at Amanda's might not be so bad after all. I'm not fully convinced, but I'm thinking.

Late in the morning, Amanda says to me, "We need to think about L-U-N-C-H. In a little bit, maybe thirty minutes down the road."

"Okay."

"Hey, I wrote you that check for groceries, didn't I? We've got plenty of things that aren't peanut butter and jelly in the house."

"I like peanut butter and jelly!" says Parker. "I like raspberry! I like grape!"

Amanda says to her, in the bubblier, softer version of her usual voice, "Yes, we all do, honey, but sometimes it's nice to have a change. Don't you think it would be nice if your aunt Ginny would cook us a lunch?"

"Yeah!" says Parker. I am starting to learn that she sounds enthusiastic about nearly everything.

"Sure, I could come up with something," I say. "I'll see what there is."

In the kitchen I start to work, setting out a pot, gathering ingredients. I poke around in the refrigerator and the cabinets. A small pile of things grows on the counter. Onion, spices, butternut squash.

"How about soup?" I call out to Amanda.

"Soup? Sure."

I have a recipe marked in one of my cookbooks for butternut squash soup. Since the recipe is in a book, I think it's safe for not calling ghosts, but just in case, I'll change a few things as I go. The flavors aren't what intrigue me anyway. It's the technique. Usually for steaming squash you peel it first. The peel can be tough, so you leave it on if you're roasting the squash whole or in halves, and then you scoop the soft flesh out, but when the squash is cut into chunks for steaming, usually the peel is removed. This recipe is different, which is why I want to try it. I want to know if it makes a difference, or if this person just wrote this recipe this way because that's the way he or she had always seen it done.

I set to the task. I trim the squash and separate the slender part from the fat bulb.

"Hey, do you need any help?" says Amanda. "Parker's so tired she fell asleep on the floor, and Shannon found your cat again, so they're good for a half hour."

I usually don't cook with help. Either Ma cooked or I did. We didn't mix much.

Amanda says, "If you don't, that's okay, but it'd be great if you'd teach me something. I know how to make about six different things, and one of them is blue-box mac and cheese, so you could help me expand my horizons."

"Sure," I say. "Take that pot to the sink and put in maybe an inch of water?"

"Done and done," she says. She also follows my directions to put in the steamer basket, turn up the burner, and put the lid on.

For the squash, I've already done the hard part, so I tell Amanda about it in gestures instead of demonstration, and then guide her through the process of cutting the whole squash into planks, then cubes. Her knife technique is clumsy, but effective. She could be more precise if she didn't move so fast. I know it's not polite to tell her so. Midnight wanders in to find out what we're doing, but when I drop a tidbit of squash on the floor for her to taste, she is unimpressed.

Once the squash has steamed through, I dump it into a larger bowl. And then my sister and I try to peel hot squash. We burn our fingertips on every single one. Pick up, drop, pick up, catch the peel with a fingernail, try to balance the cube to touch as little skin as possible, tug, drop, blow on fingers. Repeat. Make occasional noises of dismay.

"Why do we have to do it like this again?" asks Amanda.

"This is my first time peeling it this way, and I think it'll be the last," I say. "But let's see how it tastes."

When the pile of little inch-square peels and inch-cube squash are separated, we stare at the cubes of softened, naked, orange squash. Amanda's fingertips look as sore as mine feel.

"Okay," I say. "Now the easy part."

I guide Amanda through the process of heating a combination of milk and chicken broth, turning down the heat just as it reaches a boil. Drop in the cubes of squash and lower the stick blender in. Pulse gently. I veer away from the printed recipe, just to be sure, and toast my paprika and cumin in a pan before stirring them into the soup. We cook it for a while to thicken.

Amanda says, "Almost done?"

"Almost done." It feels satisfying.

"Let me go get the girls," she says.

Bubbles in thick liquids always amuse me. I could watch them for hours, and have. This one doesn't quite have the explosive *bloop* of polenta, but it's much more than just a typical simmer.

A few minutes later Amanda returns, with a yawning Parker and a scowling Shannon.

"This one didn't want to leave Midnight."

Shannon says, "I'm not hungry anyway."

"You'll be hungry when you smell this," I say.

Amanda says, "Ugh, all that cat hair, go wash your hands first, Shan," and the girl trounces off.

We put the books on the chairs at the dining room table again so the girls can sit at the right level. Once this is done, I ladle the soup into four bowls and place them on the table, one for each of us. Amanda pours milk into four glasses, two short and two tall. I set a squeeze bottle of sriracha at the center of the table.

Everyone makes pleased noises while they eat their soup. I squeeze sriracha into my bowlful until the top of the soup is more red than orange. It burns my lips in a pleasant, warming way. Amanda tries a dab of it and makes a face, and after tasting the heat, she won't let the girls try it.

A ringing phone sounds, and Amanda says, "Brennan's on a plane, so that must be Angelica. Wait, no. That's not even my ring."

"Must be me," I say, and reach over to find my phone on the mantel. I don't recognize the number. "Hello?"

"Ginny, it is Gert," says the familiar voice, all sweet dark poppy seeds.

"Gert! Is something wrong?"

"No, nothing wrong."

"Because it's not Thursday."

"No. Today I am calling for a different reason. I am calling as friend, asking favor."

"Yes?"

She says, "I need a good cook, and you are the best. Can I come get you? I will explain."

How can I refuse? Gert needs my help. No one ever needs my help. I say, "Okay. Do I need anything?"

"Only yourself."

She tells me she'll come to pick me up in fifteen minutes, and I tell her I'll be ready. When I hang up, Shannon is eating quietly and Parker is dripping soup off her spoon onto the table, but Amanda is sitting with her arms crossed, waiting for me.

"What was that?" asks Amanda.

"I need to go help Gert with something."

"With what?"

"I don't know. Something cooking related."

"How long will you be gone?"

"I don't know."

"You need to learn to ask follow-up questions," grumbles Amanda. "What if I needed you?"

"You don't, not right now," I say. "You've got the girls to help."

"Well, be back before dark, okay?"

"Okay." I'm used to that caveat. It's exactly the same as Ma's.

CHAPTER NINE

Hard-boiled Eggs

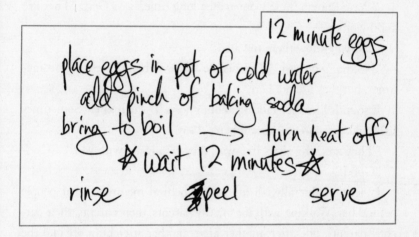

12 minute eggs

place eggs in pot of cold water
add pinch of baking soda
bring to boil ——> turn heat off
✷ wait 12 minutes ✷
rinse   peel   serve

I stand in front of the house, and though I expected Gert to pull up in a car, I see her approaching on foot. I don't recognize her at first because her hair isn't in its ponytail. Instead, when she turns to check the traffic before crossing the street, I notice it is coiled into a spiral at the back of her neck, in a neat, braided bun. It makes me think of Ma's caramel cinnamon buns, hot from the oven, melting and fragrant with the smell of butterscotch.

Gert touches my forehead and says, "Thank you for joining me. This way." With quick strides she turns right at the base of the stairs, heading back toward Ninth. I hasten to catch up. We turn southward.

"Where are we going?"

"We are going to cook."

"At your house?" I know she lives nearby, though I don't really know where.

"No, at the temple."

I start to tense up. "With other people?"

"A few. You do not need to worry. There will be no loud noises. They will not bother you or touch you."

"Are you sure?"

"I have known these women all a long time," says Gert. "They are good women."

"Did you know them in Cuba?"

"No, no," she says. "The people I knew then, I feel them sometimes, but they are not here."

It sounds like she's talking about ghosts. I play it safe. "Sometimes I feel like my parents are still here," I say.

"They are," she says. "In a way, they are always with you."

"Good."

I picture it literally, all my people behind me and all her people behind her. Walking with me are my parents, their parents, their parents' parents, one after another after another stretching off into the dark. We walk under a tree with a few last leaves still clinging to its branches. All the other trees on the block are completely bare.

Gert says, "Ginny, are you all right?"

"I'm all right."

She says, "Sometimes, when the dead are with you, it is not so good."

I think of Evangeline. "Are you afraid they'll hurt you?"

"Some. The dead are good and bad, just like the living. My husband, he died ten years ago, he is still with me, and the same as ever he was."

"It sounds like you miss him."

"I hate him," she says, "same as ever I did."

"But—" I try to process it. "How could you hate your husband?"

Pulling her jacket tighter at the throat, Gert says, "It is hard to talk about. We married very young, so I could leave Cuba. By the time I knew I hated Umberto it was too late. A woman alone in America with two young sons."

"Two? David has a brother?" I know Gert better than I know almost anyone else in the world and I never even asked her about her children. I don't know her family or her thoughts or where she lives. I don't know her at all. No one to blame for that but me.

"Had," says Gert. "He died. David does not even remember him. It is better that way, I think."

We walk in a matching rhythm, our strides the same length. I watch our feet strike the sidewalk in unison.

Gert says, "After David was born one of my brothers moved to the States also. Then his wife could look after the boys. And I started to clean houses, and started to have money. To learn the language. Once I thought I could live on my own, I tried to leave Umberto, but he would not let me."

"How could he stop you?"

"You do not understand," she says. "You are a very lucky girl. You are smart and you have money. You have a real home. When I was your age I had none of these things."

"I don't have money."

"You do. Your parents did, and they left it to you and Amanda. You may not have it in your hands, but you have it, still."

"Oh."

"For me, it was hard. I gave up and stayed. But . . . things changed. Tomas died. When I tried to leave again, your mother helped me. She gave us money, so David and I could stay somewhere else."

"And Umberto let you go?"

"For a while, no," she says. "For a while after he found out where we were living, he came every night and pounded on the door. I counted the nights until twenty, then I stopped counting. I waited, and prayed, and after many nights, Umberto found a woman he liked better. And then he let me go."

"So you got what you wanted."

"That is the truth," says Gert, "but there was much pain along the way. And still sometimes I hear him."

This is my chance to ask her about ghosts. But I can't ask straight out. "You—hear him? His voice? Like he's there in the room?"

"No," she says. "But the pounding, the sound of a fist on the door, that is enough."

I tell the truth. "Gert, I don't know what to say."

"Say nothing. I will always owe your family," she says. "Without your mother, I would be nowhere. My son would be nowhere. We owe that to her. That your father healed David's hand many years later, that is also more than we can repay, but your mother, she saved our lives. I am always paying that debt to her."

My stomach feels like there's a fist in it and I know it's not the sriracha. "But Ma's gone now."

"She is. There is much grief in the world. I am sorry."

"I'm sorry too."

"You and I, we both know much grief," she says. "But is life. When grief comes it is good that people have each other."

Gert turns left and stops at a large, squared-off building with a six-pointed star above its huge front door. "And now let us put our own grief away. We are here."

As we come into the temple, I don't know what to expect. I'm surprised to see it reminds me of church. Ma would take us from time to time, bribing us not to tell Dad. Amanda was bought off with chocolate, me with a book. But from what I remember, the sanctuary Ma loved is much like the room Gert walks me into. A high ceiling, long straight pews, tall windows to let in all the light. I remember in the church there were faces in the stained glass windows, but here, there are only colors and shapes. At the front of the room there is a squared shape in the darkness, but we don't get close enough to see what it is. Gert quickly moves out of the large open room and into a long, low-ceilinged hall, and I follow.

I trust Gert. If she says it'll be okay, it'll be okay. But I cue up the onions in my mind—white rings in the pan waiting for the heat to melt and sweeten them—just in case.

The air starts out cool, but gets warmer as we cross toward the far end of the hall. We are entering the kitchen. There are plates across all the counters, with food piled and stacked and spread out in different sections. Sheet pans of asparagus. Blocks of cheese. Three bowls each contain a white, smooth pile of eggs like river stones.

The food is so transfixing it takes me a while to notice the people.

There are three women in the kitchen, all in dark clothes. The tallest one has white hair. There are two with reddish hair and cleft chins, one older than the other, stooping slightly.

"Hello," murmurs the white-haired woman, but no one introduces herself. This suits me fine. Gert tells me how to hard-boil the eggs. Start from cold water, add a pinch of baking soda, bring them up to a boil. Turn the heat off. Time them out, precisely twelve minutes. Rinse in cold water, gently, carefully. I do two batches in small pans before Gert notices and puts the rest of them into a larger pot. She jots it down on a scrap of paper, I put it into action. Cold water, baking soda, up to a boil, turn it off, twelve minutes sitting. Rinse. Separate from the shell.

When I'm done with that, Gert gives me the task of picking through several pounds of dried lentils, checking for bad beans or small stones. The work suits my skills. If there is a stone I'll find it. I wonder, from her years of observation, just how much Gert knows about me.

Peeling carrots next to me while I pick through lentils, Gert explains.

"This is temple burial society. *Chevra kadisha*." It's odd to hear this Yiddish term from Gert. Usually her voice has a more Cuban lilt to it, but I remind myself that before she was Cuban she was Romanian, and Jewish since birth, so Yiddish is as much a part of her as anything. Just because I've never heard it, it's silly to think it hasn't always been there.

I find a black lentil among the brown ones and set it aside, to be safe. I ask her, "Burial? You . . . bury people?"

"No, no. Are many different ways to help. Some wash the body. Some perform tasks so secret we cannot discuss."

I look around the busy kitchen. "And some cook."

"Yes. We arrange meals. We decide who will cook when. Mostly after deaths, which is the saddest, but also when families have trouble or sickness. After funeral families are not to cook for themselves. It must be done by others. The community."

I consider this idea while I search the lentils for things that don't belong. Love without words. To show it by doing, not by saying. Like Amanda does for her family by taking care of them, including me, even if I don't like the way she tries to do it. Like David does for Elena, in his way, even though it's too late.

We work in silence. When I'm done with the lentils there are other tasks, folding napkins, washing fruit. Mostly Gert hands me things, and tells me in a few words what to do. At one point when I bobble a dish and two strawberries drop to the floor, the young redheaded woman hands me a roll of paper towels. When everything's done, we load trays and bowls into trunks and backseats, and drive to a house. The sun is low in the sky, so I leave a quick message on Amanda's voice mail saying I'm not sure when I'll be home, so have dinner without me. Gert doesn't say much during the ride, but everything she says counts.

"Let me explain to you the house," Gert says. "Mourners are here, the family. They are sitting shiva. Is the tradition. Family stays home, seven days. Friends and community come to sit shiva with them. Everyone comes. It is mitzvah, a commandment. To console the bereaved."

On one level, I can see why this is part of the mourning process. On the other, I am thankful that my family isn't Jewish. The only thing worse than the funeral day, with too many people paying me too much attention, would have been seven days of the same. At least with Ma and Dad it was over quickly.

Except that I'm still thinking about it constantly, so it's not really over, but I shove the thoughts away again. It's not my grief that matters today.

The car we are riding in pulls into a long driveway. We carry the food into the house. I follow Gert in, observing, keeping silent.

The five of us sort things out in the kitchen. The women move in a rhythm. Once in a while, Gert steps out of the rhythm to give me instructions. She speaks clearly but softly, in crisp words. I should keep quiet. I should follow where she goes. She will need me in the kitchen mostly. I should not use any silverware that she does not put into my hand, because kosher homes have one set of utensils for meat and one for milk, and I must not mix them, and I will not know.

"Okay," I say.

Gert says, "I will hand you what you need."

"Okay."

We get started. Women are carrying bowls back and forth. Gert continues to give me instructions while she and I unpack the food and set it out, for others to carry.

"We are here because it is the day of the funeral. The family, they do not cook this day. We serve them instead. It is called *seudat havra'ah*. Meal of consolation." Gert sets out the last of the bowls of hard-boiled eggs.

All the food is unpacked and there's nothing to do with my hands. We shift positions, and I'm next to the doorway, and I see the people we're here for. The mourners are easy to identify. They're the ones sitting on long, low benches, separate from everyone, looking straight ahead.

As other people arrive, I can tell they are looking at me. I wonder why. Not because of my clothes, because they're not so different from everyone else's. We are all dressed in dark shades. I look down at their feet and watch the slow-moving shoes. Maybe people are looking at me because I am not looking in their faces. That usually causes trouble when I meet new people. Or maybe my uncertainty is manifest in a way I can't describe. But there's something about me that's off. Not right. Everyone notices it. Except the mourners. The family. They look into nowhere.

So I watch the family. Looking at them reminds me of my own grief, my own sadness. I would have liked a meal of consolation. I suppose that is what I was trying to do when I accidentally invoked Nonna's ghost. Reaching into the past to cook the ribollita, something from a happier time. But the result wasn't at all consoling. Maybe that's why you're not supposed to cook your own. Maybe you're grieving too hard.

Behind me, Gert says, "Ginny, salt this bowl of lentils, please."

I take the bowl she offers and turn away from the main room.

To distract myself from thoughts of grief, I ask Gert, "So it's always like this? Eggs, lentils?"

"Oblong things, just for the meal of consolation. For other meals, any food."

"Why?"

"There is reason."

Someone calls to her from the direction of the oven. I start brainstorming oblong foods. Flattish, roundish things. Certain fruits must qualify. I wonder about mango. Kiwi? Papaya?

Over the next hour, we move back and forth between the kitchen and the main room, filling and replenishing bowls, clearing away things that need clearing. I only make one misstep. Thinking it empty, I reach for a pitcher of water next to the door, but Gert puts her hand on mine. I draw it back quickly.

"This is for mourners to wash," she says. "Leave it alone."

I stay far away from it the rest of the time.

There's one tradition Gert doesn't need to describe for me. I can see for myself. The members of the family are all wearing torn black ribbons pinned to their clothing. Just a small rip. At first it looks accidental, but everyone on a bench has a ribbon, and a tear in it. It can't all be accident.

It preoccupies me until it's time to leave. It seems such the right expression of grief. *I am sad, so in whatever small way I can, I will tear myself apart.* They've taken what's on the inside and made it visible. If I thought it wouldn't be inappropriate I'd do it myself.

Someone drives us back to the temple, and Gert and I walk through the chilly evening light back up Spruce Street to my house. At the base of the stairs, Gert says, "Thank you, Ginny. Good night."

"Good night."

She's walking away and it's almost too late but I want to know, so I ask, "Why did you take me to another funeral?"

"It was not the funeral," she says.

"It was similar."

It's hard to see her in the dark. We need more streetlights.

Gert says, "Ginny, you cannot stay in the house."

"No! Not you too!" I start to get outraged, try to control myself. "Amanda says I can't stay, I didn't think you agreed."

"You misunderstand," she says. "You should live in it. But you shouldn't stay there all the time. You can do more."

She puts her hand on my forehead, gives her blessing, and goes.

Maybe she's right.

I let myself in. On the first floor there are no lights on. I feel

Midnight brush against my ankles, so I walk to the kitchen and put some food in her dish. Then I go upstairs to look for the humans. They are all together. Amanda is reading the girls a bedtime story, and when I stand in the doorway she doesn't look up. But Parker sees me and says, "Aunt Ginny! Mom, can Aunt Ginny read us a story?"

"How about it?" asks Amanda, and I nod silently.

We trade places, me at the bedside and Amanda in the doorway, and the girls settle back down. I read in a small puddle of light. Parker is asleep before I even finish the second page, but Shannon watches with tiny open eyes, staring at the ceiling instead of the book. She looks like I feel. When I reach to turn out the light, she doesn't protest, and says nothing as the room goes dark.

I climb the stairs to my own room and take up the same unmoving position, arms at my sides, covers up to my chin. Downstairs a grown-up voice murmurs. Amanda must be saying good night to her husband, thousands of miles away. I catch a few stray words. I hear *vanish* and *tomorrow* and *lay down the law*. Somewhere in the house the tags on the cat's collar jingle, almost too faint to be heard.

To keep the faces of the mourners from troubling me in my sleep, I lose myself in the feel of sriracha, trying to remember every last note, to wipe everything else away. The burn of the chili heat, sharp but round. The soft, garlicky note in the back. The particular feel of the pain, not like a pinprick or a knife cut, but both blunter and sharper, a pencil eraser pressed hard against the soft meat of the tongue like a cattle brand. A taste that is somehow painful and positive. A riddle of chemical compounds, not human emotions. The only kind I know I can solve.

IN THE MORNING I am thinking about Amanda's plan for me to live with her family, and whether I should. I've been so fixated on staying in the house, not selling the house, it's hard to shift gears. But would it be so bad?

But Ma never finished that sentence. *It's very important that you not let Amanda . . .* talk me into leaving the house, maybe? Is Amanda going to hurt someone? Me? Herself? There are too many possibilities, and it paralyzes me.

Amanda looks up from her laptop at the dining room table and says, "Hey, I was just thinking about you. Do you want some breakfast?"

"Not yet."

"Parker's still asleep," she says. "And you know Shannon is wherever your cat is, she's plain obsessed with that thing. But honestly this is good. We need to talk."

"Oh?"

"I've been putting this off because we've both been so upset. But now I don't think it's right anymore. I think we just need to face it."

"Face what?"

"Your problem."

There's a soft sound behind me. I glance over at the steps and see Midnight walking down. Her white tail swishes in the air, from right to left and back, dignified, slow. I try not to let the hypnotic movement distract me.

"I've told you, I don't have a problem."

"You think normal people hide in closets during their parents' funerals? You think normal people mutter down at their shoes instead of looking people in the eye? You think normal people shriek at the top of their lungs when someone just barely grazes their arm in public?"

"I don't always do that. I hardly ever do."

"But you do sometimes. Mom did the best she could with you, I know. But I think she might have been able to help you more if she knew what you have."

"A personality."

Amanda says, "Ginny, that's not cute anymore."

"I'm not trying to be cute," I tell her.

A little trilling pattern of footsteps, muffled by the carpet, follows Midnight down the stairs. I see Shannon crouched on the bottom step, stretching her hand toward the white, soft-looking tail, just beyond her reach.

Amanda says, "Ginny, did you hear me?"

"Sorry," I apologize absently. All my attention is eaten up watching the cat and the girl and concentrating on not telling my sister to put a figurative sock in it.

"I said . . . I think . . . Ginny, I think you need more help."

"I have Gert."

"Not that kind of help."

I know that. Midnight lowers herself off the steps onto the floor and sits down to lick a paw like it's the most urgent thing in the world that her paw be licked. Shannon leans a touch too far and tips over, and she falls off the bottom step, falling too fast to catch herself, striking her head on the hardwood floor. Her howl immediately fills the house.

Amanda is on her feet. "Shannon, honey, it's all right, it's all right." She sweeps her up. "C'mere, baby. It's all right."

Shannon is sobbing as Amanda strokes the back of her hair. Amanda twists to face me and says, "You're not getting off the hook. Listen. This can be easy. All I want is for you to see a doctor. Get you diagnosed. Treated. It could make things easier."

Shannon's cry drops and rises through the octaves. I can't tell, it might be getting louder. Amanda stops stroking and just holds her head with a flat palm, pressing gently. Midnight scurries away.

"No," I tell Amanda. "No doctor."

"One of these days you're going to get hurt. That's why I worry. You nearly set the place on fire the day of the funeral. And you let strange men in the kitchen. And you vanish for hours with the cleaning lady. I mean, Ginny, it's just not normal."

"Just one."

"One hour?"

"One man."

"You're going to get hurt," she says.

I stare her in the throat.

"Those are the facts. Shannon, hush, sweetie, it's okay, all right?"

Shannon is crying some words but I can't make them out. She cries them into her mother's ear.

"Here, Ginny, you try," says Amanda. "She wants you."

I hold my hands out and Shannon comes over. She's heavy. Immediately her head drops onto my shoulder as if drawn there by a magnet. My hand goes up to cradle her without any help from my brain. I look at Amanda. She's staring at me, arms folded. I know what that means. The shoulder of her shirt is a different color than the rest, wet with Shannon's tears.

She says, "Please. I know you don't think you need it. But do it for me, Ginny. To make me happy. Just go to the doctor and get screened."

"Screened" makes me think of food getting rubbed through a screen. It's a French technique. Soups get screened, and sauces. Forced through a tamis or a chinois. Everything that comes out is smooth and all the rough parts get left behind, thrown away. I don't want to be screened.

Amanda steps toward me. She speaks in a low voice. "There's a word for it. For your condition."

"Shyness?"

"No."

"Social awkwardness?"

"No."

"Iconoclasm?"

Shannon is much quieter now, not howling, only whimpering. Amanda steps even closer and puts her hands over her daughter's tiny ears.

"God damn it, Ginny. It's called Asperger's syndrome."

I say, "I'll stick with iconoclasm."

"Hear me out." She leaves her hands on Shannon's ears. We're all standing very, very close together. "This one, at preschool, they told us she was unusually quiet. Plays alone, doesn't talk as much as the others. I'm sure she's fine. But I started doing some research on the Internet, and when I saw this list of symptoms for this syndrome, Asperger's, I was like, oh my God! That's Ginny."

I snap, "I don't have a *syndrome,* Amanda."

"Just think about it. Just consider it."

"No." If I weren't holding Shannon I would bolt for the closet right now.

Amanda won't stop. "And I talked to Angelica about it and she said she had a cousin who has it, or something like it, and all he had to do was take some pills and now he's fine."

"I don't want to take pills."

"Don't be mad. I'm trying to help."

Parker comes thundering down the stairs, and Amanda runs to the bottom of the staircase in a flash. The little girl is unsteady on her feet. My arms are getting tired, so I move in the direction of the chair by the fireplace, thinking I'll set Shannon down.

Amanda yells back at me, "We're not finished!"

Shannon puts her hands over her ears.

"Are you okay?" I ask her.

"Mommy's loud," she says, speaking into my shoulder.

"Everything's all right," I tell her. She says nothing, but my arms have gone from tired to tingling. "Do you want to get down?"

"Okay."

I set Shannon down. She immediately heads toward the couch and lies down on the floor in front of it, her head on a throw rug.

"Why is she doing that?" asks Amanda.

"It's where the cat went," I say. Parker walks over to her sister and mimics her, lying down with her head against the floor.

Amanda speaks softly to me. "Just go to the doctor. It's one little thing. For me."

"No."

"Come on. After all I'm prepared to do for you."

"What is that?"

"Open my home to you. Let you stay with us."

I think about it, and I say, "But I don't even want to stay with you."

"This is how I know something's wrong with you," says Amanda. "Because I can't make you see reason."

Parker says, "What's wrong with Aunt Ginny?"

I say, "Nothing at all." But that's not what Amanda thinks. Amanda wants to label me. Like a piece of fruit. A cut of meat.

Shannon says, "The cat won't come out."

"Just let her be!" shouts Amanda, too loud again.

My sister wants to put a word on me. *It's very important that you not let Amanda* . . . "put a word on you"? Is that what Ma was saying? It makes sense.

Amanda says, "God, are you even listening to me?"

I tell her the truth. "No."

"This is your future we're talking about!"

"You're talking about it. I'm not."

"This is the bottom line," she says. "Will you go to the doctor to make me happy?"

"No."

"That makes me unhappy."

"Then be unhappy," I say. We're all unhappy sometimes. I don't see why Amanda should get to be exempt.

She says, "Oh, I'm unhappy, believe me. Believe me."

Parker says, "Mommy, why are you unhappy? You should be happy instead!"

"I know I should, sweetie," she says, "but sometimes people just won't listen. Hey, tell you what. Do you and your sister want to go out for breakfast?"

"Yeah!" says Parker.

"Shannon, do you want pancakes?"

"Pancakes!" says Shannon, getting up off the carpet.

"That's silly, I can make pancakes here," I say, but Amanda's already walking out the door, taking her daughters' winter coats off the coatrack as she goes, and they scurry out behind her.

Okay. She's upset. She needs space. That's fine, if that's what she needs. But I'm not going to do what she wants me to do, and not just to be contrary. Because I think I've finally figured out what the ghosts are warning me about.

If Amanda puts a word on me, I won't be equal anymore. She can run the show. She can take the house, and kick me out, and sell it if she wants. If I have a disorder, she's in charge.

It doesn't matter what the disorder is—I don't have it—but I should probably educate myself anyway. That way I can prove it. I've heard the word, I don't remember where—maybe at school? But I only know how to spell it. I don't actually know what it is. In that way Asperger's is like fregola, or kohlrabi.

I go to look up Asperger's in the dictionary, but it's not there. The page it would be on is a good one, with lots of food words. *Asparagus. Aspartame. Aspic.*

Then the words turn bad.

Asocial.

Asphyxiate.

I close the book and walk into my parents' room and kneel down on the floor of the closet and put my hands inside Dad's shoes. I stay there for a long while. I break one of Ma's cardinal rules. (*Cardinal* is on a page with *cardiology* and *cardoons*.) I let the one-hour battery recharging turn into two hours, even three. She would be aghast at the indulgence. She would say, *Ginny, my word!* But she isn't here to say it.

When I come back out again, Amanda and the girls are still gone. I go upstairs to my room and sit down with my laptop in the alcove facing the back of the house, and I pull up Kitcherati. I read a thread about kitchen injuries. I have countless little cuts and burns and bruises, but nothing serious other than the cut across the pad of my thumb that Dad was too late to fix. Even that one isn't as bad as what a lot of people on Kitcherati are writing about. People talk about burning themselves on spun sugar, which is extremely hot and dangerous. Or they cut off parts of their fingers in meat slicers. They swallow pure wasabi, sit down on griddles, step somehow into boiling stock-pots. The kitchen is a place of sharp and hot and deadly things. Ma never would have taught me to cook if I hadn't kept going in there, over and over. But either she taught me right or I learned right, because I never hurt myself that badly again. Amanda thinks I'm not capable, but I am.

After Kitcherati I pull up one of my favorite advice columns and read the day's quandary. The writer complains about something hurtful her mother-in-law said, something she let pass at the time but has never forgiven or forgotten. The columnist counsels her to either address it head-on or let it go, because the pent-up resentment is harmful. *Channel negative energy into something positive*, says the advice.

I decide to give it a try.

I'm on the Internet anyway, so I look up Asperger's, for Amanda. Maybe I can tell if Shannon has it. That's how Amanda said she starting thinking about it, wondering what syndrome might make a girl unusually quiet in preschool, enough that her teachers would remark on it.

Lots of sites come up. Blogs, discussion groups, the whole smorgasbord. I go for something that looks clinical and not homemade. That way it's likely to be more precise. I've learned this over time. You can learn from the Internet but you can't be sure what you're learning is true. Same as life. Be careful.

I pick a white-and-blue site with a consistent font, not too large, not too small. The definition comes in bullets. *Difficulty with eye contact. Inability to read emotions. Lack of empathy. Inappropriate social reactions.* Doesn't sound like Shannon so far. I read on.

Tendency to obsess on particular topics that may not be of interest to others. This symptom has the opposite problem. In short, it reminds me of everyone I've ever met. Everyone has something they like to talk about. I remember a boy in kindergarten who only ever talked about caterpillars, and a girl in the fourth grade who was the same way about butterflies. The girls who sat behind me in college classes only ever seemed to be talking about beer and sex. Even Dad talked nonstop about surgery. And Amanda—unicorns. When we were kids Amanda obsessed about unicorns for more than a full year. She bought unicorn stickers and unicorn shoes and begged Ma to sew unicorn appliqués inside every item of her clothing. Does that mean Amanda has Asperger's? I know she doesn't. She wouldn't have made a big deal out of telling me she thinks I have it, then. But do I? I don't want it, so I push that idea away, and keep reading.

As part of the autism spectrum, can be more or less severe. May also include facial tics, repetitive behaviors, aggression, poor gross motor coordination. Key distinguishing characteristic from autism is lack of speech delay. Like autism, more common in males.

More common doesn't mean only. And the more I think about this list, the more I think it fits Shannon more than it fits me. And Amanda did say she didn't know for sure if Shannon had it.

I copy the list of symptoms into an e-mail and send it to Amanda's address, with just a one-word comment, *Shannon?*

Maybe she has the syndrome, maybe she doesn't. Of course she is normal. We are all normal. I wonder if Shannon would like her own version of the Normal Book. Maybe when she's older.

I can't think about it anymore. I need to think about something else. I look over at the closet and remember what's hiding under the carpet there.

I turn up the corner of the carpet in the closet and pull out the pictures of Evangeline. I put the one I showed Amanda back with the others. I haven't really looked at the whole series since I saw Evangeline's ghost. I was too shocked, but as time passes, I think I can control my feelings now. I think I can look at them in the right way. Analytically, instead of fearfully.

The woman in the photographs looks nothing like the ghost I saw. Maybe it wasn't even the same Evangeline. I consider the differences. The ghost's bald head and huge sunken eyes. The wrinkled skin of her neck. Those gaunt toothpick arms. The woman in the picture is round and soft and young. But when I look at her face—it isn't pleasant but I can do it—I begin to see the similarities. The eye shape, the ear shape. A faint discoloration on her left temple. There's more here than I've already seen, I know it. I just need to figure out what it is.

Could Dad have loved this woman? Run his fingertips along that neck and kissed those lips? Why would he, how could he, when he had Ma?

I line up all twenty-nine pictures in a long row on the floor of my room. The gray sky stretches above her head and the white collar marks the spot under her chin. It is all the same, the same, the same.

A nurse at the hospital, Ma said. The white collar is part of her uniform. I can't tell if they were taken at the hospital or not, but it was definitely outdoors. Maybe in the courtyard out back.

I remember thinking maybe she was looking at something, something she was holding in her hand. She is looking down and to the right.

Not always.

Her eyes are looking down in some pictures, but in others, she is looking directly into the camera.

I change the order of the pictures. Getting up and moving from one end of the line to the other gets tiring, so I kneel in the middle of the room and spread the pictures out in a circle around me. I start with all the ones where she's looking down, then all the ones where she's looking up. There's some kind of pattern there but it's not quite right. I try a different approach.

I stack all the pictures and straighten their edges to make them match, straight up and down. I hold them at the bottom with a one-handed grip and put my thumb at the top, then flip through. Evangeline's eyes flick back and forth. I scatter the photos around me again and put them back in a different order, checking the tiny variations between each to make sure each one follows from the next, then stack them neatly again, then flip through again, fast.

The effect is this: her eyes slowly look toward me, then slowly look away.

It's uncomfortable at first. I hate it when real people look toward me, and because of the motion, it's like she's looking at me that way. But I remind myself. This is not a person. This is a series of photos. I flip through it again. She looks toward me and away again.

Did he keep these as a reminder of her? Does this mean they had a relationship? That Evangeline, as terrifying as her ghost was to me, was once a tender young woman my father loved?

"Are you feeling more reasonable now?" comes Amanda's voice from the doorway. My back is to the door. I've been so absorbed in the photos, I didn't even hear her. I hunch over to protect them. I don't think she can see.

I make myself be calm. I couldn't do it earlier.

As I turn around and look up at her, I make sure my eyes connect with hers, and I say, "I don't know how to answer that question."

Her eyes are on mine. With a flick of the wrist I toss the stack of photos under the bed. I finish turning, standing up, to face her.

She says, "I'm sorry if I came on too strong, but I'm really frustrated. It could really help you, to deal with this. Knowing what you are."

"I know who I am."

"Let's not fight," she says, and holds her hands out for me to take. I can't tell if it's a genuine gesture or a test. I offer her my hands and she gives them a quick squeeze, a friendly action.

"Okay."

Amanda drops my hands and says, "Sorry I didn't call. Brennan got back early, so everything was a madhouse. I drove the girls home, and now they're with him. I thought you and I could get a little more done in the peace and quiet."

"Sure."

"The library is next on the list."

We pack another wall of books in the library. As I put them away, I shake each, just to see if there's anything in it. If she notices what I'm doing, she doesn't say. But there's nothing. No letter, no recipe, no hint about the past. The most interesting thing I find is another book of Dad's with a strange title, *The Man Who Mistook His Wife for a Hat*. I show it to Amanda.

"Haven't read that one," she says. "I haven't had much time to read lately."

"You love to read."

"I used to. These days, I can't find the time."

"You can always find the time," I tell her.

"No, Ginny," she says, shaking her head. "You can. I can't. Actually, that— You know what, let me show you something."

We walk down the hall to her old room, the one painted buttery yellow, and she walks to the stack of labeled boxes along the wall. She opens the AMANDA KIDHOOD box.

"Unicorns," she says, flipping through a notebook, pointing. "All over the place. Here I'm copying a recipe for chocolate peanut butter balls from the Mini Page. Here I'm in love with Trent Dillinger." She picks out another notebook, "Here, this one's high school, this is only ten years ago. Here's backward writing that Angelica and I used to write notes to each other during study hall. This one says, lemme see, 'JW has great big zit on nose.'" She flips a few pages forward. "Here I was writing SO BORED in the margins and practicing to see how tiny I could write 'Mrs. Amanda Davis' because I wanted to go to prom with Greg Davis so bad I thought I'd die. And he didn't ask me and I didn't die. But at the time that was the most important thing in the world to me. That feeling. Now I can't even picture him."

I can picture Greg Davis—she brought him to the house once that summer—but I don't mention it. I don't know what she's trying to tell me, but I know what she doesn't want to hear.

"He's buried under years of details," she says, talking faster, "all the things I did and had to do, paying bills, for years, figuring out how to get our security deposit back when we moved to a new apartment, the little things like making reservations on our anniversary, the big things like deciding on a hospital to give birth, the time we had to drive in a snowstorm to get to Brennan's parents' house by Christmas and how scared I was and how sure I was we were going to drive into a ditch and die, I mean, it's thousands of things, it's millions of things."

She picks up a notebook in each hand and says, "You know what all this tells me?"

"No."

"I've changed," she says. "A lot. Getting older, getting married, being a mom, moving from house to house, all that has changed me. I've grown up."

"I know."

"You haven't," she says.

I'm stunned for a moment, then I say, "That's not true."

She says, "It's not your fault. I see that. Mom and Dad took care of things so you didn't have to. You live here and it's all so comfortable. And the question is, can you even be an adult? Because you didn't grow up. You've never had to."

"I am grown up!"

"Are you?"

"Yes!" I'm done being stunned. I'm angry.

"A person who hides in a closet is not a grown-up," she says. "That's not normal."

"Just because it's not what you would do doesn't mean it's not normal."

"Grown-ups finish college," she says.

"You didn't," I snap back.

"Because I got pregnant! That's not the same thing at all!"

"Then why'd you bring it up?"

"Whatever. My plan got derailed because real things happened to me. Real things. Nothing real ever happened to you because Mom wouldn't let it."

I yell, "Do you think I wanted that? I hated that!"

"Bullshit," says Amanda. I have never heard her swear.

I'm so furious I realize I'm starting to lose control, and I can't do that, especially because Amanda will just assume that means she's right. That I'm not a grown-up if I can't even handle an argument. I know I can't slap her so I slap one of the boxes, it makes a loud sound, I know I'm about to break apart.

I focus on food. I need it.

I pick the slick nuttiness of sesame oil. I don't know any other words for what sesame oil tastes like. It tastes like toasted. It tastes like brown. A drop of any oil on the tongue will spread and slide, except sesame oil. Canola, sunflower, grapeseed, olive, they all slide. Sesame oil stays where you put it.

"Don't you have anything to say?" she says.

I say, "Yes. No matter how much you push me, I am not going to any doctor. A lawyer, maybe."

"What for?"

I work hard on keeping my voice soft, keeping the anger out of it. "This house is half mine," I tell her. Logic is all I have. "Legally. And if you insist on trying to sell it, I will make sure that doesn't happen."

"It's half mine too," she says.

"Yes. Only half. Not all."

"Yeah, exactly half. That's how things work. We're supposed to be equal, even if we're not."

"We're equal," I say.

"Yeah," she sighs, tossing the notebooks back in the box. "We're equal. You know what? I have two little girls who depend on me for everything. I had friends, really good friends, back in Los Angeles. But I wanted my girls to know their grandparents. Dad was retiring, I knew they'd both have time on their hands. So I talked Brennan into getting transferred back to the East Coast. I gave up that life to come back here and then the rug got pulled out from under me. They *died,* Ginny."

She slams the lid onto the box.

"I know you're sad," I start, but she holds up her palm.

"Don't even try," she says. "You don't know how. You don't have a clue what it's like for me. Did you get the call that they were dead? Were you the one who made all the arrangements? Headstones? Flowers? Coffins? Did you have to go and identify their *bodies?*"

She looks at me and I know she wants an answer and I look at the cardboard box and give her the only one that's true. "No."

"No! That wasn't you! It was me. You, you're standing here helpless with no one but your stupid cat in this big empty house and I am your *sister* and you can't even look me in the face when you talk to me and you're saying we're equal? You're saying we get to go halfsies? Bullshit, equal. I'm leaving. You're on your own."

I chase her down the stairs, but I don't know what to say to her. I'm angry and scared and a lot of other things.

At the front door she says, "And don't think I haven't noticed. They're not coming back, Ginny. They're not going to need their shoes."

Instead of slamming the door she leaves it hanging open, and I watch her get smaller and smaller as she goes down the street, cold air blowing in around me.

Then I realize she didn't even mention the e-mail I sent her, with the list of symptoms, asking, *Shannon?* Which might make her angry but I can't imagine her any angrier than she already is.

My sister hates me. She's right. I didn't do anything, I never do anything. I'm helpless. Maybe I do have a syndrome. Maybe I am not normal.

My vision's going black, which doesn't usually happen unless I'm being physically threatened, but no time to analyze now I just rush inside, upstairs, the closet, the shoes, the dark. Sesame oil, sesame oil, sesame oil. Think of everything wonderful made with sesame. Tahini, therefore hummus. Benne seed wafers. Cold sesame noodles. Pasteli. Halvah. Creamy and shattering all at once. Grainy but round. A contradiction. I lose myself inside the thought of food, go in as deep as I can go, retreating from the light and the world and my sister's fury.

. . . .

WHEN I AM calmer I step out into the light and let my eyes readjust. I look back into the closet, at the shoes. That's one thing Amanda's right about. I don't just put the shoes back in the closet so I can put my hands in them when I'm retreating from the world. I like seeing them there, imagining my parents' feet stepping into them. All these boxes don't matter if I can just make contact with the shoes. It may not be logical to the rest of the world but it makes sense to me.

But I can't force everything into the arrangement I'd like. I can't use denial to make everything simple. I'm furious that Amanda thinks I'm no better than a child, but I also can't imagine life without my sister. With no family at all. She's all I have left. But it's more complicated than that. My family is dead, but I can bring them back, at least for a short time, through their recipes. I tell myself that power would confuse anyone. I don't know why I have it, but I do. Something about the way I cook their recipes calls to them. I tell myself it doesn't mean I'm crazy, or not normal, or that I have a syndrome. I'm flawed. I never said I wasn't.

Difficult, Ma called me. It cuts both ways. Difficult for her to deal with me, sure, but difficult for me too. Difficult to feel like I'm always a little bit on the outside. Difficult to launch myself into activities everyone else seems to take for granted like a school day, a lecture, a lunchroom, knowing that I might have a reaction I can't control.

Difficult, but not impossible. I am not impossible.

CHAPTER TEN

Chicken Soup

When the phone rings later, without any hello or anything, Amanda says, "I've been thinking a lot about what you said."

"What did I say?" It's not that I don't remember. In a sense I remember too well, I remember everything I said to her and everything she said to me. *That's not normal. You don't know how. Their* bodies. *Bullshit.*

Amanda says, "I want to give you a name."

"I have a name."

"Someone else's name," she says. "Someone you can go to."

Now I think I know what she's talking about. "A lawyer?"

"Why not," she says. "You need someone to look after your interests. I've been thinking a lot about that. This turned into a big fight and it doesn't need to be. I meant what I said. I really think we should be sticking together."

She's not quite making sense, but no one does all the time.

"So you'll go?"

"To a lawyer? Sure."

"Here's the name and address," she says, and rattles it off. "I made an appointment for you. Four o'clock."

"Today?"

"No time like the present," she says. She is biting off the ends of her words. I think I know what this means. She's not happy. But right now it's not her happiness I care about. It's mine.

"Thanks."

Amanda says, "Well, I just want us to get along. I want you to figure out what you want. And I guess maybe I haven't been taking that into account. So, you get things figured out, okay?"

"Okay."

THE OFFICE IS on Broad Street, not far from the Kimmel Center. I walk straight along Spruce. It's the most familiar way, the most familiar street. I could get there just as easily on Locust, and that route would take me past the community garden that Ma loved so much, but I don't turn. Instead, when I get to Broad, I pause and look up the street toward City Hall. I love that building. All bizarre and lumpy and way too huge. From one direction it's a big square behemoth. From another, an oddly slender tower. It is both things, mashed together. And at night the clock has a glowing yellow face. Right now, the clock is just the same color as the rest of the tower. And William Penn is facing away from me, northward.

It's time. I go to the address Amanda gave me. I take the elevator up to the eighth floor, practicing. *I'm here to see Ms. Stewart. I have a four o'clock appointment.* This won't be hard.

But I notice that the nameplate on the door says Dr. Stewart, not Ms. Stewart, and if I weren't already in the process of pushing the door open . . . but then it's too late, because I'm looking the receptionist square in the eye. It's almost a physical pain.

I look down.

I say, "There's some kind of mistake, I'm sorry."

She says, "Are you Ms. Selvaggio? Her four o'clock?"

"Yes."

"Please, just go right through that door."

I don't want to. I want to run.

"Please," says the receptionist again, politely. "Right through that door."

So I do what she says. Authority really screws with my head.

I expect a cold, clinical, all-white doctor's office, but apparently, Dr. Stewart is not that kind of doctor. The walls are warm beige, like sugar cookies. The lighting is gentle. There's an overstuffed chair, and a more streamlined leather one. This is much worse than a regular doctor. Much worse.

"Hi, Ms. Selvaggio? It's great to meet you." Gray pants with barely visible stripes, an open-necked shirt. Round-toed shoes.

Dr. Stewart says, "I know your sister well."

"I bet," is all I can manage. I can't tell if her shoes are high heels. The toes are all I can see. I keep my eyes on them.

"Why don't you tell me about yourself?"

"There's been a mistake," I say. I wish I thought it was a mistake. "Amanda told me you were a lawyer. That's why I came to see you. But you're not a lawyer, are you?"

"No. I'm a psychiatrist. I think you know that."

"I saw the sign. I'm not stupid."

"That would be judging language. I didn't say that."

"Not in those words, no."

"Okay, that's okay." She gestures at the soft, deep chair. "Since you're here anyway . . . ?"

"No." I stay on my feet.

"You sound angry."

"You'd be angry too."

"You're right," she says. "I probably would. But I'd try to keep an open mind."

"My mind is open," I say. "Wide open." I sit down, just to show her it doesn't scare me.

She has skinny fingers that pluck at her collar. "But you don't want to talk to me. Even though there are people who care about you, who think it's the right thing for you. Why? You have nothing to lose."

"Nothing to gain, either." It's a reflex.

"Do you really think that's true?"

"I have to," I say, suddenly aware I'm whispering.

"Your sister says you don't like people."

"My sister is a liar."

"You do like people?"

"Well—no—that's not what she lied about."

"So she told the truth in this respect. You don't like people."

"Yeah," I say. "I don't."

"Well, why not?"

I consider it, and my answer surprises me. "Because I never know what they're thinking, that's why."

"You could learn. Figure out how people do it, read the signs."

"I've tried, actually."

"Tell me more about that."

"No."

"Well, I can imagine. It must be frustrating."

"You have no idea," I say, and have to try to pull myself back. I'm on the verge of getting truly furious. It's a shame that anger is pretty much the only emotion I can identify in myself for sure. A few black freckles swim at the edge of my vision but they pop and vanish like bubbles. I sink back in the overstuffed chair and it surrounds me. It looked soft but it feels firmer than it looks. I think of peppercorns in a mortar and pestle, grinding around in a circle until they finally yield and crack.

Dr. Stewart says, "Maybe I do."

"I doubt it."

"Ginny, one of the hardest things about Asperger's is the isolation. But that's in your power to change. You can do something about it."

"Pills? Brain magnets?" I remember what I saw on the Internet. It didn't sound pleasant.

"That's what some people choose to do, yes. But you don't have to choose that. You have options."

"Hey," I say. "Hey! I don't even have it. Why are you assuming I have it just because my sister says I do? My sister is a proven liar. She lied to get me here."

"I don't want that to affect how you view me. I didn't know that."

"But she told you I have a problem and you took her word for it. That's lousy medicine. I don't think you're very good at your job, Dr. Stewart."

She says, with lots of space between the words, "Ginny, it would be premature of me to diagnose you. But just talking to you, I can see that you aren't meeting my eyes. That's a key symptom."

I look her in the eyes and it hurts but I do it so I can say, "I do not have *symptoms* because I do not have a *disease*."

"Your sister is scared for you."

"My sister wants to control me." And take my home away and probably all my money too, but I know I don't need to say everything I'm thinking.

"I don't think that's the case."

I say, "Well, I've known her longer than you have."

The doctor plucks at her collar some more and says, "I just want you to know that there's help for you if you want it. What we're seeing now with younger children is if we start encouraging them to participate, to socialize, that they don't put up these barriers—"

I cut her off. "So if I had it, and I don't, but if I did, you're saying it's too late for me anyway? Great motivation, Doc."

"No, no, I didn't say that. It's just, that's when patterns get set, and probably by the time you were seven or eight you'd already developed your own understanding of what was normal. And—"

"Normal" makes me think of it. "Seven or eight?"

"Around then, yes."

"So, Shannon is still young enough to do this—what are you talking about, socializing?"

"Oh, Amanda's never thought that Shannon has Asp—" She stops in the middle of the word. I feel a surge of pride. She should have pretended she didn't know who Shannon was at all. For once, for a moment, I know what it's like to have what the advice columnists call *the upper hand*. It doesn't mean anything, but it helps, just for a second.

Then she says, "We're just talking about you, Ginny, and how I can help you. You can work on understanding what people are thinking. I'm sure you feel lonely. Especially with your parents gone."

"They're not gone." *Shit*. "It feels like they're with me, I mean, since I live in the house. With everything of theirs still there. I know they're dead, of course. Anyway, I don't feel lonely." I qualify it in my mind to make it true. Not right now. Not every day.

"Maybe you could tell me some of what you're feeling, then."

"Maybe," I say, crossing my arms deliberately, "you're just trying to sucker me into staying here longer and talking to you longer so you can report back your conclusions or whatever to my conniving sister."

"I'm not going to report anything to her at all," says Dr. Stewart. "This conversation is between you and me."

If that's how she's going to play it, then I will too. "So tell me," I say. "How would my parents have known? Say I was five years old. How would my parents know that I had this syndrome? What would I have acted like?"

She says, "Certainly that's an age when a neurotypical child would be socializing, reaching out, learning to interact with other children. While an Aspergian child is more likely to withdraw, be private."

"That just sounds like a normal kid," I say, and I word it that way on purpose, and I think of Shannon standing on the bottom step and reaching out for Midnight's soft, swishing tail.

"The definition of normal is a lot more expansive than most people think," she says. "I would never say you're not normal."

"We're not talking about me," I say. "We're talking about a hypothetical five-year-old."

"You're right, you're right. The hypothetical five-year-old might have an exceptional memory, beyond what's typical of a child that age. The ability to recite an entire page of a book or a conversation she had three months ago, word for word. And as I said, there's the avoidance of eye contact, which is common, and often there's a tone of voice too. A way of speaking that sounds less natural to a neurotypical person, who would describe it as emotionless or robotic."

I think about Shannon's voice. She sounds like a little girl. "And that's how you know? The tone of voice?"

"Again, there's so much variation, it's hard to say."

"If it's so hard to say, then how do you know? If this hypothetical five-year-old is just a five-year-old like all the others, or something else?" I'm getting nervous now. I tap my fingertips in patterns on the table, one two three four five four three two one two three and so on.

"Largely, it's a matter of degree. Most children get deeply interested in certain things, and most of them become attached or averse to certain tastes and textures. But an Aspergian child's interests are deeper, their aversions are stronger. Here's another way to look at it. A neurotypical child might refuse to eat white food. An Aspergian child might react with anger when a plate of white food is placed in front of him, and either scream or throw the plate or cover it with something so he doesn't have to look at it."

I notice something. "You keep saying 'might.'"

"It's a spectrum, Ms. Selvaggio," she says, uncrossing her legs and leaning forward. "It manifests differently in different people. It's the same spectrum as autism, and some cases are right on the line. The example of white food, let's keep looking at that. An autistic child is less likely to be able to express that he doesn't want the white food, he's more likely to express himself by throwing and pushing the plate. That's one end of the spectrum. But because Aspergians can express themselves in words, they have more ways to deal with their aversions or indulge their interests. Some of them use their interests to become very successful, actually. There's a very popular theory in the Aspergian community that Albert Einstein had Asperger's. But that's neither here nor there. Aspergians can often find a way to deal with their aversions and interests, either through accommodation or behavioral modification. I generally recommend behavioral modification."

"What does that mean?"

"In a sense, you can train yourself out of certain behaviors. Especially if you start young. If you accommodate too much, the person's behaviors, even the more unusual ones, just become part of the fabric. Like if a child has a tantrum. You can allow them to have tantrums whenever they want, or you can teach them that a tantrum won't get them the desired goal, and eventually, they'll stop throwing tantrums."

"So I'm like a child?"

"That's not what I said, and remember, you said we're not talking about you."

I take a deep breath. And in my mind, a leap. I say, "Okay. Let's do it. Just for a minute. Let's talk about me."

"Okay. The tantrum example is just that, an example. Tell me about a coping behavior you have. Don't worry, we're not putting you in a box with this. Everybody has coping behaviors. I do, your sister does, so does the president of the United States. When you're uncomfortable or unhappy, how do you cope?"

"Food."

"Eating?"

"No, I just think about a food. Its flavor and shape, or the different ways you can use it, or the process of cooking something."

"Give me an example."

I tell her about caramelized onions. How heat transforms. How they go from white and raw and crunchy to soft and melting and sweet. I describe the whole process.

She says, "That's great to work with. So you're uncomfortable, like maybe someone tries to touch your arm? And you don't like that, so you close your eyes and in your mind you walk through the process of caramelizing onions. Is that what happens?"

"Yes."

"It interrupts the conversation, right? If you're feeling this way with other people around and you need to soothe yourself with this thought of food, it takes a few minutes?"

"Yes."

"One behavioral modification would be training yourself to get all the benefit of the coping mechanism without going through the whole process. Finding a way to just close your eyes and think 'caramelized onions' and be calm. Then you could open your eyes and continue the conversation. The other person wouldn't even notice."

It sounds so reasonable.

Now's the time. I brace myself. "So, Doc, do you think I have it?"

There's a long, horrible moment when she says nothing and I feel like a skinned side of beef in a meat locker hanging, hanging, hanging.

"It's not like that," says Dr. Stewart. "It's not like a rash or a broken bone. I can't just spot it. I'd have to go through some screening questions with you, which I'd be very happy to do, either now or at some other time." I tense up at the word "screening" but let her continue. "You're obviously a very intelligent young woman. I'd ask you questions about how you perceive certain things, how you react in certain situations. As I said earlier. This conversation between us is private. Your sister made the appointment, but my allegiance isn't to your sister. It's to you. If you want to come back, we can talk about hypotheticals, or we can talk about you, and behaviors that you have that you'd like to change, and some ways that you might modify those behaviors."

"You make it sound so easy."

"It is and it isn't. Everybody struggles with this stuff, you know. With social discomfort and grief and fitting in. People with syndromes, people with disorders, people with diagnoses and without. People who would be classified as neurotypical. Idiots and geniuses, maids and doctors. Nobody's got it all figured out."

"Not even you?"

"Not even me."

"So . . . it doesn't actually matter whether I have it at all?"

"I didn't say that," she says. "But you want my personal opinion? It matters a lot less than some people think it does."

WHEN I LEAVE Dr. Stewart's office I have a warm feeling, but when I step outside and the cold hits me things change. She was nice, but she didn't have to be. Amanda didn't know she would be. Amanda sent me there blind to be analyzed and found wanting, and I don't know if I can forgive her for that.

All the way home I make promises. Ten, twenty, thirty. I will never speak to Amanda again. I will curl up on the kitchen floor and stay there for three weeks. I will take a vow of silence and keep my hands in my pockets so I can't speak even in signs. I will take a shower for a thousand years. I will dial up some ghost with a grudge and send it like a hellhound against all who have wronged me. Amanda, for suckering me like that. Brennan, for not stopping her. Angelica, who would be happy to help take my house away. Ma, for abandoning me by dying. Dad, the same. I didn't realize I was angry at my parents until now. And it's not their fault, but that doesn't change how I feel. They could still be here. But they're not. Things would be better if they were.

By the time I'm home, and the gray sky has begun to drizzle rain over what's left of our snow, my anger is gone. Drained out. No one really deserves my fury but Amanda.

I look at the closet, a small, dark refuge, and I think about what Dr. Stewart said. Is it that easy? Just find a way to get the effect without indulging in the behavior? Or is she, like Amanda, just trying to sucker me in? That happened. People taking advantage of me just because they could. Maybe that's it. Maybe she's just pretending to be on my side so she can get me diagnosed and put a word on me.

If that's the case, I've screwed up something awful. Even the little bit I told her feels like too much. But the words won't go back in my mouth once spoken. Food can't be uneaten. A precious few things in this life are reversible.

Instead of sitting in the closet I go up to my room and stare at the piles of paper. This is who I was as a child. This is what I thought, what I did, how I felt.

I go over my piles again. Second grade, third grade, fourth, fifth, sixth. Six five four three two.

One?

There's got to be another box.

I go down to my old room on the second floor and I get down on my knees to look and I stretch my arm into the back of the closet, feeling for an edge.

Against the back wall I find a suitcase. It's easy to lift because it's empty. Behind the suitcase, I see another square corner, and it makes me sit down hard on my heels. The other cardboard box. The other half of my childhood.

This one is pushed all the way back to the deepest reaches of the closet. It's been sitting here in the dark for years. It might as well have grown mushrooms.

One, and everything that came before one. That's what this box is. Everything, all of it, all the way back to the baby book. If I remember right, my baby book wasn't particularly well filled out, but at least I had one. Amanda didn't. But I don't want to think about Amanda right now.

I'm tempted to pull the box out and open it right there, but I take it down to my parents' room instead. It's the largest room, so I can spread everything out on the floor all together. I bring in all the piles from my room. Two, three, four, five, six. I open the top of the new old box. The ancient masking tape protests, crackles, and gives way.

As I'm drawing out the first of the papers, I hear what sounds like the noise of the front door. I sit back and wait, listening.

No feet in the hall, no feet on the steps. Must have been a car door slamming outside. Midnight scratches at a door somewhere, lightly. After that I hear no sounds. I quickly become absorbed in the contents of the box. Then there is nothing but the childhood me that I can think of.

This one is the opposite of the other. The layers of age run in reverse. So the oldest thing is the one on top. The baby book. The cover is checkered pink and blue, indecisive. I open to the first page, the first entries. My weight and length at birth. The hospital where I was born, Pennsylvania Hospital, Dad's hospital, just a block away. More pages, more notes. A lock of hair. A picture of me with Grandma Damson, somewhere, smiling. Ma's handwriting, neat. She's entered the dates when I first held up my head, first sat up, first rolled over. My first word was *da-da*. Everything after that, blank.

I dig down through successive layers. My childhood self moves through the years. Handprints in clay, one of them broken across the weak middle. An ornament I clearly had some help making, red and green foil layered into a star. A coloring book, some pictures colored inside the lines, some not. I have to smile when I see a house with a purple roof and a yellow sky. Even then I had my own ideas.

A tiny figure made of homemade Play-Doh. There was a flour paste we used to make, I remember that now. Amanda loved the commercial stuff because of the bright colors. I preferred homemade, because it looked more natural. Never mind that my tiny Play-Doh people didn't look like people and my clumsy Play-Doh horses didn't look like horses. They were all blobs with more legs and arms than necessary. Dad had always praised them but they were far from accurate. And he always made things out of the Play-Doh too. Models of nerves and hearts and other parts of people. Impossibly detailed. But then he always let me mash them up into my less perfect works.

Tucked into the corner of the box, flattened and crumbly with age, is one of these tan animals. I don't know what I thought it was at the time. Right now, it bears a faint, equal resemblance to a dog and a cat and a horse and a lion. I'm pretty sure it's not supposed to be a person, because the ears are atop the head instead of on the sides. But this is very early work. I might have made a mistake on anatomy. The perfect understanding of how bodies are constructed, how they come apart and are put back together, I never learned that from Dad or anyone.

I continue making piles. First grade, kindergarten, preschool, younger. The box slowly empties out.

The last thing in the box is a square of folded paper. Badly wrinkled, squished by the weight of all these years. I try to unfold it without damaging it as best as I can.

Dad's handwriting. I recognize it because it's the only handwriting familiar to me that's even less legible than mine. Tailless As that look like Os, strange half-cursive Fs that too closely resemble Ps.

Dad's handwriting.

Familiar, powerful words. *Flour. Water. Cream of tartar. Salt. Oil.*

A recipe.

Something that was his. Something I'd forgotten. That homemade Play-Doh recipe. Whether he made it up himself, whether he copied it out of a book, I have no idea. And it wasn't in the kitchen because it hasn't been needed there for nearly twenty years. So it went to the back of the closet, with the memories.

It may not be food, but it's a recipe. Something of his I can make.

He might come.

I can hardly breathe.

Carefully, I lay the recipe aside. I step back from it. I've never held anything more precious. Really, I don't trust myself to hold it at all.

I have to think about this. Something I wanted so much and now it's here, and I don't know what to do.

Who can I talk to? Not Amanda, not right now. Angelica's phone number is on the refrigerator but since Amanda's cut me off she's worse than useless. The list of people I actually know is a very short list. I think of David, but I don't have a phone number for him, only the address in the kitchen drawer I sent the check to, and I think the only thing he knows about my dad is the evidence of his own healed palm, impeccably stitched.

But Gert. Gert knows more. I'll ask Gert what she thinks. I can't tell her the whole truth of it, but I can ask her about my dad, and maybe that will help me figure out what to do. She knows him. Knew him. She can advise me. Someone needs to. Once I do it, it can't be undone.

I call her.

"Gert?"

Her familiar voice says, "Yes, it is Gert."

"It's Ginny."

"Ginny! I was just wanting to call you."

"Yeah?"

"Yes. Well, I had hoped you would help me cook some more again."

"Oh," I say, remembering the family sitting shiva for their dead relative. It feels like a year ago. It was the day before yesterday. "For the burial committee?"

"Not quite the same. No one is dead."

"Good."

"It is still a sadness, though. I can explain more when I see you. Will you come to the temple now?"

"Now, okay."

"Do you know the way?"

"Yes, I know the way. I'll call if I get lost."

I mean to leave right away but it takes me more than half an hour. First I can't even get out of the hallway. Every time the recipe is out of my sight I have to turn back to look at it again. Each time I see it I'm reassured, but when I look away I worry that I've misunderstood it, that I'm somehow mistaken. But it's still there. It's still something my dad wrote that I can cook.

I want to see him.

This is the way.

So then I stare at the recipe for a while trying to decide if I should take it with me. I get downstairs with it but then decide folding it is a bad idea. It's weak and might crumble away, losing a letter somewhere important. I don't want to just leave it sitting out so I look for somewhere to hide it. I don't want to slide it up into the chimney with the other things I'm hiding there, nor slide it under the mattress with the envelopes of cash, because it's so fragile. I open the top drawer of the bureau where I left Ma's Bible, but the Bible isn't there. Amanda must have put it in a box. I don't know anywhere that's safe. In the end I tuck it into the back of a cookbook, the same one Nonna's recipe fell out of, *Tuscan Treasures*. I put it on the top shelf and close the doors over it.

When all this is done I walk to the temple. I remember the turns. Right, left, right. When I see Gert I can ask her advice.

I walk through the large darkened worship room. I don't know what it's called. In the church they called the room like this a sanctuary, which I always liked. *Sanctuary* is on a page with *sanitize* and *Santa Claus*. As I approach the kitchen, I walk into waves of smells. I'm late.

Gert says, "Come in, I was beginning to worry about you."

The red-haired woman is there, and another woman too. They only glance at me, then go back to their work. Chicken broth is bubbling on the stove. I smell raw flour, beef, thyme.

Gert explains, "Remember I said death is not the only cause for grieving. This family has a five-year-old daughter. She is having bone marrow transplant, and keem . . . keem . . ."

The red-haired woman says, "Chemotherapy," and then goes back to shaping small balls of dough.

"So they have no time to cook. But they must eat. So we help them."

The women are working mostly from memory, but I see a scrap of paper here and there. I can't be completely sure they're not recipes. I don't know if it's possible to invoke a ghost anywhere other than my own kitchen, but I see no reason to chance it. So I help the others. I cut garlic in slivers, onions in half-moons. Chop shallots. Make carrots into coins. I slice scallions straight across and on the diagonal. I'm distracted, wondering when and how to catch Gert's attention so I can ask her advice. Slicing too fast, I cut off one of my fingernails but manage to catch it and drop it down the drain before anyone notices. It would have been a disaster otherwise. Once sliced, a fingernail and a scallion are not easy to tell apart at a glance.

We make casseroles and soups. Things that will keep. Things that will freeze. Things easily retrieved and reheated. Chicken soup with the matzoh balls the red-haired woman makes. A vegetable-filled lasagna with carrots and peppers and cheese. Beef stew, heavy with garlic and thyme and tomatoes.

For once, I don't disappear into the recipe. I enjoy the feeling of cooking, and everything comes out as it should. But there's a whole process running in the background. The whole time the thought of my father's ghost is bubbling up like the air in the simmering broth, *dad dad dad,* filling every moment.

Mix dough. Cut noodles. Poach chicken. I try not to think of Dad, and put my mind on the little girl whose family we're helping. She's a sick little girl, and I hope what we're doing is enough to help her be just a little girl again. I don't know what she looks like, so I guess it's unavoidable. When I think of her, I picture Shannon.

We pack the trunk of the car with food in coolers, and I ride in the backseat to a brick two-story house, larger than I expected. The first thing I see is a tricycle in the flower bed and then I just look at my lap. I don't get out of the car. Gert does, but only to stand on the porch for a moment. This time, we drop off the dishes without going inside. Our food pays the visit on our behalf. Being there in person would be less welcome. We would be a distraction, and they don't want a distraction.

I look up at the house and see the shape of the father in the window, looking out at me. I don't have to read his face or talk to him to know how he feels. I put myself in his shoes. He has a small daughter who loves and trusts him, and he wishes more than anything he could help her, but he's powerless. I realize I don't need to talk to Gert, I don't want her advice. I already know what I'm going to do.

CHAPTER ELEVEN

Homemade Play-Doh

combine
1 c flour   1 c boiling water
2 t cream of tartar
.5 c salt
1 t oil

Everything is sitting on the counter, ready. Flour. Salt. Cream of tartar. The boiling water, already rolling, will soon start to boil away.

I can do this if I want. I can put the dough together. And maybe, if I do that, Dad will appear on the stool in the corner of the kitchen. I will see him in the clothes he was wearing when he died. I won't be able to put my arms around him but I could pretend. If I let my arms hover in the air near where he appeared. It might be almost as good as a hug.

The recipe is set far away from anything that might stain or stick. Next to it is Dad's letter to Ma, the one asking for forgiveness. Next to that are the pictures, all twenty-nine photographs of Evangeline, in the right order. Ma said she was just a nurse at the hospital and nobody important. Now I can ask someone else's opinion.

Quick as I can, I pour in all the powders. A cup of flour into a cup of boiling water. The cream of tartar, the salt, the oil. The powder swirls in the water, at first separate and then coming together. The salt cuts down and through. The oil bubbles and fights and pulls into itself before surrendering into the rest of the ingredients. The recipe only says to combine. I don't have instructions. So I stir and stir in the hope everything will come together into a paste.

I breathe shallowly, up in my throat, and look at the stool.

Nothing.

I look back at the recipe, checking over it, though I've checked over it a dozen times. A dozen feels like a thousand. I check it once more. Concentrate. Read it out loud. Two teaspoons of cream of tartar. Half a cup of salt. One teaspoon of oil.

I stir again. I look over the spoons and the half-cup measure and the spatula and the pot. The heat. It's all what it's supposed to be.

But the dough won't come together. And on the stool, nothing. No one.

There must be a mistake somewhere.

I wake up the computer, tap one two three four five four three two one while I wait for Kitcherati to load. Even the moment it takes feels too long, and I try to settle myself down with the thought of brown, rich, nutty sesame oil again, but the mental image of the vegetable oil dripping into the failed dough keeps intruding. I search for a thread that talks about homemade modeling clay, hoping maybe that will give me a clue.

There are several, and I read them all. Advice on what to do, what not to do. Don't add too much salt. Don't add liquid food coloring because it throws off the proportions, use gel or paste instead. Don't let your pets eat it. I find a recipe that's very similar to Dad's, but instead of teaspoons of cream of tartar, it calls for tablespoons.

I look at Dad's scrawled recipe again.

It looks like a small t, which means *teaspoon*. Big T means *tablespoon*. I only confused the two once, when I was nine. But maybe Dad didn't know. How would he? This is his only recipe.

I can picture his handwriting perfectly, but right now, I don't need to. I reach for the letter.

> *it's not so great*
> *can't pretend it's not*
> *take responsibility*
> *anything between us*

The crossbars on his Ts are high up, sometimes all the way on top. Most of the time it wouldn't matter. In this case it does. If these are tablespoons, it makes all the difference.

I boil the water again. Set the powders out again. Try to control my breathing again. Fight the ache and the rising panic again.

A cup of boiling water swallows a cup of dry, soft flour. Drinks in two tablespoons of cream of tartar, blazing white. Absorbs half a cup of salt and turns grainy against the stirring spoon. A tablespoon of oil sits on top of the paste and then, with repeated stirring, slowly starts to sink back in. The spoon is pushing against something now solid.

It's sticky and unpleasant. The smell of the flour isn't a delicious one. It's functional. But it's a smell.

Dad resolves on the stool.

He is wearing an old pair of his scrubs, soft with age, most of the blue rubbed right out of the fabric. Ma could never get him to wear pajamas. He is solid. Feet and legs and arms and hands and head. All there. Dad.

He says, "Hey, *uccellina*."

Cropped white hair, small ears, tomato juice voice. Exactly as I remember. My father, here in the kitchen.

I can barely put the words together to say "Hi, Dad."

He says, "I'm so sorry, Ginny. I hope everything is okay. I hope you are okay. I didn't mean to leave you for good."

I know his voice so well but this is the first time I understand it. His voice reminds me of tomato juice because there's a metallic note to it. His words are even, measured. I look into his face and he doesn't meet my eyes.

I never realized.

I can't spare the time to think about it. I don't know how long he'll stay. I thrust the pictures in his direction and say, "Dad, who is this?"

"Why would you want to talk about her?" he says. "This was a very long time ago. Twenty years."

"But who was she?"

"She was a nurse at the hospital. Evangeline."

"Why did you take pictures of her?"

"She was nice, she let me," says Dad.

"Let you what?"

"Take the pictures of her. Isn't that what we're talking about?"

"But why did you want to?"

Dad puts the heels of his hands down on his knees and stares at the floor between them. His lips are moving slightly and I think he may be counting the squares.

"Dad?"

He says, "It was for practice. This is how I pretended there was someone looking at me, and I practiced looking back, until it didn't feel so strange anymore. I never got to like it, but it bothered me less."

I've gotten it all wrong. The pictures are important, but not for the reason I thought. Ma was right. I didn't understand.

"So . . . you weren't unfaithful to Ma?"

"I was faithful, always!" he says. "I was full of faith! Caroline loves me and I love her. Other women, they thought I was being mean to them on purpose, or I was stupid, or other things. I never got it quite right."

"Because you're . . . you were . . . like me."

"You always knew I was like you. We were like each other." He smiles, mouth closed, lips turned up at the right corner. I love that smile.

I say, "But not in this way."

"Not in what way?"

I clarify, "The syndrome." It's exhausting to lead the conversation. I feel like I'm dragging him along, word by word.

I can't tell if he's even heard me. His gaze is on my shoulder, the cabinets, the doorway, anywhere but my face.

He says, "I guess that's right. It didn't exist when I was a kid. They hadn't come up with it yet. So I never had a diagnosis, and they never put a word on me, and I turned out fine."

"Better than fine," I say.

"Caroline helped me," he says. "She was everything. Still is."

I have to stay focused. He could disappear at any moment. I say, "Dad. I have something else to ask you."

Dad says, "I could never say no to you, *uccellina*."

"Okay," I say. I hold the letter up, right in front of his face, so I know he sees it. "Why did you ask Ma to forgive you?"

He says, "Ginny."

"I just want to know what happened. What did you do?"

"Ginny."

"Dad."

He glances at my face for just a moment and then settles his gaze back on my shoulder again. "It's hard to talk about things like this. I don't like it."

"I don't like it either."

"THEN DON'T ASK!" he shouts, louder than I've ever heard

before. The words echo around the tiles and metal and up to the glass of the skylight.

We're both silent for half a minute. I can't stay quiet longer because I'm so afraid he's going to disappear.

"Dad," I say, "this is hard for me too."

He seems to consider this. He taps his fingers on his thigh, in a pattern, one two three four five four three two one two three four five.

I say, "Dad, please tell me. What were you sorry about?"

"I don't want to tell you."

"Tell me."

"Ginny."

"Dad."

"You," he mumbles down at the floor.

I don't know what to say. "Me?"

"You," he says, "I was sorry about you. That you're like me. Instead of like your mother."

"Instead of . . . normal?" I ask.

"No, you know, your mother never wanted to say it like that. She knew things were hard for me when I was young. So she was afraid for you and that's why I was so sorry I messed you up."

"Dad," I say, "you didn't mess me up." If he messed me up it means I'm messed up. Wrong. Not normal.

"I was afraid of it when I wrote the letter. But that was so long ago. You were only a year old then, but you were so sensitive to being touched, like I am, I thought it meant that you'd turn out exactly like me."

"It wouldn't be so bad to be exactly like you," I say, my voice coming out strangled.

"But I was lucky," Dad says. "I kept skipping class because I never saw the point of school, and they were going to kick me out, I was on my last warning and I went to science class and we were doing a dissection and it was all so clear to me. I could look at any part of any body and I could see how it fit together. But I especially liked hands. The superficial transverse ligament, here, the synovial sheath of the palm and the slip of the superficial fibers. It's very plain to me but everyone kept making me repeat it and then I realized it made me special. They said I was a genius, and I went through medical school, and your mother fell in love with me and taught me how to be more comfortable. And the hospital was very good to me because I'm so good at what I do and I made a lot of money for them. I got to a good place. But I didn't start out there."

"Dad—"

Dad says, "You seem okay, though. Maybe I didn't mess you up too much. I hope I didn't."

And then, terribly, too soon too soon too soon, he is fading.

I say, "Dad, I'm not messed up, Dad—"

And too soon, he is gone.

HEARTBREAK IS STUPID and impossible. Hearts don't break. Hearts squeeze, they wrench, they ache, they shrivel. Hearts pull apart in wet chunks like canned tomatoes. I go as deep as I can into the closet. It isn't enough. I wish there were a closet behind the closet, somewhere deeper to escape to. I turn my body toward the back of the closet and place my hands and forehead against the back wall. Turn my back on the world. Hide from the slightest hint of light.

I don't cry, but I ache. I ache because my father was sorry I was born, because I'm the way I am, and that's what he needed my mother to forgive him for. Me. I ache because I feel hopeless and sad that people were keeping so many secrets from me and I never knew. I ache because Ma spent all that time with me making sure I was okay and now that she's gone I'm falling apart.

I don't know how long I'm in the closet. Minutes. Hours.

But it doesn't matter. I don't leave the closet because I feel better. I don't feel better. I leave the closet because I need to take action, and there's only one way to do it. I make up my mind and squint into the light.

I may be strange and hopeless. I may be a disappointment to my father, the one person I thought always loved me exactly as I am. But now I know something I didn't know before, and I know who else needs to have that information. Dad had the syndrome and he found a way to succeed anyway. He found something he was good at and he used it. Maybe I could do the same. Cooking, I'm good at it, maybe I could use that to connect with the world instead of hiding away. But it's Shannon I'm thinking about. It may be too late for me. It's not too late for Shannon. If Amanda can help her, if she thinks about possibilities instead of diagnosis, Shannon could be okay.

My dad was normal in his own way and so am I and my heart is wrung out like wet cheesecloth and I am going to do something normal about it.

I dial Amanda's number, and it seems like it takes a long time for her to pick up. When she does, she asks, "Are you calling to apologize?"

"Apologize for what?"

"What you said about Shannon."

"I didn't say anything."

"You said you think she has the syndrome."

It takes me a few seconds to remember she hadn't read the e-mail last time we talked. It seems like forever since I sent it, so much has happened since. "I wondered if she might, and it wouldn't be so bad if she did maybe, and that's not the point."

"Oh, it's not? Then what is the point, Ginny, since you know so much, tell me, what's the point?"

"I don't know whether I have this syndrome or not," I say. "But if Shannon has it, you should—"

"If what? If Shannon what?"

She doesn't understand. And I'm so exhausted I don't know if I can make her understand anyway. I want to curl up on the closet floor. I find words. I don't know if they're the right ones.

"If Shannon has Asperger's."

"She doesn't," says Amanda. "My daughter is not . . . like that."

"If she is, it's okay."

"Okay?"

"It's no big deal."

"No big deal?" Amanda's laugh sounds red and raw like ground beef. "Spoken like someone who doesn't understand . . . who just . . . you don't understand anything at all. Not what it's like to deal with you, and not what it's like to be a mother."

I can't tell her what I want to tell her if I can't make her listen to me. I have to defend myself. "Of course I don't know what it's like to be a mother. I'm not one."

"That's right. So don't try to interfere with how I raise my children."

"I'm not trying to interfere. I'm just trying to—"

She cuts me off. "You know what? You're so all-fired excited to be left on your own, I think that's what I'll do. I'll just leave you on your own for a while. Like maybe forever. Maybe you can just live in that house that you're so attached to, and you can leave my family alone, and you can forget about me trying to help you get better and have a better life because I am just done with this, you understand me, Ginny? I am done with you."

She hangs up.

I'm scared, that's for sure. I know rage when I hear it. I heard it in Evangeline's voice and now I've heard it in my sister's voice, and it's so far from anything I've ever heard from her before.

It takes everything I have not to run straight to the closet but I clench my fists and plant my feet and don't let myself. Instead of giving in to the anger I analyze it. Take it as a given. If the milk goes sour, you use it like buttermilk. Pancakes, biscuits, things that need its acid. She's angry, I'm angry. She's furious, I'm furious. She doesn't know what's best for me and I can't communicate with her. If we were calmer I could tell her.

This syndrome, it affects our family, but it doesn't make us helpless. I'm not helpless. Dad wasn't helpless. If Shannon has it, she doesn't have to be helpless either, but the way to deal with it is to deal with it, not to hide her away from the world. I got hidden away and now it's harder to break out. I think I can. I don't think it's too late. The Normal Book had the right message, but I can't just read the message. I have to live it.

I go upstairs and retrieve the pictures of Evangeline from under the bed, and I leaf through them. She's not who I feared she was. My father didn't have an affair with her. Her ghost was terrifying, and I don't know what kind of person she was all her life, but once she was a young nurse who did someone a favor. She stood in the courtyard behind the hospital with an awkward young doctor she knew and looked toward him, looked away, let her picture be taken, because she wanted to be nice. There are people like that everywhere. People who will overlook my awkwardness. People who understand, like Dr. Stewart, that the word *normal* is inclusive. Maybe I can live in the world, and be who I want to be, after all. But what about Amanda? If my sister hates me, and my whole family's gone—

A memory comes to me. Five years old. Sitting on Nonna's lap and leaning against her soft angora sweater. I am telling her all about round things, *a biscuit cutter is round and the sun is and so is the moon, and a ring like you wear on your finger,* and picking bright, crunchy, candy-covered sunflower seeds out of her outstretched hand. I remember how much I loved that sweater. Six months after that she didn't wear the sweater anymore and I asked her why. She said, *When you cut yourself, you remember? The hand you cut. You went looking to find your father, you were hiding in the hospital. But anyone who try to help you, you no let them touch you. They tell me, after. You are so quiet until they try to look at your hand, and then you scream and run. They call me, I come. I hold you on my lap. And we wait until your father come. Hours we wait. But you are happy because of the sweater. And then when your father look at you, your hand, it is too late. He clean it out, sew it best he can. On the sweater, after, there is too much blood. It never come out.*

I had already learned to apologize. *Nonna, I'm sorry I ruined your sweater.*

And she said, *Oh,* uccellina, uccellina. *No you worry. Always there are other sweaters.*

Nonna is gone. Her sweater is gone. That memory, there's no part of it I can ever have back again, except the taste. I want the sunflower seeds, that exact kind. The kind in waxy, clingy chocolate with an unnaturally bright candy shell around the outside. I want to shake the long plastic package and hear the rain-stick sound it makes. If I can't have anything else from the past, I can at least have its taste.

So I grab the credit card and walk down to the Korean grocery, and it looks like it's going to be one of the nine out of ten uneventful trips. I get my sunflower seeds and a Fresca, and set them on the counter.

The woman behind the counter picks up my card, and I read the long list of ingredients on the back of the package of sunflower seeds while she handles it, *dehydrated cane juice cocoa butter whole milk powder chocolate liquor soybean lecithin carnauba wax*, and my attention is elsewhere so when she speaks to me I'm startled.

"No," she says.

For a moment I think she's trying to stop me from buying something she knows is bad for me. For a moment it's touching. Then she says "No" again, and taps the credit card, and I realize she's saying the card won't work.

Amanda.

She said she would leave me alone and see how I liked it. Apparently she's done more than that. Alone doesn't just mean without people. It can mean without anything else. And maybe, even without putting a word on me, she's found a way to take away things I thought were mine. If this is the start I have no way to know when it will stop.

I leave the candy on the counter and walk out, hoping hoping hoping no one will touch me as I leave because I don't think I could take it, and no one does, and I walk straight home almost running and the closet downstairs still has Dad's rain boots in it and thank goodness for that.

AN HOUR LATER, I go upstairs to my parents' room and find Midnight on the window seat. She blinks when I turn on the light. I lean back against the wall, and stroke the cat's soft fur, and take stock of the situation. I could take the cash from one of the envelopes, and pay for the sunflower seeds with that, but the short-term problem is not the real problem. It's the other things Amanda might be able to take away. She is cutting me off, cutting me out. I try to apply logic. On one hand, I can deal with that. I can get the card reactivated, I'm sure that won't be a problem. My name is on it. There's a number on the back. I can call. And maybe, if she leaves me alone for a while, that's okay. Because I've done what Nonna and Ma told me to do, what Dad tells me he and Ma were very careful to do my whole life. I've kept her from putting a word on me. She can live with her family and I can live by myself, and we'll all be happy with that, won't we?

But it's not all about me.

Do no let her. It's very important that you not let Amanda.

Maybe it's not me I'm not supposed to let Amanda put a word on.

Maybe, by trying to figure out what the ghosts want and blocking whatever it is they want blocked, I've actually made the thing they don't want come to pass. I was the one who suggested Shannon might have the syndrome. If Amanda puts a word on her, it's my fault, not hers. Mine.

I call Amanda, call her, call her. She won't pick up. She knows it's me. After ten o'clock at night I realize I need to stop calling, it's getting late, and when I try one last time she's turned her phone off anyway.

There is a kind of sleep where you're absolutely certain you were awake all night. That's the kind of sleep I have, waiting for morning, hoping tomorrow isn't too late.

CHAPTER TWELVE

Hot Chocolate

First thing in the morning I call the only person I can call.

"Gert, I need a favor."

"Of course. I will help you if I can."

"I need you to drive me somewhere."

"I am sorry, Ginny, this is something I cannot do. I have no car. I do not drive. I do not need to."

"Oh."

She says, "A few years ago David used to drive me where I needed to go."

"Does he still have a car?"

"He has it," she says. "He does not like to drive it, but he has it."

"Thank you," I say.

I try calling Amanda again, but the situation is the same. The first few times she lets it ring through to voice mail, then later, she turns the whole phone off.

I can't reach her this way, but I have to reach her. I'll have to try something else. List the options, figure out what's possible, make it happen.

This is one of Ma's lessons: *Sometimes you have to cut toward your thumb.* It was a hard lesson for me. It was a cut toward my thumb that scarred me, and all the books say not to do it. After I hurt myself, she took charge of me in the kitchen. She wouldn't let me touch the knives unless I promised to use them only on the cutting board. But when I was nine, she taught me a new lesson that contradicted the old one. She was showing me the secret of her potatoes au gratin. First, she taught me that au gratin doesn't mean cheese, like everyone thinks it does. Then, she taught me that everyone else slices their potatoes, but she chips them. And so I learned to chip.

You slice off a bit of the potato. It'll leave a point. See this here, this point? Then you cut that off. It makes this little kind of triangle shape. But now you have another place where too much potato sticks out. So you cut that off too.

I do as Ma says. In my mind, I chip the potato. Cutting off any part that sticks out. Cutting toward my thumb, though I had learned always to cut away. Cut, turn, drop, cut, turn, drop. Until my hands are sticky with starch. The starch makes them slippery, like oil, but white and powdery, like chalk. The heap of chipped potatoes grows on the cutting board. Cut, turn, drop. Cut, turn, drop.

In my mind the knife slips so fast I don't feel the pain until long after I'm cut and bleeding. A fat, thick, wet red bubbles up out of the gash. It isn't real but it still hurts.

It's time to cut toward my thumb in another way. I dig through the kitchen drawers until I find the scrap of paper bag I'm looking for. I look up the address on the Internet, and just put my feet on the sidewalk, and go.

THE HOUSE AT 114 Pine Street is a brownstone, flat and imposing, not as large as my parents' house but in the same classic Philadelphia style. I swing open an iron gate and go down a short set of stairs to the door marked 114A. Cold air settles into the stone. I knock. He answers, brown hair sticking up all over. I try to read his face. I can't imagine he feels anything but surprise.

"Oh, it's you!" he says.

"It's me."

"I got the check."

"That's not what I'm here about." I realize I'm not responding the way he expects. I add, "Good."

"Come on in before all that cold air ends up in here," he says, and I go in, and he shuts the door behind me. "You know, no one has ever visited me here before."

"Gert hasn't?"

"I always go to her apartment," he says. "She's come here once, maybe. I go over there, we have dinner, I stay overnight in my old room from when I was a kid. If she came here, she'd have to see what I have left of Elena. I'd have to be who I am instead of the one she wants me to be."

My eyes are still adjusting from the bright sun glinting off the snow outside. All I can tell is that the apartment is small and dark and warm.

He says, "Sorry, sorry. Pretty heavy conversation for me to lay on you first thing in the morning. But for some reason I always want to tell you everything. You're a good listener."

"I don't know if I'm that good," I say.

"Well, anyway. Sorry. My issues aside, how are you? How do you like the place?"

Now that my eyes have adjusted I can see that the apartment is a small room made smaller by the stacks of cardboard boxes lining each wall. Each one is labeled in Spanish, which I can't read. There's only enough room for a bed, a chair, and something that looks like a lamp with a brightly patterned cloth draped over it. The cloth on the lamp is the only color in the room. The only window I see is here, high up, near the door.

"It's like being in a 250-degree oven," I say to David.

"Is it that hot?"

"No, I mean, it's dark, and warm. Two hundred and fifty degrees is a good warming temperature. It's the lowest a lot of ovens go." I'm struggling to make conversation, to be polite, not to let what I want override everything else. It's hard. I don't think I'm doing it right. But if I just tell David what I want from him with no conversation at all, I know he's less likely to help me. We need to go through this process.

"Oh."

He says, "Well, let me show you around the place."

"I think I can see everything."

"Everything but Tambo," he says, and reaches for the cloth I thought was covering a lamp. It isn't a lamp at all. It's a birdcage.

Inside is a single bird, very small, drab in color. Black on the top of its head and under the beak where its chin would be if birds had chins, white on the sides of the head, tan on the breast. Not much bigger than David's thumb. Not an exotic bird. Just like the ones I see flying around outside. It looks like it has soft feathers. It flicks its black-and-white tail from side to side.

"She was Elena's," he says. "Her favorite kind of bird."

"What kind?"

"Chickadee. She just loved that word. It was her favorite English word. When she found out we had chickadees in Pennsylvania, she was so excited, and we'd go out biking to try to spot them. So when she found an injured baby one, you should have seen her. There was no question. She was going to save that bird. And she did. She didn't let Tambo die, and I haven't either."

I can't wait any longer. "David, I have a favor to ask you."

"What is it?"

"I need you to take me to my sister's house."

"Where's your sister's house?"

"Out in Haddon Township." I keep looking at the bird. It shakes its wings, in a tiny rippling motion, a kind of shiver.

David says, "What, you want me to ride the train with you?"

"No."

"We won't both fit on the bike."

"No, I want you to drive me," I tell him.

Silence at first. Then David says, spitting the words out like cherry pits, "You want me. To get behind. The wheel of a car."

"Your mom says you still have the car."

"You asked her first?"

"Yes."

"And she sent you to me."

"Not really." I tell the truth. "She said you have a car."

"She's not stupid enough to think I'll drive it."

"Why not? Why do you have it if you don't drive it?"

"Do I have to spell it out for you? Do you remember this?" He thrusts out his hand toward me and I see the thick scar where my dad sewed his fingers back on. As much time as he's had to heal, it still looks raw.

"Your accident," I say, realizing. "You were driving."

"And that was the last time I drove, and I killed my wife doing it. So you'll understand why I'm not exactly eager to hop behind the wheel." His voice is the darkest I've ever heard it, all the chocolate notes smothered under seething, spreading mud.

"Just this once," I say, desperate. "It's a beautiful day. The weather's fine. It's an easy drive."

He says, "You have a sick sense of what's easy."

"I'm sorry," I say. I force myself to look away from the bird, at him. I get as far as his chin. "I'm not good at this. I know that. I know I'm weird and quirky and I don't act the way you expect polite people to act. I'll never really know all the rules. So I say things wrong and I do things wrong. But I'm a person and so are you and I just need this one favor. It will make a huge difference for me. I need to see my sister, and I need you to take me to her."

He says, "No."

"No?" My stomach feels like it's full of cookie dough.

"Look at it from my position," he says. "You're asking me to do something I am really terrified of doing, and you haven't even given me a good reason."

"I have to tell Amanda something."

"Call her."

"I have been. Since yesterday, over and over. She won't answer. She doesn't want to hear what I have to say."

"What's it about?"

"It's private."

David snaps, "Be private and take the subway, then."

"The subway doesn't go to her house."

"Call a cab."

"Amanda put a hold on my credit card," I say. "And all the cash I have isn't enough to pay for it." I've put several twenty-dollar bills in the pocket of my jeans, but I know they'll only cover the trip out, not the trip back. And I have to come back. I don't know what I'll find there.

"You can find a better way. A different way. Don't ask me to do this. Not unless you can give me a really good reason."

My heart is beating so hard I can hear it. I need something to calm me. Something sweet and rich and decadent. Not chocolate, not pie. There it is. Tres leches cake. A white cake waiting in a white porcelain baking dish. Cream pouring down, not a drizzle, but a thick, steady, heavy stream. Soaking into the dry sponge of the cake. Being drunk up hungrily. Seeming to disappear, but changing everything. Texture. Taste. The cake can't stay the way it is. Without all three milks it's too dry. It has to change.

I open my eyes. I'm willing to risk everything.

"I can help you see your wife again," I tell him.

"What did you say?"

"Just what you think I said. It sounds crazy, but it's true. I can help you see your wife again."

He sits hard on the bed, springs up again, clenches his fists, unclenches them. It's too much motion for a tiny room. I take a step back toward the door. "That is sick, Ginny, just sick. My wife is dead. You know that."

"I do! That's why I'm the only one who can help you. I can see ghosts."

"That's ridiculous."

"I know. I know. It is." The air in here is getting hotter, harder to breathe. It feels even more like I'm inside an oven. I scramble to make myself make sense. "I never believed in ghosts either. Not till I saw one. But ever since my parents died, I can make something from a recipe, and I can see the ghost of the person who made it."

"That is . . . I don't know . . . it's ridiculous, that's all I can think, ridiculous."

"But it's true."

"But it's ridiculous."

I ask him, "Do you have a recipe?"

"For what?"

"Doesn't matter. Anything. Anything of Elena's. Any recipe she wrote."

"Yes."

Everything is uncertain. I am running out of strategies and he doesn't believe me. I don't know how to make him. "Tell me about it. The recipe."

He gulps in air and says, "Okay, yes, I have her recipe for aji de gallina. It's a Peruvian dish, her favorite, with chicken and potatoes.

In a yellow sauce. When we were dating she gave it to me and said if I could make it I would impress her. I never made it but she married me anyway."

I still need to know one more thing. "And is it . . . from a book, or—"

"She wrote it down for me," he says.

He fumbles with his wallet and drops it on the carpet. I don't bend to pick it up, we are too close in here. He opens the wallet and pulls out a folded piece of paper. The chickadee softly chirps three notes.

Carefully, David unfolds the paper and spreads it out on the bed. He beckons me over, and I cross the short space to look.

A handwritten recipe. Sharp slanted letters and numbers, all leaning right. Faded, but whole.

In a quiet, hard voice like a brick, David says, "Is this what you need?"

"Yes. Her handwriting. I'll make the recipe, and she'll come. I promise."

"You promise?"

"Yes."

"It's not enough," he says. "I can't believe you, it's just not possible."

He lifts his hand quickly and I think for a second he's going to hit me, so I step back, but I trip on a box and land hard on the bed, on my side. Without thinking about it I hold up my hand as if that will keep him from hitting me if that's what he wants to do. This is why my mother wouldn't let me get into these situations. I can't read them. I can't save myself if someone has bad intentions.

David says, "Don't be afraid," and I realize I shouldn't be. He isn't going to hurt me.

He grabs my extended hand.

"Your dad," he says.

I wonder if he wants to know if I've seen the ghost of my dad. I start, "Yesterday, he said—"

"Don't," David interrupts. "I don't want to talk about ghosts."

I don't know what he's saying.

He places the palm of his hand against mine. His hand is dry and firm. I feel the warmth of his skin. One scar against another.

David says, "For your dad's sake, I'll do it. Because he helped me."

I sit up. "You'll do it?"

"Yes," he says. "I'll take you to your sister's."

IT TAKES A WHILE to find the keys, but I don't rush him. Any minute he could still change his mind. It's a terrible thing to ask of him, but I need his help. And I've promised something in return that he needs. Even if right now he doesn't believe me, or doesn't think that's what he wants. I promised. We won't know for a while who made the more dangerous bargain.

The garage is in back. It's musty and cobwebbed. The car is covered under a cloth, and when he pulls the cloth off, I see its silver sides are smooth and unmarked.

He answers my question before I ask it. "That's the worst part. I made her let me drive that day, it was her car, I shouldn't even have been behind the wheel. And if you ask me to say one more word about it we are not going anywhere. Okay?"

"Okay."

We get in the car. I hand him the directions. He nods, three times, and hands them back to me. We drive in silence, his hands high up on the wheel, my feet jammed hard against the floor. My legs are tense and straight as celery sticks.

The streets are familiar at first. Brick from the 1830s mixed with tall modern glass boxes, everything colorful and close together. Narrow, one-way streets, packed tight. Then things open up a bit more. We take the parkway, moving north. Roadways blur into one another.

Wide, gray streets. A long bridge, soaring upward. With the gray sky there is little to see. The warm, dry air of the car makes me sleepy. I almost give in to it. My head lolls against the window.

From the other side of the car, David says, "Ginny? You all right?"

"I'm okay."

"You don't look okay," he says. "You look awful."

"You look awful," I say. It's a reflex.

"I suppose I do. This isn't easy for me."

I apologize, not as a reflex, but because I mean it. I shouldn't have put him through this. "I'm sorry."

"Me too," he says, his eyes on the road.

We arrive before I realize we've turned off the parkway. The house is large and white. I don't know how to describe it. I never learned the words for architecture. With all the things I threw myself into between my childhood and now—round things, and ESP, and Turkish rug patterns, and letters written by nuns, and food, so much food—I was never all that interested in houses. I've only been here twice before. It looks big and comfortable. It looks like a place real people live.

"Okay," he says. "I'll wait here."

I remind myself, this is what I wanted. Before I can second-guess myself into inaction I push the door of the car open and stride up to the front door, rapping on it with my knuckles, rap rap rap a steady rap.

Nothing happens.

I turn my fist to the side and instead of rapping I'm pounding, and I realize how desperate I am to see Amanda's face appear at the door, so I pound, and I pound, slamming my fist into the wood of the door like I'm crushing a bagful of graham crackers, but the firm wood doesn't yield, not even a little.

"Amanda!" I shout. "Amanda!"

I think I see little faces at the window, but it could be my imagination.

Someone is coming up next to me on the porch, and I think for a second it's David, but he's still in the car. Brennan must have come out of a side door, or the garage, maybe. He steps up onto the porch with me and I back into the only space left, against the door.

"Stop shouting," he says.

"I'll stop shouting when she comes out. Amanda!"

"No, stop shouting," he says, and reaches for my mouth with his hand. I smack his arm, hard. He yanks it back.

He glares at me and I make myself glare back at him, gaze locked, silent.

Brennan says, "Ginny, she doesn't want to talk to you."

"It'll only take a minute," I say.

"She's not coming out."

I try to tell him. "I just want to explain to her, it's the family, she doesn't know about Dad, and the syndrome, and me, if it's Shannon, there are so many different points on the spectrum she shouldn't be afraid—"

"Listen. Don't tell me either. I'm trying to deal with two scared little girls and their hysterical mother, she is so worked up about this, I can't even tell you. Yesterday instead of putting the girls to bed she locked herself in the bathroom and sobbed on the phone to Angelica for an hour. Maybe two."

He turns and looks in the front window. I follow his gaze but no one is there. He says, "I don't know if she even slept last night. I've never seen her like this. She said all she ever tried to do was help, and now you've gone crazy, and she's washing her hands of you."

"I'm not crazy," I say. "I'm normal."

He pauses and puts his fingers and thumb across his forehead, pinching, like he's trying to press through to his brain. "I'm not going to debate this with you. Honestly, this whole thing is awful. I think you're both having a lot of trouble dealing with—you know, your parents. And you really need each other, but you don't know how to handle what's going on, and you just can't see straight. So go home and cool off. And try this another day."

"But it's important."

"It'll still be important tomorrow."

"It's about Shannon."

"Shannon's fine," he says. "Shannon's inside the house right now. Nothing's going to happen to her."

"But I want to tell—"

"Ginny," he says. "Please. Whatever it is you want to say, Amanda's not ready to hear it. The longer you stay here the more the neighbors will stare. And the more the neighbors stare the madder she'll get. She cares how things look and this looks bad. You want to give her some time to calm down."

I say, "Is that what I want?" I intend it to sound defiant, but it comes out in a soft, questioning voice, and that's how I find out I don't really know. I don't know what I want. I don't know who I am or what's going on or what to do.

Brennan says, "Go home, Ginny."

And I go. I climb back into the car. I close the door and the sound of it closing is too loud. I look up to see if Brennan is still on the porch, but he's gone inside. The house presents a blank face. Nothing in the window but a curtain.

David asks, "Did it work?"

"No."

"I'm sorry."

I say, "Not your fault," but even the effort of getting those few polite words out undoes me, and I drop my head down to my knees and reach for some kind of food memory but I can't find anything, my brain won't put it together, matambre lungo fleur de sel zeppole. The rush of the car's engine as it starts. Blood orange, think of oranges, think of citrus, lemon, lime. We're in motion. I can't get food and I can't get in the closet so I hug my knees and rock and I don't know there's a noise coming out of me until David says something.

"Shhhh. Easy, Ginny, easy," he says. "It'll be okay."

"No it won't! It won't be okay!"

David says, "It might."

I press my head against my knees and feel the horrible ache in my stomach. Rocking gets me nowhere. Things are black. I keen but David doesn't tell me to be quiet so I keep keening and I try to find something, anything, to think about. We're in a car. A car. What's on a page with *car*?

Carpaccio. I latch onto it. I clutch my hands around the idea as if I could touch it. I think about all the different things a person could carpaccio. The only true carpaccio is beef, though it was an invented dish anyway, named for a painter, so *true* is a misnomer. Now it's anything sliced thin, usually raw. Scallop carpaccio. Portobello carpaccio, an invented dish from an invented mushroom. Sometimes chefs even extend it to dessert. Pineapple carpaccio, very difficult, since when you slice the outer layer of pineapple it tends to fall apart so you really need to slice it from the tender flesh right next to the core. People don't realize the heart of the fruit is often a different texture from the edge. Almost everything has its own kind of grain. You can only get a feel for it by handling it yourself. You have to learn to recognize the difference, feeling it resist your knife. What happens when you push, what happens when it pushes back, how you refine your approach to get just exactly the right amount of pressure. That's the only way you know.

"Ginny," says David's voice from far away. "Ginny."

I open my eyes. My right hand is stretched in front of me, bent at the wrist with the fingers curled together, as if I were holding a knife. I let the hand drop. We're sitting in front of my house, its stone steps reaching up to the portico, looking like a mile's climb.

"Let's get you inside," says David. "Okay?"

"Okay."

I push open the door. I expect my legs to be unsteady, but why should they be? It's my heart that's injured, not my body. Squeezed dry like a lemon wrung for juice. Collapsed like an overbeaten egg white. One foot in front of the other. Up the steps to the door.

When I get to the top of the stairs I notice his hand is on the small of my back, supporting me. Strange that I didn't even feel it. Amazing, even.

"Come on," he says, "inside. I'll help you."

"No more help," I say, and he takes his hand away, but as I walk inside he walks along behind me, until we get to the living room.

He says, "Sit down, you look like death. There's the couch."

I want to protest but I fall down onto it instead. I can't remember the last time I sat on the couch. For the first six months Ma wouldn't let us sit on it, and although that must have been at least ten years ago, it never felt right to disobey.

When I open my eyes again David is standing with his back to me facing the mantel, staring at a scrap of paper there. The recipe, of course. I know what he wants.

"I wasn't lying," I say. "I promised I'd bring her. I can do it right now."

"You can barely stand up right now," he says. "Stay there."

I stand up, just to prove I can. The edges of the plaster molding high above me swim a bit, then settle into place.

He says, with a biting, mineral edge, "Ginny, what's going on? Are you really just crazy, like your brother-in-law said?"

"No," I say firmly. I hadn't realized he heard the conversation. I hadn't thought about it. I play it back: *All she ever tried to do was help, and now you've gone crazy, and she's washing her hands of you.* "I'm not crazy."

"Did you tell your sister you can see ghosts? Is that what this is all about? And that's why she won't take your calls or see you?"

"No," I say, "she wants me to go to a doctor."

"Are you sick?"

"No. Well, she thinks so, that's what it's about. I won't get a diagnosis like she wants me to and I told her that her daughter might have the same syndrome she thinks I have."

"You have a syndrome?"

"I have a personality," I say, but it's just a reflex. Right now, I don't believe it.

"But it has nothing to do with the ghosts?"

"No, I haven't told her about the ghosts. But the ghosts, they had warnings, they warned me about her . . ." I trail off, because now I'm not sure I understood the warning. It was about Amanda, but was it also about me? Or Shannon? I don't think they know about Shannon, but even if that's not what the ghosts meant, she's more important. However I succeed or fail, it's up to me now. Shannon is so young. Her happiness depends on her mother.

"Tell me about the ghosts," David says. "No, wait. Let me make you some hot chocolate first."

My instinct is to say no—if I wanted some, I'd make it myself—but he's right. Drinking something warm might help this cold, hollow, exhausted feeling.

In the kitchen, I reach for the cocoa, but he says, "You let me do that, okay?"

I pull my hand back. "Okay."

He starts opening and closing cupboards, looking for things. He roots around in the junk drawer, not realizing right away that he won't find what he's looking for among the hammers and phone cords and index cards. I stay silent. Instead of wasting time disagreeing, I go over to the glass cabinets and take out *Drinkonomicon,* which I place on the counter next to the stove and open to the right page. In case he needs it. While he is knocking pieces of silverware together in a different drawer looking for the right spoon, I open the cookbook to the Hot Chocolate page.

"Oh, I don't need that," he says. "I'm going to make you my specialty."

"I thought you were going to make hot chocolate."

"I am. But mine is special."

"Okay."

"It's hot hot chocolate," he says. "There's a secret ingredient."

He holds up a spice jar he's taken off the shelf. Ancho powder.

"Okay," I say.

"Just wait till you taste it."

As David heats the milk on the stove, he says, "It's not just different, it's better. Amazing. After this you'll never make hot chocolate any other way."

"Won't I?" He's distracting me. Thank goodness.

"Well, if I were you, I wouldn't. Because it's the best. But if things that aren't the best are fine with you, by all means, go ahead."

He stirs the milk, which isn't boiling yet.

I say, "You can do that in the microwave, you know."

"I know."

"I don't think it tastes any different if you use the microwave."

"Hush. You have your methods, I have mine."

We stand in silence, his attention on the milk, my attention on him. I shift toward the refrigerator so I have a better view of what he's doing, and watch his hands. When little bubbles foam around the lip of the saucepan, he spoons in the sugar first, a spoonful at a time, then the cocoa, the same way. The milk goes tan, then brown, then almost a red-brown, even before the ancho powder goes in. This last spoon he tips in with a flourish, and stirs gently, the spoon not touching the bottom of the pan.

When it's all done, he fills two mugs, one green, one brown.

He hands me the brown one. The brown of the cup is a different, less interesting brown than the brown of the chocolate. I put both hands around the mug and inhale. The smell revives me.

"Why don't you hold it by the handle?"

I raise my face from the hot cocoa long enough to say, "Because I don't," and deeply inhale again. I am trying to discern the heat. The spice, I should say. It's in there, but deep.

"It's not poisoned," he says. "Drink it."

"I'm savoring."

"Oh. Well. That's okay then."

I take a sip. I open my mouth. I learned this from a Kitcherati thread on wine tasting, but it works on all the other kinds of tasting too. The air circulating in your mouth helps things land differently on your taste buds. You taste better with air.

"It's delicious." The cocoa is dusky. The milk, rich. The ancho adds an earthy note. The whole thing together is perfectly bitter and perfectly sweet.

"I knew you'd like it," he says.

We drink our chocolate, standing up in the kitchen. I can feel the cold trying to get in through the windows, but the warmth holds it off.

When I am halfway through my chocolate, David says, "Now. Ginny. Tell me about the ghosts."

I tell him everything, simply. The ribollita that brought Nonna. The shortbread that didn't bring Grandma Damson. The water and the wine and Necie. The brownies that brought Evangeline. Trying again with the ribollita to see Nonna, failing. The biscuits and gravy that brought Ma. The homemade Play-Doh recipe that brought Dad. All of it. Their warnings. My mistakes. I even tell him about Dr. Stewart, even though she has nothing to do with the ghosts. Once I get started talking it's hard to stop. I trust David and I have already opened the door. There's nothing to hold back. I tell him about everything, even the syndrome.

After a long pause, he says, "I really . . . I thought . . . I really don't know."

"Don't know what?"

"These ghosts, this ghost thing. You say you can bring them."

"By cooking."

"By whatever way, it shouldn't matter," he says. "There's no such thing. So I shouldn't believe you at all. Not even a little. Because it's not possible, and because it doesn't make any sense."

I say, "When you see it for yourself you'll believe me."

He says, "That, that right there. The way you say that. So sincere. Not even any hesitation. And then I buy it, I buy it all. Because you sound so sure."

"I am sure."

"And you don't sound crazy."

"I'm not."

"It even makes sense, why you can do it," he says. "Why you can bring the ghosts."

"It does?"

"Sure," says David. "You're making other people's recipes, right?"

"Right."

"And because of this syndrome, your memory, your obsession, I bet you're making things *exactly* as the recipe tells you. You're doing Nonna's recipe exactly like Nonna would, or your mom's recipe exactly like your mom would. So that connects with them in some way."

He's right. It does make sense. But that's not really what I want to know.

"And you don't think I'm crazy," I say.

"No. I don't think you're crazy."

"What do you think I am?" I ask, desperate for an answer.

"Just someone trying to get by," he says. "Like me. Like any of us. There are lots of people who think ghosts exist, and I've never been one, but . . . I don't know. Mom always says she feels spirits, but that's a feeling, right? I guess I feel Elena's spirit, in the things she left behind."

"Her chickadee."

"Chickadee," he says, and smiles.

"You still love her," I say.

"I can't stop. I know she's dead. I mean, it's a fact, I know it. But I can't let her go. I can't move on. So when you said I could see her—maybe that's it. Maybe if I saw her ghost I could say good-bye and I can let go of this feeling, this guilt. You don't know what it's like."

"Losing someone?"

"Being responsible."

"It was an accident."

"It was my accident," he says. "If I hadn't been driving, if we hadn't gone out that night, if I hadn't this or that. You don't know how many times I've thought, 'If only I'd done one thing different.' Even if I hadn't ever met her, hadn't brought her from Peru to Philadelphia. I wouldn't have ever loved her, and that would have been my loss, but how bad is a loss you don't know about? You can't mourn all the people you could have loved but didn't. You mourn the ones you loved and lost."

David finishes his chocolate. He rinses his cup and leaves it in the sink.

He says, "Okay, let's do it. I've got nothing to lose. If you're imagining it, fine, that's that."

"I'm not imagining it," I say. "Besides, I told you I'd do it. I promised."

"You did," he says. "I heard you. So. I'll buy the ingredients. I'll bring them here. When?"

"Now?"

Shaking his head, he says, "Whatever power you have, whatever you can or can't do, I don't think you're in any shape to try right now. Tomorrow. I'll come back tomorrow."

"Tomorrow."

He lets himself out. I stay in the kitchen, cupping the mug with both hands, savoring the soft burn of the ancho. Even when the chocolate itself has gone cold, and there's no more heat for my fingers, my belly is warm, my lips lightly stung.

Afterward, I cross through the rooms of the first floor. Hard to believe it's still daylight. The noises from the street are soft, muffled. A siren whoops far off. In the living room, I notice something out of place.

David left the recipe for aji de gallina on the mantel, resting against a picture in a frame. It isn't a family picture, not exactly. Amanda put most of those away, and they're boxed up with the books and clothes, their fate yet to be determined. Dad used to take vacation pictures without us in them ("Let's get one of the scenery"), and those are the ones I've kept in sight. So I can remember Charleston without having to look at my awkward, seven-year-old self, in lopsided braids. Boston without my ten-year-old tears. Christmas in Macon, all those lovely strings of lights that blinked in a precise sequence, without the family picture that didn't have me in it because I couldn't be pried away from timing them with Grandpa Damson's stopwatch, even for a minute. Especially not for a minute. The interval timing for a complete cycle turned out to be fifty-three and a half seconds. It took me the better part of a day to figure it.

I read the aji recipe. It's complicated and long. I don't have most of the ingredients for it. Certainly not the yellow pepper, because it's not regular yellow pepper. But as I do every time I look at a new recipe, I sort it out, and analyze. Where would I get the aji? The Korean deli on the corner isn't likely to have it. If Ma were here she'd look at the spice store in Reading Terminal Market, Whole Foods, Trader Joe's. Most of the other ingredients are easier. It doesn't specify a type of rice, so Arborio should do, though what's authentic is probably short-grain.

I am, in my head, already cooking.

I'm terrified of calling Elena's ghost, but at the same time, I feel strongly that it's the right thing to do. I can help, and I said I would, so I will. Besides, love is a powerful force. More powerful than reason. Even if that love, as strong as it is, isn't yours.

I feed Midnight, then I decide to go out for a walk. I don't want the walls to close in on me. I'll go somewhere without walls. While I'm walking, the cold wind stinging my face, I try to imagine this situation from Amanda's point of view. I try to put myself in her shoes.

She thinks I am a mess and that the only way to fix me, if there is one, is to get a diagnosis. When I told her that her daughter might be like me, she heard that as me saying that her daughter is broken. That upset her. She's also trying to take on Ma's role, to be the protector, to keep me safe. She isn't thinking about how much protection can feel like imprisonment. She doesn't know about Dad. It might help to tell her. She isn't seeing things from my perspective, either.

I decide to walk to the garden. I've been avoiding it, but there's no reason. It's not going to remind me of Ma more than living in her house is. A block up on Tenth, a block over on Locust. When I get there, there's nothing to see. Inside the fence everything is snowed over. I can't even see the dirt, and if I could, I know it would be frozen. It is just a blank space with iron around it. Someone has opened a cupcake place next door.

I turn left and get back onto Spruce, and play an old game: looking for boot scrapers. Especially in this part of town they are everywhere, and with nothing else to look for, all my attention is on the ground.

Next to any old set of steps you might find one. They are all iron but in all other ways they vary. Flat, plain, snapped-off bars sticking up out of the sidewalk, or bowing, flowered scrolls that look like they should have broken years ago. All variations. No pattern.

I follow the sight of one boot scraper after the next, and turn, and turn again, losing track of the streets. That's how I find myself on an unfamiliar corner, and I look up through an ironwork gate and catch sight of row upon row of low, dark headstones. A cemetery.

Headstones? Flowers? Coffins? shouts Amanda in my mind. *Did you have to go and identify their* bodies?

No wonder she won't talk to me.

What if she never does?

I speed up, veer away, turn at the first corner I get to, trying to get my mind to settle on some kind of food that will comfort me, meat loaf, gelato, pumpkin soup, cherries. I settle on the bitter intensity of espresso, a taste so powerful it wipes other tastes away. I imagine stroking the lip of the cup with a lemon peel, the Italian way. In sipping the imagined espresso everything slows down, my pace, my mind, my heart.

That calms me enough so I can at least get inside my own house and close the door.

I'm already heading toward the stairs to get to the closet but the noise stops me. I hear someone moving around on the ground floor. My first thought, oddly, is that David has decided to go ahead without me. That he thinks the magic isn't in me, but in the kitchen. This is of course ridiculous. It is also not true. Then I think maybe Amanda has sent Angelica back to show the house to invading strangers again, but thank goodness, that isn't the case either.

Gert is in the downstairs bathroom, on her knees, sponging out the bathtub. I can see her, at least part of her, through the doorway. The familiar sight helps me calm down. Gert is a constant. I can depend on Gert. I call out "Hello" but don't go in. I think it's rude to stand behind someone while they're on their knees. Especially in a small space.

I think of familiar things. I think of routine. I bring my laptop down to the dining room table and pull up Kitcherati to look for new recipes. Nothing that's on a card in the kitchen. Nothing that has anything to do with ghosts. Certainly not the one recipe I know I have to cook to keep my promise. Just something I want to cook because it sounds interesting or delicious. The way I would if everything were normal.

While I click and read and click again, I hear Gert coughing in the other room, a deep, hard cough. It reminds me she's older. Older people's coughs sound different. It subsides to one cough every couple of minutes, then nothing.

I've bookmarked recipes for clementine cake, tarragon vinaigrette, and bacon-wrapped dates when Gert says, "Ginny, do you need this?"

I look up. She is holding the aji recipe. It must have gotten in the way of wiping dust off the mantel.

"Sure," I say, putting my hand out. "It's David's, but I'll hold on to it."

She looks at it more closely. Reads it for real. "Not David's. Elena's."

"Yes, that's right."

Gert looks at the paper and folds it along the preexisting line. I notice for the first time how soft the paper is, how worn around the edges.

She says, "Ginny. Why is this here?"

"David brought it."

"He has been here? He did not mention."

"Yes, he has been here," I say, trying to figure out how much I can tell her. I don't want to tell her everything. David has a reason to believe. Gert doesn't. She also has my sister's phone number, and the last thing I need right now, literally the last thing, is for Amanda to find out I've been seeing ghosts.

"What is my son to you?" she asks.

"A friend," I say. "He did me a favor. He gave me a ride. That's it."

"He is a good son," she says. "I have told you that before. But I worry about him, I have told you that too."

"Yes. He's still having a lot of trouble with his grief."

"He does not know what to do with it," says Gert. "I do not want him giving it to you. You have enough grief of your own."

"It's not what you think."

"Did he ask you to cook this?"

The truth is easier than a lie, so I say, "Yes."

She says, "I cannot tell you what to do. But if I were you, I would not do it. He does not need reminders of her. He has reminders of her, everywhere. What he needs is not to be reminded."

"Why?"

Gert hands me the paper, saying, "She was never good for him, from the beginning. And now it must be worse. She is gone. He must let her be gone."

"Okay."

She says, "Curiosity killed the cat, you remember."

"I remember."

"Good," she says, giving a short, sharp nod.

After she leaves, I ponder the paper, and unfold it. I put it back where it was. I let it lie, propped up on the picture of Charleston, a pineapple-shaped fountain in a bright green park. A family vacation, but no family to be seen.

I remember the picture before the picture. Amanda and me on the right-hand side, all braids and braces. Ma in the middle, with a floppy hat shading her eyes. Dad on the left, too tall to match the rest of us, his right arm slightly blurred. He always set the timer and then ran into the picture, so more often than not, when the shutter clicked he was still in motion.

This picture, of course, has no family. But the family was there. Before.

I go up to my room to read. The piles of childhood artifacts are still sitting there. I don't know what to do with them, if anything. I can't deal with them right now. I don't want to think about my smaller self struggling. Because it makes me think of Shannon struggling, and I can't protect Shannon right now. I can't make my sister listen. Not today. Probably not tomorrow. Once she has calmed down and is ready to listen, I'll reach out to her again. And I'll keep reaching out until we connect. Until she hears me.

Today all I can do is wait. And tomorrow, when David comes back, deliver a ghost.

CHAPTER THIRTEEN

Aji de Gallina

aji de gallina

1 chicken
1/4 cup oil
1 lg onion, chop
4 cloves garlic, chop
4 tsp aji amarillo paste
4 slices bread, crusts cut
  off, soaked in milk

1/2 cup walnuts, chop

1 can evap milk
1/2 cup grated parm chs
salt and pepper

black olives
boil rice
boil potatoes
boil eggs

Roast chicken while potatoes and eggs boil, tear
from bone. Heat oil and fry onion and garlic with
aji paste until all is golden. Add soaked bread.
Cook slowly, then add chopped nuts, grated cheese,
and evap milk. Add chicken. Put rice on plate, cover
with chicken in sauce, and decorate with peeled
potatoes, half eggs, and olives.

When David arrives, I am sitting at the dining room table looking over the aji recipe, a stack of books beside me. He lets
himself in, and sets two grocery bags on the table.

"I have it all," he says. "What are the books for?"

"I just like to cross-reference different recipes to see how things are going to behave," I say. "Don't worry, I'll make it exactly like hers."

"Is that important? For the ghost?"

"I think so. I made my dad's recipe with teaspoons of something instead of tablespoons, and he didn't come. But then when I made it with the right amounts, he did." I think of him sitting on the stool, looking away from me. I don't want to think of that.

"And can you bring him again?"

I shake my head. "It gets used up, I think. The magic. Whatever it is that tethers them to the original recipe in the first place. Brings them back."

"And how long—how long do they stay?"

"As long as the smell stays, I guess. I don't know how long you'll have with her."

"I don't know what I'll say, either, when she comes."

I notice he says "when," not "if." One way or another, now he is convinced. I suggest, "Tell her you love her?"

"She knows that. She always knew that. I think I just need to tell her I'm sorry. That I know if it weren't for me—"

"Maybe because of you she was the happiest she could have ever been."

"Maybe," he says. "We can guess all we want. Or we can ask her."

He carries the bags into the kitchen and starts unpacking. Raw chicken on the bone. A bag of potatoes. A can of evaporated milk. A loaf of white sandwich bread in a plastic bag. Black olives, with pits. Walnuts, cheese, eggs, rice. A squat yellow jar, its label in Spanish, *aji amarillo*. While he counts out how many of everything is called for and puts the remainder in the fridge, I copy the instructions from the recipe in large black letters so I can be sure to follow everything exactly, and I put the original in a clear envelope and tape the envelope to the cabinet at eye level, where it will be safest.

David helps me set everything out, a roasting pan, a large pot, a small one, all the ingredients, everything in the right order. I'm not used to help. I can't find a rhythm this way. It would probably be easier for me if I put my hands on each thing myself. But, I realize, it wouldn't be easier for him. And this dish is for him, not me, despite my reasons.

"Are you ready for this?"

He nods.

I open my mouth to ask him if he's sure. But we both know he is. So I don't ask.

The recipe is complicated and time-consuming. Once I start the first step I do it all myself, just in case that matters. I slide the stool over a few inches to make sure it's exactly where it has been before. David stands against the wall next to the shelves of cookbooks and watches in silence.

I put the chicken in to roast, without preheating the oven, because the recipe doesn't specify preheating. I boil a pot of water that will serve for eggs and potatoes. Another pot boils water for rice. The time adds up. An hour for the chicken, twelve minutes for the eggs, the potatoes have to be boiled whole in their jackets so another forty-five minutes for them, half an hour for the rice. Some things overlap. Smells surge up and fade away, each in its own time, blending unequally. The raw, starchy smell of the rice beginning to cook gives way to the last sparkling golden waft of the chicken, its fat spattering and browning against the baking pan. I know it isn't possible to feel someone looking at you, but I become conscious of David, watching me, in the minutes when there's nothing to do. I want to reassure him but it would be empty. My work at the stove is the only reassurance I can give.

The chicken isn't cool enough to shred yet when I peel the eggs, running them under cold water to separate the shell from the smooth, glassy cooked white. Their sulfur smell rises up while I move on to the olives, laying them flat on the cutting board and smacking them with the side of a knife, then working the long pit free with my fingertips, stung by salty brine. Then I tug the peel off the potatoes carefully, in long strips, with my bare fingers. Their warmth makes them feel as if they're somehow alive. Then finally the chicken is ready, and I pull it apart with my hands, stripping flesh from bone, my fingers slick with fat. Twist off each drumstick at the socket, detach the wings, strip away the long fibers of the thigh with their thick fat pockets. I pop the oysters out of the chicken back with the back of my thumbnail and have one halfway to my mouth before I remember none of this is for me. None. I set it with the rest of the meat.

The work at this stage is the work of separation. I'm surprised to find that I am also separate, in a way. As absorbed as I am in the process, a small part of me is thinking, watching, worrying. Have I done it right? Will Elena be drawn by the smell? Will she appear?

The heap of discarded things grows: the chicken skin and bones, the pits of olives, potato peels, eggshells, everything left over.

As each component finishes, the peeled eggs, the peeled potatoes, the pitted olives, the shredded chicken, I dome each of them up on a separate plate. Last, I make the sauce. I chop onion and garlic and start them frying in the oil, then I spoon out the right amount of *aji amarillo* paste and put the jar back in the fridge. I pinch wads of white bread from the loaf and soak them in milk. Once the contents of the pan are browned to golden, I build the sauce with the soaked bread, the nuts, and the cheese, then pour in the evaporated milk slowly, until the gold liquid and the white liquid blend to a consistent color.

Consulting the recipe, I move into the last stage, and begin to assemble all the separate pieces together. I lower shredded chicken into the sauce, and stir gently, keeping the pieces somewhat whole.

On the plate I heap a cup's worth of white rice, its grains tumbling over each other as they slip out of form. On top of that, a ladleful of the thick yellow sauce, smothering the rice underneath a creamy rich layer, the soft striped texture of the chicken showing through. On one side of the plate I arrange the clean white ovals of skinless potatoes, and on the other, I mirror them with the white ovals of hard-boiled eggs cut in half, their yolks bright yellow and perfect, circles inside ovals, yellow on white on yellow on white. Then the last touch. A row of deep black olives. The recipe doesn't specify exactly where they go so I put them down the center. Like punctuation in a sentence, the pupil of an eye. A perfect blackness.

It's done.

David and I both stare at the step stool in the corner, looking for her shape. Elena should be there, looking back at us.

Instead we stare at emptiness.

He whispers, "Shouldn't she . . . be here?"

"Yes."

"Why isn't she?"

"I don't know."

Louder, David says, "You told me you could bring her."

"I can," I say, "I mean, I could, I thought, I thought she'd be here. I thought I did everything right."

I grab the copied version of the recipe and hold it next to the original version. Everything's the same. The ingredients, the timing, the order. I pick up the plate and look at it, examining every detail, it's right, it has to be right, I did it exactly.

David says, louder again, "Then what's wrong? Why isn't she here? Where's Elena?"

"I don't know."

"What do you mean, you don't know?"

"I mean I don't know, that's what I mean!"

David moves so quickly I flinch, but it's not me he's reaching for. He scoops up a clump of aji de gallina in his outstretched palm, curling his fingers around it. The heavy plate tips in my hands, I struggle to right it. Yellow sauce drips onto my arm. A skinless potato rolls off the plate and hits the floor, landing with a soft but audible thump.

David crams the food into his mouth, and works his jaw, chewing fiercely. Rice spatters down across his shirt, trailing yellow stains. I assume he thinks it will make a difference to eat it. Maybe the smell isn't enough and the taste is essential. I have no idea. I don't know if he's desperate, or right.

Still nothing.

"Fuck!" screams David. "Where is she?"

"I don't know!"

"What did you do wrong?"

"I don't know! I tried!"

David rips the plate out of my grip and flings it hard with both hands.

It smashes straight into the cabinet full of my family's cookbooks. Glass shatters with a crackling boom. Thick yellow paste streaks down the broken glass. Over the cookbooks. Toward the recipes.

My fist strikes David high on the cheekbone, almost square in the eye. I feel the impact in the bones of my knuckles, the sound becoming vibration becoming sound. David staggers back and I turn away.

I kneel down and yank the door open and grab for the Japanese tea box of recipes, everyone's handwritten scraps, everything so important and so irreplaceable. I'm so startled and disoriented it takes me a few seconds to register that the things I want are safe and dry in my hand, the box would have protected them anyway, and it takes me another few seconds after that to see that I've knelt down in the broken glass.

It doesn't hurt yet, but it will.

On the way out of the room I catch a glimpse of David hunched over on the tile. His arms and head are draped over the empty step stool. There is a noise coming from him. Crying, but not a soft, private crying. Sobs that come from all the way down in his gut. He sounds like a wolf.

I lock the door of the bathroom and crouch down in the bathtub, picking the glass out of my knee with a set of tweezers Ma used to use to pluck her eyebrows.

They say the best way to treat yourself when you're injured is to pretend the body is not your body. I am barely pretending. I lift the shards of glass as if they were bay leaves I needed to retrieve from a finished tomato sauce, nothing more. Lift them off, set them aside. The shards of glass pile up on the edge of the white tub. When I don't see any more glass against the bleeding skin, I turn on the faucet and run the water over my knee, letting it run until the tub is half full.

There is a knock on the door of the bathroom and I don't answer. It's locked. There's nothing to say.

Eventually, the bleeding stops. The water goes from lukewarm to cool, then cold. I sit on the edge of the tub, wrapped in a towel. There isn't another knock. I hear the front door close. That doesn't mean anything, really. He has a key and could come back in, but I doubt he will. He doesn't want to be here any more than I want him here. We've failed. I've failed. I made a promise that I couldn't, didn't, keep.

From the cabinet in the bathroom I fish out a roll of gauze. I wrap the knee up tight. There isn't anything to secure the loose end with. I go back into the kitchen, stepping carefully around the broken glass and ruined food with my bare feet. I sew the trailing end of the gauze to itself with kitchen twine and a larding needle. Dad was the one who taught me to sew. I couldn't match his surgical precision, but I learned by imitating the technique. Imitation is as close as I can get.

Thinking of him, I reach for the bottle in the back of the cabinet. I leave the mess in the kitchen for tomorrow, and take the scotch upstairs to bed.

. . . .

It's late in the morning when I wake up, dry-mouthed and disoriented. A shot of the Lagavulin was enough to seal my eyelids for longer than I thought. I'm startled awake by the thought that Midnight could be injured by the glass in the kitchen, but she is sleeping peacefully on both my feet, so I go down to take care of the mess first thing. The creamy smell has gone stale and unpleasant. I open the kitchen windows and let the cold fresh air in. I sweep up the glass and carefully scoop it all into several layers of paper bags. Everything is still on the kitchen counter, the eggshells, the chicken bones, olive pits. All that waste. It goes in the trash. I twist the neck of the bag tight shut. The cold wind is blasting now, so I close the windows. I pour Midnight a bowl of food, close the sliding doors to the kitchen, and set it outside them, in case I missed any glass. Then I put my coat on and haul the mess away.

When I go home I'll be just as uncertain, so instead when I leave the alley I walk south, heading down through Society Hill and Queen Village, going the long way around. When I was little Dad used to take me down to the Italian Market, until Ma made him stop. Now that I know what I know about him, it must have been hard for him too. Crowds on both sides of the street, loud voices, constant motion. But he dealt with it somehow. Maybe he just got used to it, or maybe he did what Dr. Stewart was talking about, some kind of technique to help himself tune it out without having to withdraw completely. Hospitals are loud and hectic too. But he handled it. He got through.

What could I get through, if I tried? Anything? Everything?

I turn left off Christian down Ninth and walk up to the first produce stand in the market. In winter there isn't much variety, but here I see onions, root vegetables, kale. The rusty orange of gnarled carrots next to tiny white onions like eyeballs next to dark greens that feather out in wavy patterns like the fins of some deep ocean fish.

"What you need, lady?" calls a voice.

I reach into the pocket of my jeans and find a twenty-dollar bill, one I tucked there for the trip to Amanda's. No, don't think of that. Think of something else.

"Onions," I say.

"This kind or this or this? How many?"

I look at the variety on the stand, all these boxes spilling out onion after onion. Yellow ones, and white, and red, all here, all possible.

"Lady, I ain't got all day."

I breathe in and breathe out and think how lovely these onions will be, on my stove, transformed from biting sharpness to sweet brown jam. A short, simple thought to ground me.

"Two pounds, these red ones," I tell him. In a flash he scoops things up and makes change, and when he drops coins and bills onto my outstretched palm I just tell myself to think of the sweet smell of the onions and not the feel of his flesh brushing my flesh, and my hand trembles, and a few of the coins drop, but he doesn't say anything else. I bend down to pick up the coins, and tuck them back in my pocket, and walk away.

After that I walk over to the Whole Foods on South Street. The door slides open for me without a touch. It is bright and very nearly overwhelming. Pyramid after pyramid of vegetables and fruits. What do I want? I reach for the closest thing, a ten-pound bag of Yukon Gold potatoes. This will do. Feeling reckless with my success, I decide I can do more. The feeling is energizing. I'm almost giddy. I put more things in the basket. Humboldt Fog cheese. Marcona almonds. Honey tangerines. When the basket gets heavy I stop.

I wait in line for a cashier, and set everything on the conveyor belt, and hand him my credit card. He's already running it through the machine when I realize it probably won't work. It didn't last time, with the sunflower seeds. So I'm surprised when he hands me the slip to sign.

"Oh—it worked?" I blurt.

"Yep, they generally do," he says. "Do you need a bag?"

"No."

"Then just sign that and we'll be golden."

"But . . . I . . ." I pretend he's someone I already know, like Gert. Focus on his cheek. Speak to that. "Last time I used the card they wouldn't take it."

"I don't know," he says. "Works fine here. Some places have a minimum, like you need to buy ten dollars' worth of stuff? Could be that?"

"Oh."

"Anyway." His hand makes a flickering movement. "Could you just sign that?"

I do, and I take my groceries, and I go home.

I CLOSE THE front door behind me and hear a noise from inside. First I assume it's Midnight, but then I look up and she is descending the stairs toward me. I must be rattled. I know the sound my cat makes on the stairs and it is not this sound.

A tapping. From the kitchen, I think.

I call out, "Gert?" before I realize that isn't possible. She came yesterday. She wouldn't be here.

A man's voice calls my name and I stiffen. Then he says, "It's only me, David, don't be afraid," and I'm not once he says it.

I stand in the doorway of the kitchen and look in at him. He's on his knees in front of the glass cabinet. Near him on the floor are stacks of small glass squares, and lots of tools I don't know the names for. Knifelike things, razorlike things, gluelike things. And an open bottle of wine.

David says, "Don't be mad, okay?"

"Okay." I look at the cabinet. He is replacing all the broken panes, and is almost done. There is only one empty rectangle left, one last gap.

"I'm sorry," he says.

"Me too."

I look down at his upturned face. My fist left a solid bruise on it. The purple of a Concord grape. I'm not good at reading emotions on faces but the bruise changes his. He doesn't look as angry as he has before. There is more sadness. Maybe it isn't the bruise.

"It wasn't fair to you," he says. "To bring you into it. Nothing's permanently damaged, right? Your recipes are okay?"

"Yes." My knee is still bandaged with gauze under my jeans, but he can't see that. Besides, it's healing.

"Good, I'm really glad to hear that."

"Thank you for fixing the glass."

"I'm just trying to make things right," he says, his voice heavy like coffee grounds and wet sand and earth.

I heave the bag off my shoulder and onto the butcher block, out of the way. Then I watch David finish the work, slipping the pane into a waiting sill, and then the glass-front cabinet is whole again. He taps and presses and reassembles. He folds up his leftover supplies in newspaper and pushes them across the floor toward the garbage can. He gets up and washes his hands in the sink, dries them on the towel, and sits back down on the floor. He looks up at me, so I sit down with him, not too close.

Sitting on his right, I have a closer look at his bruise. From the grape center it fades to green at the edges. The color changes a little over the contours of his face. It's a deeper purple near the bone. From the core of the bruise, without meaning to, I look to the eye. It is a warm brown, with a little bit of dark gold in it. Milk chocolate, dappled with dulce de leche.

He grabs the wine bottle by the neck and drinks. When he sets it down I can see it's half empty. "Unseemly, I know," he says. "Middle of the day and everything. It's just, I'm, you have no idea, I'm falling apart."

"I'm sorry," I say. "I'm so sorry she didn't come. I don't know what I did wrong."

"Maybe nothing," he says. "Maybe she didn't want to come. I don't know. Maybe it's better this way. If I got that angry—Ginny, I've never been that angry before. I'm so sorry. If I'd hurt you—I'm just so sorry, I can't even tell you."

"You don't have to tell me anything," I say. "We both got very upset. You're sorry and so am I."

"Is it that simple?"

"Maybe it's not really," I say, "but let's make it that way."

The corner of the eye crinkles up, everything on the face shifts, it's almost a smile. David says, "Let me pour you a glass, huh?"

"Just one."

He looks around and says, "But one of us will have to get up for a glass."

I reach out for the bottle. He hands it to me and I drink. The wine is much easier to drink than scotch. It has a pleasing bitterness, an interesting balance of sharp bite and sweet fruit.

David says, "Don't fall in love, Ginny."

"Why not?"

"It hurts too much. Honestly."

"But there's the good along with the bad." I'm thinking of my parents, who loved each other, no matter what.

"I don't know if the good was good enough," he says. "I've had a year of bad. A year where I can't even get my head above water. You think I'm depressed because Elena's ghost didn't come, but honestly, it's made me realize that I don't know what I would have done if she had come. I wasn't totally truthful with you, Ginny. It wasn't just because I loved her that I wanted to see her. I had a question I wanted to ask her."

"What question?"

"I wanted to know if she was cheating on me. Before. I mean, we're both jealous people, I mean, we were, you know?"

He holds the bottle out and I take another drink.

"I don't know," I say. "Tell me."

"You don't know what it's like," he says. "You get so tuned in to another person, you notice even the slightest change. If she starts coming home at a different time than she used to. And she says she's going for a bike ride but she doesn't take her helmet. And she mentions this guy, this one particular guy, almost every day for a while and then never again all of a sudden. It might not be anything at all. But it might. And if you let that thought in, you can't ever get it back out of your head again. You understand?"

I admit, "Not really," and drink the wine.

He leans his head against the wall and says, "Hold on to that. I love that about you. You can still think the best of people. I wish I could be that way, I really do. But once you lose that, you can't ever get it back."

"How did you lose it?"

He says, "Innocence isn't a set of house keys. You don't just up and lose it one day. It's a process."

"What was your process?"

"Over time, I just stopped trusting people," he says. "I got hurt too many times and I started to anticipate it. Expect it. And that applied to Elena too. I didn't trust my own wife. What kind of person does that make me?"

"Normal."

"That's nice to think," he says, and drinks again. "I thought you could save me from myself, but that's not your responsibility. I shouldn't have put it on you."

"I could try again. With the aji, I mean."

He shakes his head. "No, don't. I have my answer. If she was faithful to me, I'm a horrible person for suspecting her. If she wasn't, I was an idiot to trust her. And either way, I killed her. I killed her! Not on purpose, but that doesn't matter, if it weren't for me she wouldn't be dead. Regardless, I still have to live the rest of my life without her. I can't stand it, I can't."

He is crying now. He grabs my hand, the one with the scar, and holds it in a firm grip. It isn't an unpleasant feeling. He starts talking and the words spill out of him. He murmurs them into the palm of my hand.

He tells me about Elena. Little things. Important things. The smell of her skin, almost currylike. The beaten-up shoes she refused to get rid of because of all the places they'd touched earth. When they went shopping for a new bike the week before she died, the way she ran her fingers across the handlebars of every single one, in a caress. Her favorite Spanish word, *desafortunadamente*. The sound she made when the back of her neck was kissed. After he tells me that one he is silent for a full minute, maybe a little longer. It is not the pleasant kind of silence.

He says, "She deserved better than me."

I tell him the only thing I can think to tell him, which is what he said to me after I left Amanda's house. "Easy, easy. It'll be okay."

"It won't be okay."

"It might."

David says, "It might not."

I say, "No promises."

He presses his face into the palm of my hand again and says, "I thought the problem was her. But the problem was me."

I say, "Everyone thinks that. Everyone thinks they're messed up. Everyone struggles. You're normal."

"I'm not."

"You are. Come on, come upstairs, I'll prove it."

I pull on his hand to bring him upstairs after me. We climb.

In my parents' room, he watches me while I move the red geraniums out of the fireplace and reach up into the chimney.

"What's that?"

I say, "It's called the Normal Book. I read it when I need to know that I'm normal. Because I am. You are too."

I show him the window seat and gesture for him to sit down. I sit down next to him, book in hand. His head is down and everything about his body shows his sadness, so I reach out. Without thinking or weighing or planning. I reach out and stroke his hair, to soothe him, the way I always find most soothing. Fingertips at the hairline, smoothing the hair back over the top of the head, all the way down to the bare skin at the nape of the neck, in a long, unbroken movement. And I read to him from the Normal Book, telling him all the broad and wide and far-reaching definitions of the word *normal,* the way people use it as a placeholder, a code word, a Band-Aid. The way it means nothing, and everything.

raised in a normal home, I probably would be a much healthier person

to a point where I felt like it was normal to exercise three hours each day, on the

think it's normal to obey rules, like RSVPing for a wedding by the date

no problem with the gays as long as they act like normal people the rest of

what I consider a normal amount of drinking. But my boyfriend thinks I'm

So I guess the question is, what I consider normal for Americans might

Yakima, why let *him* define what's normal? You're letting him control

cold day in hell when this girl gets to tell me what's normal for my own son

I say, "See? Normal means a lot of things to a lot of people. You're normal. Don't worry. It's okay."

My hand is lingering at the back of his neck and he puts his hand over it to keep it there, and then brings his mouth down on mine, firmly. His lips are full and warm.

The first feeling is shock, but then another feeling crashes over it like a wave, blots it out. All my nerves are singing and all my wires are crossed. I am tasting and feeling but nothing that I am tasting or feeling is here. His kisses are honey. His tongue is like a ripe slice of mango, firm and slippery, irresistibly smooth. It's hard to breathe. A soft, spreading warmth descends from my neck down my body to my toes, spreading out like milk in coffee, rolling in curls and waves and currents. Both of his hands are in my hair now, grasping.

I want to be closer so I push my body against his.

He leaps back as if scalded.

"Oh, God, Ginny," he moans, "I'm sorry, I'm sorry."

"It's okay," I tell him, but it's too late for that, he's out the door and down the stairs and the slam of the front door comes so quickly it seems impossible. I kneel on the window seat and look out the window of my parents' room and see him unlocking his bike from the No Parking sign, moving so quickly he fumbles and drops his helmet onto the sidewalk.

I work to open the window, I've never tried this one before, I fumble with the latch. It rides open with a whoosh of cold air. I call to him from the window, "Wait!"

He turns and looks up at me and pain is written so clearly across his face it takes what's left of my breath away.

Then he throws one leg over the bike and rides off, so quickly the helmet is still rocking back and forth on the sidewalk, unsteady, left behind.

I would say it was a bad idea, but it was never an idea.

I never thought about it before it happened. Now that it has happened, though, I can't stop thinking about it. For that reason and many others, sleeping is out of the question. Cooking too. I can picture the wine bottle sitting on the floor of the kitchen. It can stay there.

I sit in the window seat and read one of Ma's southern romance novels. The cover is barely cracked. The woman in the story falls in love with her neighbor, an older man. Her parents disapprove. There are scenes. There is disowning. There is forgiveness, and a tearful reunion. It all sounds unpleasant.

I am not a fast reader. Midnight curls up on the seat next to me for part of the night. Later she tires of that position and disappears. Before I've finished, the sun comes up. When I can see it's light out I go outside and pick up David's helmet from the sidewalk. I bring it in and set it on the dining room mantel, next to the picture of Charleston.

Then I nap a few hours, though the noises of the day wake me up from time to time. A car door, a horn, an alarm. Someone swearing at their lack of quarters. Gossiping nurses, a shriek of laughter. The last time I decide there's no point in trying anymore. I get up, get dressed, make myself coffee. The coffee is to force me back into alertness, or something close to it. Making myself be awake is always a possibility, in a way making myself be asleep is not.

The helmet sits on the mantel in the dining room, white and webbed like tripe. I don't know what to do about it. I can take it over to his apartment, but if he's not there, that's pointless. I can't just set it on his steps and leave it. It hasn't been that long since I showed up at someone else's door unwanted, and I'm still reeling from that.

The bag of groceries is still on the butcher block. Potatoes and red onions and almonds and tangerines. It seems silly now. I felt so proud, like I'd achieved something. People do these things every day, all their lives. When I can do them with no fear, then I'll have something to be proud of.

On the kitchen floor is the empty wine bottle. David, poor David. I couldn't help him get what he needed. The ghost didn't come. I didn't keep my promise. Why did he kiss me? Was he just seeking comfort, responding to kindness? I don't know what he was feeling, but I know what I felt. Some kind of intimacy, some kind of tenderness. At the time it felt like a breakthrough, something I'd never felt before. Connection. Acceptance. And what I feel now, I think it's guilt. I should have pushed him away before the kiss even happened. But I didn't. I was selfish.

I think about how sad he was, how overwhelmed. How he went so quickly from mood to mood. I always thought other people were more sure of themselves. When I think about Amanda, the way she wants to help me but can't figure out how to do it, I realize she must be unsure too. David always seemed that way, but now I guess he isn't. He isn't acting sure.

David. I really don't know what will happen next. But this will all unfold the way it will unfold, whether it's yesterday or today or tomorrow. If David never speaks to me again, that's what happens. For someone who didn't even know him a month ago I find myself caring a lot. I learned the word *fatalism* at a young age and after I got over the idea that it meant something about death, I grew very attached to it. It's like realism, but even more so. It's also on a page with *fastidious*, and *fatback*, and *father*.

I'll feel better if I cook. Something that will completely absorb me, push everything else out of my mind.

Flipping through the recipe cards, I notice the yellow stain on the corner of Ma's recipe for chicken and dumplings. When I was a kid I loved chicken and dumplings. She would open the can of Golden Mushroom Soup and it made a satisfying splat. The yellow stain reminds me of the yellow aji de gallina, how I was afraid it would ruin the recipes. It failed to bring Elena into the kitchen. David grabbed it out of my hand and threw it at the wall. I never got to taste it.

There is still plenty of *aji amarillo* left in the jar, and potatoes from yesterday's bag. I open the refrigerator to look for the rest. Yes, olives, evaporated milk, chicken, bread, everything I need. David bought extra of everything. I know why. He was trying to be sure.

It's always hardest to make something the first time. So much uncertainty, in any unknown recipe. Will the dough come together? How much liquid will the fruit give off? Will the potatoes be cool enough to peel by the time the sauce is thick? That's part of why the recipe seems to go much more quickly this time, even though it takes just as long, nearly two hours. There are so many things to cook and to peel, to heat and to cool, to stir and tear and shred. I lose myself in it.

At the end, the aji comes together as it should, its yellows and whites correct, the black olives like punctuation. I lower my nose to the dish and inhale. It smells like creaminess. There's a slight heat in the yellow pepper, a sweet note, and of course the blooming color.

I lift my head.

A blur of brown and white, resolving, and there she is. I see her form come together.

On the stool sits a beautiful woman, skin the color of buckwheat honey. She wears a thin white hooded sweatshirt, zipped up to the neck, with black yoga pants that end midcalf. On her feet, white slip-on sneakers, almost like Nonna's Keds. No socks. Her ankles are bare above the lip of the shoe. I look at her face. Around the eyes there are lines and shadows. She looks sadder, and older, than her picture.

"Hello, Elena," I say.

"Who are you?" She clings to the stool as if the floor were ocean. "*¿Quien eres?*"

"Please don't go," I say. "I'm a friend."

"Not my friend."

"I'm a friend, I promise. Of David's. And his mom's. You know his mom? Gert?"

"Yes, I know her."

"She's been a friend of my family. For many years."

"That doesn't explain."

"I know it doesn't," I say. "But the truth . . . the truth is kind of hard to start with."

"It's easier if you just say it," she says.

Maybe she's right.

I tell her, "You're a ghost."

"I know I'm a ghost." It's a statement, flat. She says, "I remember. I remember dying."

"I'm so sorry."

She says, "And why you? Who are you?"

I say, "I invoke ghosts by cooking from dead people's recipes. Your husband asked me to bring you. I made your aji de gallina."

Her voice cracks as she says, "I told him I'd love him if he made it. He never made it. I loved him anyway."

"Did you?"

"What a question," she says, "when I don't even know you."

"I'm sorry."

She says, "So you're not . . . with him? You're his friend?"

"I try to be," I say.

She says, "I didn't understand."

"Understand what?"

"I didn't come before. The last time, when you made the aji. I didn't come, because I didn't want to."

"What?"

"I was close—I smelled the aji—I could see him—but it was David and a strange woman in a strange place, what was I supposed to think? It was too surprising."

"But you came this time."

"I was lucky to get a second chance. I didn't want to wait for a third."

She kicks her foot, points her toes. She makes circles on the kitchen floor. We both watch her toes making one circle after another in the same clockwise direction. Around and around. Half hypnotized, both of us.

"There's so much you never think about," she says. "Before you die."

"Like?"

"We were never outside ourselves," she says. "We should have been. We should have tried."

"What does that mean?"

"I can't even tell you, I'm sorry. I know it in my mind. But I can't find the words to explain."

I hope that she will find some of them, but she goes back to making the circles with her foot again. She carves the air and it heals behind her.

If I only get the chance to tell her one thing, I want it to be the most important thing.

"Stay," I say. "David wants so badly to see you."

"Where is he?"

"I don't know exactly where. I'm sorry. If you wait . . . I didn't mean to have you come this time. It was an accident."

She says, "There are many accidents."

I say, "Please stay until I can find him. He misses you."

"I miss him too," she says, "but I think it is too late."

She's right. The smell of the aji is already fainter, already disappearing. She'll be gone, and soon.

I say, "But—for David—won't you tell me anything?"

"There's nothing to say, not now," Elena says. "Too late for some things, too soon for others. I will tell him all myself, eventually."

The palest parts of her, the arms, the shoes, go first, but it doesn't take long before her whole form becomes mist and then nothing. Then the bare stool sits there, empty again.

I TAKE DAVID'S helmet and walk to his apartment, cursing myself all the way. I'm useless, worse than useless. I can't bring a ghost when she's needed, but I can invoke her by accident, and in doing so, give up the one way I could have been useful. I can't help David, I don't know why I thought I could. I don't know why I thought I had the right to touch him. He barely even knows me. I pound on his door but he doesn't answer. I assume he's in there, hiding. Staying away. In a sense it's the smartest thing he can do. The only thing other people can do is hurt you, so, forget it.

But I can't. What if he's not at home because he's with Gert? Will he tell her what we did? What I did? I don't want her to not like me anymore. That's frightening. Did I seduce him? I didn't mean to, but how would I know? I've never been a siren. Not that kind.

I carry his helmet home under my arm and put it back on the mantel. I look at the picture next to it, the one of the fountain, a vacation picture without the family. The scene is most beautiful without people in it. People just screw things up.

Forget the whole thing, the world, all the living people, I tell myself, and it has a ring of truth to it. The dead are better, aren't they? The dead don't betray or harm. They've already done all they can do. I can't figure out what people mean or who they are or whether they can be trusted, so, forget them. Don't even try anymore.

For now at least, forget the living.

CHAPTER FOURTEEN

Hot Chocolate

My world has turned upside down again and again, which should mean it's right-side up now, but it isn't. Everything's different, everything's the same. Midnight still basks in the window seat and there are still seven piles of childhood artifacts sitting on the floor of my parents' room. Neatly spaced at regular intervals. If I were a civilization, unearthed by scientists of the future, what would these artifacts say about me?

Then I think about Elena, and what she said. *We were never outside ourselves.* Maybe I should try to get outside myself. Think about someone else for a change. I look down at the piles of paper. Change the question. What would these things say about my parents?

Sixth grade. A five-page paper on "The Initial European Resistance to and Later Culinary Assimilation of the Tomato." Was I the one who chose the topic? The grades are okay on the report card but the comments section says things like *occasionally disruptive* and *needs to participate more*. Nothing here about anyone but me.

Fifth grade. Quarterly reports on my performance. The grades dance. In the first quarter I get a D in Earth Science. The next quarter Earth Science is up to an A, but English has fallen to a D, and Social Studies to a C. Then English takes the A, and Social Studies the D, and Earth Science back down to a C again. It's almost like music. I remember Ma showing me flash cards on all these subjects. I hadn't remembered each one took turns.

Fourth grade. A unicorn notebook, pink. The names of nuns who wrote letters repeated in varying orders down the left-hand margin. Only the left. Class notes alternate with excerpts that even now I know are from Heloise's letters to Abelard. It's a jarring effect now. At the time I'm sure I could read it easily.

Third grade. Precise, repetitive drawings of fruits from every angle. The delicate spotting at the base of a ripening Anjou pear. Shading to emphasize the round fullness of a muskmelon. A note from the teacher: *Goal for the summer—let's try to expand Ginny's focus! Needs to make more progress next year to keep up, and if she'd work as hard on math as she does on her drawings . . .* And then it trails off.

Second grade. Those Turkish rug patterns. Some in margins. Some taking up an entire page. The page-size ones even have a perfectly regular border of knotted fringe drawn at the bottom and top. Declining grades on the report card. A note from the teacher: *Ginny failed to turn in a completed assignment, please acknowledge you have received this notification.* Signed by Dad in his scrawl. Another note, same message, different date. Signed neatly, Caroline Damson Selvaggio. After that the grades nudge upward again.

First grade. A picture of the whole class, all thirty of us. Mrs. Mitchell in the middle. I remember her, she was my favorite. I'm nearly hidden in the picture, tucked half behind the boy to my right and half behind the girl to my left. Only one of my eyes is visible and it's looking down. My grades are all Satisfactory. There is a thank-you note from Mrs. Mitchell thanking my mother for the Christmas cookies.

Kindergarten. A drawing of a family. Curly-haired Ma holding baby Amanda, whose face is colored in pure red. Dad is wearing scrubs and a surgical mask. Two words in an adult hand: *Where's Ginny?* Rows and rows of perfectly formed capital and lowercase As on an exercise sheet intended for the whole alphabet. *Come in for a conference* written on the first report card, and grades are better on the second.

Preschool and before. Crayon drawings and practice pages covered with Gs and Vs. The teacher's note says, *Let's get Ginny to come out of her shell! Needs to share more with the other children.* The drawings of the house with the purple roof and yellow sky. The broken handprint.

The baby book, where it all started. I flip through every page, even the blank ones, this time. A scrap of newsprint falls to the floor. What's on the page itself is nonsense. Part of an article on lumber prices, one of those legal ads announcing an auction. I turn the scrap over. What's important is what's gone. This side is an advice column, with a small rectangle missing. Just about two lines. Maybe I wasn't the one who cut the first bit of newspaper for the Normal Book after all.

Now it's clear. I sit back on my heels.

Ma had to work hard, so hard, to keep me unlabeled. It would have been so much easier to let someone else tell her what to do with me. To accept help, to accept the suggestion that I be moved down a grade, or into a special class. Instead she went back to each teacher, insisting I could get by with a little help. I know Ma. I'm sure she charmed them. I'm sure every teacher thought *Oh, no* when she came in but by the time she left was thinking, *Caroline's right, maybe I am a little too hard on Ginny. She's just a little shy is all.*

And that was just the dealing with other people. She also had to deal with me. And I was difficult. I didn't want to be protected, and I made it hard on her. But she chose her battles. She protected me, maybe too much, but she didn't let me retreat from the world completely. And no matter which way she leaned, protecting me or pushing me, I fought her every step of the way. I was mad because she wouldn't let me stay in my room by myself. I was mad because she made me go back to school, again and again, after every failure. She gave me what I needed. The evidence is stacked up here on the bedroom floor. And Dad loved me, but he wasn't the one who helped me get by. He was just a person too, with flaws, not the hero I made him out to be.

It took their ghosts to do it, but now I think I understand who my parents were. And who I am.

Usually when I get excited my body heats up, but in this case the opposite happens. I get cold all of a sudden, deeply cold. I stare out the window toward the sidewalk. I wonder if the whole winter will be like this. I put on another sweater. I consider draping Midnight around my neck like a scarf but assume she has other plans.

Hot chocolate comes to mind. That'll be perfect. I take milk from the fridge, cocoa from the cupboard. It's Ma's cocoa, one of the cans that Amanda tried to throw away that I reclaimed and put back up on the shelves. It seems a long time ago now. I understand a little better what Amanda meant that day. She didn't want to feel their presence. And it's confusing that I can. Until I let go of them I'm not going to be able to move forward. I have to think about it, but I think that's what I want.

I heat up the milk on the stove instead of in the microwave, so I can stand by the lit burner and feel its warmth. I know the right proportions by heart, one cup of hot milk to one tablespoon of cocoa and one tablespoon of sugar. I feel like there's something missing. Maybe salt? I take *Drinkonomicon* down from the cabinet and flip it to the right page.

The recipe is there, and it does have salt in it, but that becomes less important when I see the change. In tight red block print someone has added *1 TSP ANCHO POWDER* to the recipe in an unfamiliar hand. I know who it was. On one hand, it wasn't very polite of him to write in my cookbook without asking, but on the other hand, it makes me smile. It's a form of conversation. And he was right, it makes it better. I stir in the sugar, wait for it to dissolve. Add a little cocoa at a time. The pinch of salt. And yes, a swirl of ancho powder, for that bitter, smoky tang.

I take a long sip out of the mug. Delicious.

There's a movement in the doorway, and I start. A little of the cocoa slurps up over the edge and falls to the floor. I bend down toward it, thinking I'll wipe it away, but then my eye is caught by something else. Someone else.

David.

"Oh," I say, trying to sound nonchalant. "Did you let yourself in?"

He shakes his head, saying nothing.

"I'm making your cocoa. It's the best, just like you said." This probably sounds fawning and horrible. I shouldn't be allowed to talk to people. I don't make any kind of sense.

He's just standing there in the doorway, shaking his head, shaking his head.

Finally, he says, "I'm sorry, Ginny."

"You shouldn't, I mean, I'm not mad or anything, but you know, it doesn't have to—" I look at his face. I read what I see there. I've gotten it wrong.

So I backtrack, and I start over, and I ask David, "Sorry for what?"

He sits down, almost in slow motion, on the stool in the corner of the kitchen. He puts his head in his hands.

I go get his helmet from the mantel and hold it out to him.

"This is yours," I say. "I tried to bring it back to you."

I stand there holding it out, but he doesn't reach for it. He doesn't move at all.

"Don't you want it?"

He doesn't want to look at me, so I won't look at him. I look down. At his shoes. They're caked with slush and salt, with the by-products of a Philadelphia winter, icy and salty and messy. But there is no water pooling on the kitchen tile, and in the dining room, the hardwood floor is clean. Between here and the door there isn't a mark. It's not possible. He didn't walk in.

It's David, but it isn't David.

I should have realized it, but how could I?

How could I recognize David's ghost if I didn't know, never thought, he could be dead?

That can't be it, I tell myself. This is something else, a spirit displacement thing. Somewhere he is fine and living. Maybe asleep. And his spirit has come here, like the ghosts come here, only not like them at all.

"David?" I want to ask him more. But I can't put the sentence together.

He says, "Make sure you don't blame yourself, okay? It's not your fault."

He lifts his face up out of his hands and looks at me. The bruise is still there, a crescent-shaped smear on the right side of his face. His eyes are tired and sad.

David is dead.

When Amanda was ten years old she used to fake faint at every little thing. She has always been dramatic. Somehow I feel this is what I should do. My eyes should roll up into my head. I should collapse.

Nevertheless, I stay on my feet. I feel sick. I am sick.

I say, "I'm sorry too."

He looks me in the face, but I don't even flinch. He says, "I know."

"What happened?"

"I couldn't. I just couldn't anymore. Tell my mom it was an accident."

"I can't tell her I saw you—she doesn't know—"

"I'm right next door," he says, pointing down the block with an arm that is already growing faint.

"I'm sorry," I say again, because I don't know what else to say, he is less solid and more translucent by the moment, and as I rack my brain for the right thing to ask him or to tell him he is gone.

. . . .

I DON'T KNOW what to do. I can't process it. First I'm mad at myself because I didn't think to tell him about Elena, then I realize it wouldn't have mattered, nothing would have mattered. Of all the impossible things that have happened to me, this is the one I get stuck on.

What do I do?

It doesn't make any sense, but I do it anyway. I walk to the front door and open it and look out in the street. Ice and brick and bare brown trees. Nothing there. No one there.

The hot chocolate goes cold on the kitchen counter before I realize the one obvious thing I absolutely have to do.

I have to call Gert.

I dial her number. Too fast, too soon. I shouldn't have called her, I realize too late, I don't know what to say. I hold the phone away from my ear. I stare at the buttons, not sure what to push. How will I talk to her? How will I tell her?

Faintly, I hear the phone ringing. But it's not the sound of my phone ringing hers. It's the sound of her phone ringing. On the other side of the door.

I open it. She's here.

"Gert," I say, and she puts her palm on my forehead, and I reach out to do the same, placing my hand against her forehead like a blessing, because I know she needs a blessing, and I say, "I know, I know, I know."

We stand in the open doorway with our heads bent down, searching for comfort.

PENNSYLVANIA HOSPITAL is only a block away, and that's where he is. *Right next door,* he said, and he was right. They called Gert, and she was coming to see if they'd made a mistake, and she needed someone beside her, so she stopped to ask me. Everything else fades to nothing. Gert needs me, and besides Amanda and the girls, she's the closest thing I have left to family. She grips my hand and doesn't let go.

The doctor—a gray-haired man with lines in his face and gentle, clasped hands, like Dad's—explains things to us in a calm, quiet voice. David was on his bike. We know how tight the streets of Center City are, no room for error. One car turns, another brakes, but not fast enough. David, caught, knocked into the next lane.

It was fast, he says.

We are escorted into a room, a cold one, where a body is covered with a sheet. I hang back, letting my feet get heavy, delaying the moment.

"Don't be scared," Gert says, so I try not to be.

Her hand clutches mine so hard it aches. She can break it for all I care. I never had to look at Ma's and Dad's faces. No one made me.

When the nurse exposes David's face I force myself to look where she looks, and follow her gaze down.

The dulce de leche eye, the bruise, the cheek the color of Arbequina olives. It's him.

Gert makes one loud sob, and her grief unlocks my own, and my sob follows hers like an echo. My throat narrows until I can hardly breathe. My cheeks are wet, then wetter. I'm crying, hard.

Still holding on, Gert gasps, "Yes," and there's the swish of the sheet lowering again, thank God.

Now that my tears have started flowing they won't stop. I'm not just crying for David, but that doesn't matter. Today has an all-encompassing sadness. My grief is pouring out over everything like spilled salt.

Afterward, I try to keep my wits. They're needed. Just as we worked our way into the hospital, step by step, we work our way out. From the place where they keep the dead to the place where they break the news, then to the place where people wait, then to the place where people have just arrived and aren't even sure what they're waiting for.

I have to guide Gert so she doesn't run into anything or anyone. As we work our way to the outer circle the other people around us are becoming more frantic. They're not watching where they're going. We're islands in a river, in our way. There's so much movement and noise I shouldn't be able to do it. But Gert needs me to do it, so I do. I walk with purpose.

Finally, on the sidewalk outside the hospital, we break clear of the crowd. I stop leading Gert, and turn to her.

I try to read her face. I know she's in anguish, her whole body tells me that. But I look at her face because I hope it will tell me what to do.

Mostly, Gert just looks lost.

"Come rest at the house," I tell her.

Her look doesn't change.

"It's so close by, and you should sit down. Come on, come over," I say. "Just for a minute."

She nods just slightly, and next to me, shuffles along. But I'm afraid she might fall, so I have to take her arm. She accepts it with no indication she knows it's there.

It's the coldest day in Philadelphia that I can remember. The sky is cloudless and bright, and in the half block between the hospital and my house, my arms go numb and my face freezes into a mask. I left without a coat. Even with this, I have no desire to stay inside. If I need to stay out here for an hour I will. I only want to be helpful.

We make our way slowly, but we get there. Up the steps. Through the door. Down the hall. I get her seated on the couch. I make tea for her, mint tea, heavily laced with honey.

"Is there anything else you need?" I ask her. "Anything you want? Anything I can do?"

She cups her hand around her tea but doesn't drink it. She stares down into the cup.

I gesture toward the fireplace. "I could make a fire."

"Oh, Ginny," she says. "Do not be helpful. Not just now. Right now, please, just be here."

So I reach out for her hand, and hold it. It's neither warm nor cold, wet nor dry. I squeeze and she doesn't squeeze back. If she wants me to be here, I'll be here.

We sit on the couch, facing the empty fireplace. Facing nothing. The smell of the sweet mint tea slowly disperses through the room.

The two of us stay that way for a long time, until someone from the temple comes to take Gert, and David, home.

MY PARENTS ARE dead. David is dead. What comes next? Gert's grief was all I could think of while she was here. If you don't know how to deal with emotion, other people's feelings can hit you like a drug. But now that I'm alone here it's my own grief I'm obsessed with. How my mother did so much for me, and I never thanked her, not once. I begin taking ingredients out of the cabinet for a recipe to summon her ghost, and then realize I am crying so hard I would never be able to form words, so I put them back again.

Did he want to be dead? Did he say to himself, *I can't take this,* and shove his handlebars toward the left at a crucial moment, and end his life on purpose?

I can't imagine him doing that. But I don't have a very good imagination.

It hurts, knowing I couldn't help him. We both reached out. The ache in my body shifts, encompassing my lost parents, my lost friend, my lost life. And in another way I've lost my sister, but there's a chance, some chance, that I might be able to get her back.

This is why Ma wanted to protect me. This is how much life hurts. But even now, even in this pain, even in knowing that, I'd rather be living it than hiding from it.

My stomach is growling with hunger when I hear another noise, faintly.

Knock-knock.

Not spoken, but rapped: knuckles on wood. The sound, an everyday sound, but full of mystery. *Let me in.*

It's a knock on the front door.

I think hard about it. Is there anyone alive I want to see right now? Is it someone alive who's knocking? What makes me answer the door is the fear that it's something important, and they would be persistent. It's easier to answer than not to.

The woman at the door, the hood of her jacket raised against the cold, is familiar.

I've only seen her twice, but the circumstances were memorable. I recognize her right away. Reddish hair. Slender build. She was at the temple. She made matzoh ball soup for the family with the sick daughter.

"I'm Miriam," she says. "From the *chevra kadisha.*"

"I remember."

She says, "I'm sorry to bother you. I would have called. But I knew only the address. May I come in?"

"Of course."

She comes in and stands inside the door. She places her feet firmly on the welcome mat, so any melting snow will be caught.

I don't know what to say to her. I don't know why she's here. My thoughts are in the kitchen, and with Gert, and under that hospital sheet.

Miriam says, "We would like you to help us with the meal of consolation for Gert and her family."

I can't believe I didn't think of it. All those mourners and mitzvahs. All those meals Gert made for others in grief. The oblong foods, the separation of meat and milk, the casseroles for the freezer. Kugel and soup and muffins and cakes. All lovingly prepared. Now, she is the one grieving. Hers is the family that needs consolation.

Miriam says, "It is unusual to have someone help who is not Jewish. I think you understand why?"

"Of course."

"But this is an unusual case. She brought you to help us because you're a very good cook."

"I'll be very happy to help," I tell Miriam, because Gert needs me. I will help the burial committee make the meal of consolation. I will take a new approach to death, because what is important about death is not the dead. It's the living. Those of us left behind.

I ask Miriam, "Could I bring another woman with me to help?"

"It's unusual."

"But it's okay?"

"It's okay. You know she'll help?"

I say, "I'll call her and ask."

"Tomorrow morning at the temple," she says. "Ten o'clock?"

"I'll be there. I hope we both will."

"You are good daughter," says Miriam, putting her hood back up, and walks off into the snow.

I HOPE AND hope that Amanda will answer her phone, but she doesn't. So much has changed for me in only a couple of days, but she doesn't know that yet. For her it's only been a little time. She still thinks it's worth holding on to her anger. She knows a lot more than I do about a lot of things, but there are still things she doesn't know.

I figure it out. I look up at the scrap of paper on the refrigerator, a few precious digits. I dial a different number.

A woman with an orange juice voice answers, "Hello?"

"Angelica, it's Ginny Selvaggio, please don't hang up," I say, and she doesn't. I tell her that someone has died, it's hard to explain why this is important but it was our cleaning lady's son, our friend Gert's son, and I need Amanda to come help me tomorrow morning, and I need her to forgive me and won't Angelica please call Amanda and let her know that we shouldn't be fighting anymore and she's right that Ma and Dad would want us to work together, and that I love her, she's my family, that's the thing that's important, and everything else we can figure out how to deal with together.

There's a pause, and I'm afraid I've lost her.

A sound, a swallow, a gulp of air. Then she says, "It's me, Amanda, I was having dinner with Angelica so I answered her phone while she was in the bathroom, it's me, Ginny, baby, are you okay?"

"I will be."

"I'm sorry about all this, I'm sorry," she says. "Is Gert okay? What happened? What do you need from me?"

I tell her what she needs to know, not everything, but enough. She agrees to meet me at the house tomorrow so we can walk over to the temple together.

After I hang up, I give Midnight extra food because I feel like feeding someone, but go to bed without dinner myself.

IN THE MORNING I decide to sit and wait on the steps. It's still cold, but with layers and the sunlight, protected from the wind by the portico, it's warm enough.

When I see Amanda walking up, I stand and come down the steps to meet her.

The first thing she says is, "I'm sorry."

"I'm sorry too," I say. "Let's go." I point her in the right direction.

As we walk I tell her about David and his wife, her death, his inability to deal with his grief.

"Scary," says Amanda. "That's not going to happen to us, is it?"

"I don't think so," I say.

"And do you think—I mean, it sounds like it was, but the way you're talking about how he was feeling before it—do you think it was an accident?"

"Yes," I say, because that's how he wanted it. And if I couldn't give him what he was looking for while he was alive, I can at least give him that.

She says, "Do you really need me? For this?"

"I'll feel better with you there."

"Okay."

"Besides, you want to learn to cook, don't you?"

"This isn't what I had in mind," says Amanda.

"Not what I had in mind either," I say, "but we have to make do with what we've got."

We walk into the temple and I guide her through to the kitchen.

Miriam says, "I'm glad you're here."

I say, "Us too," and we start to work.

First I have Amanda pick through the lentils, making sure there are no stones, and she is diligent. When she has finished with the lentils I show her how to make hard-boiled eggs, the twelve-minute technique, the same one Gert taught me.

She says, "You're good at this."

"Thank you."

"No, really. I'm impressed. I hadn't realized, you have this teaching quality, that's something you should, like, work with."

"Thank you," I say, which is the same thing I always say, but this time I mean it.

After the meal is prepared, we go with Miriam to Gert's apartment. It is very neat, neither small nor large, with brown carpet and pale yellow walls. I wonder if they are Chardonnay. I've never been here but Miriam knows the way to the kitchen. We set things out. Eggs. Lentils. Bread. After this I think I may never eat a hard-boiled egg again. Their smell is the smell of grief to me.

Gert is the mourner now. She sits, in black, low to the ground. She wears no shoes. The mirrors in the house are covered. There are other relatives, uncles and cousins, I think, who have attached the ripped black ribbons to the lapels of their shirts. I wish someone would give me a ribbon. I miss David. He was a friend. The first one I'd had in a long time. I'd been dividing my world into family and not family, but the truth is so much more complex.

Gert isn't wearing a black ribbon. Gert's fine dress itself is ripped on the left side. Everyone else has a neat, separate grief that they can unpin afterward. Her rip looks hasty and rough, jagged as a serrated blade.

A little boy, maybe a cousin, knocks over the pitcher of water near the door. I right it, mop it up, refill the pitcher. Whatever needs to be done.

I know from previous shivas that it isn't allowed to engage the mourners in conversation. If they want to speak, they will. And at last, after a while, they do.

Gert says, "He was a good son. Always so much energy."

"Yes."

She says, "When he was little, he used to wear me out. Just running all over the place, all the time. Back and forth. I said, hummingbird, you drive me crazy! And he would hum. Because I had called him hummingbird. A bird that hums."

I say, "He was a good person."

She nods, and looks down, fingering the hem of her shirt.

"We'll all miss him," I say. My cheeks are wet again.

Gert says, "I thought I would be angry. I am not angry. I am just sad. Later I will get angry, I think."

I nod. Everything I want to say sounds stupid.

"Thank you for knowing him," she adds. "This last year, he struggled. These last few weeks—he needed, I am glad he had, someone who was on his side."

I put my hand toward Gert and she lowers her forehead. I press my palm against it. She pushes forward and lowers her forehead against my shoulder. I touch the back of her head, gently, and say, "Rest."

She clings to me. I wish I could do more.

In front of the candle the mourners come together. Gert joins them, huddled over, looking small. Men's voices mutter a prayer. I find Amanda in the kitchen and squeeze her hand. We're strangers here, but we have each other.

The evening is long. People come in and out of the front door, silently, because ringing the bell would make the mourners feel like hosts, which they're not. So many relatives, more than I thought people could have. And friends, so many friends. So many people, but they move quietly, respectfully. I let them flow around me like water.

And gradually the crowd gets smaller. Eventually it's only the mourners, and Miriam, and myself, and my sister. She gives us a ride home. Her car is small and clean. It smells, unfortunately, like hard-boiled eggs. This will fade.

When she drops me off, she says, "Thank you both."

I say, "Thank you for asking me to come. It means a lot."

Amanda echoes, "Thank you."

"There are meals after the meal of consolation," says Miriam. "The family will need more care. I hope you will help."

"Of course," I say, and mean it.

Inside the house Amanda sets down her purse and sighs heavily. I look at her posture. Her shoulders are slumped downward. She looks exhausted.

I say, "Why don't you stay here tonight?"

"I think that's best," she says, "I'll just call Brennan and let him know."

When she's done with the call, I make peanut butter and jelly sandwiches and pour two tall glasses of milk. Amanda stares at her milk and says, "This looks great. Do you have anything stronger?"

I bring her Dad's bottle of scotch. I pour us both a shot.

She drinks hers down and starts coughing. I clap her on the back. The coughing slows down and then stops.

When she speaks her voice is husky. She clinks her glass against the bottle and says, "Like he's right here."

I say, "We have to remember them and let them go."

"It's hard," she says. "It's so hard. But you're right. They're gone. I just—thought we'd have them for longer."

"Me too," I say, and sip at my scotch. It burns, but after the burn, I like the warm feeling.

"Listen," says Amanda. "All this aside. Today aside. I understand why you're mad at me."

I remember Dr. Stewart, and how betrayed I felt, knowing my sister sent me there unaware.

She says, "But you have to see where I'm coming from."

"Don't *have* to," I remind her, wondering if I sound impatient.

"Yeah, okay. Sorry. Maybe I should have said that differently."

"Maybe."

"I just want what's best for you," says Amanda.

"You say that," I tell her, "but what's best for me is not being tricked by my own sister. What's best is being able to trust you."

"I hear you."

"So can you be patient with me?"

"Yes."

"And trust me?"

"I'll try."

One of my professors in college used to say *As the wise man said, Do or do not, there is no try,* but the advice columns generally say the opposite. If someone promises to try, and you're happy with that, don't push. It can backfire. You can get yourself in a lot of trouble asking for too much.

Amanda says, "I just worry about you."

"Please, could you stop? Don't worry about me."

"So you're doing all right?"

"Yes," I say, because that's easiest. Once I started telling her the ins and outs and ups and downs I'd never be able to stop.

"I just hope you understand, Ginny, I have your best interests at heart."

"I guess I do."

She says, "And I think you have my best interests at heart as well. What you were trying to say about Shannon—I know you weren't trying to hurt me."

"I don't know what she's like all the time," I say. "You do. I wasn't saying I know something you don't. It's just, if she's like me, she's going to need to be helped along some."

"I just don't know, if she does have a problem of some kind, I just don't know how I can be sure that everything would be okay. And that's all I want for her. That's all a parent wants for her kids."

I realize I meant to tell her about Dad, but maybe now isn't the time. I ask her, "Did you ever think Dad was odd?"

"No," she says. "I mean, yes, but, he was just Dad. He wasn't around much, and when he was, he didn't want to see me. You were always his favorite."

"Well, you were always Ma's favorite."

She says, "The grass is always greener."

"Grass?"

"I just mean, since Dad liked you better . . ." She pauses and starts again. "I always felt like there was something wrong with me, right? Since I wasn't his favorite?"

She's crying.

"He loved you," I say.

"I know."

"He loved both of us, and so did Ma."

She says, "I miss them so much."

All I can say is, "Me too."

She puts her face down in her hands. There isn't anything I can say, but there's something I can do. I wrap my arms around my sister, and hold her.

We're not going to settle everything, heal everything, in one day. But at least we can get started.

After Amanda goes to sleep in her own room down the hall, I fill Midnight's dish, and walk through the darkened house. I have one more thing to do before I go to bed.

They're not coming back. I know it. I accept it.

I take the rain boots and Dad's dress shoes and Ma's bedroom slippers and I place them neatly in the box labeled *SHOES*, and I close the top.

CHAPTER FIFTEEN

Ribollita

GINNY'S RIBOLLITA

SALT · 4 CLOVES OF GARLIC · 4 SHALLOTS CUT IN RINGS · OREGANO · BLACK PEPPER · 1 14-OZ CAN WHITE BEANS · 1 14-OZ CAN CHICKPEAS · 1 28-OZ CAN TOMATOES (TORN BY HAND) · CHIX BROTH · 1 BUNCH STRONG GREENS SUCH AS KALE · 2 CUPS CUBED ONION FOCACCIA · OLIVE OIL · ½ CUP PARMESAN CHEESE

The garlic on the bottom of the shallow pot is turning golden. I need to act before it's brown. The broth goes in, covering the garlic and shallots and oregano, hissing with the heat. Just as it should. Everything in order. Pepper. Two kinds of beans, soft to the tooth. Tomatoes, torn by hand. Greens sliced in ribbons, stirred in after everything else has collapsed together. Clap the lid on, to keep the moisture from evaporating, and let it stew until the flavors meld.

In a separate pan I carefully toast the focaccia croutons in olive oil, turning them so each side gets its turn, then set them on paper towels to cool. Just before serving I'll add the cheese, and scatter the croutons on top. I have read and tried a dozen different recipes for ribollita since last December and this is my favorite way. I take the bits and pieces I like. The end result doesn't belong to just one person. There's some of Nonna. Some of other cooks I don't know at all. And some of Ginny, in the end.

Out of habit, when I complete the last step of the ribollita, I glance toward the corner where the stool used to be. I've taken it out of the kitchen, moved it over to the front window. There isn't a need for it. I didn't move it to discourage the ghosts from appearing. It seems they've already left on their own.

On one level this is sad. No more espresso voice of Nonna's, calling me *uccellina*. No chance to tell Ma that I understand and appreciate her, and nothing more to be learned from Dad. No more satisfaction or disappointment from David and Elena. But in a way, it's better. I couldn't just hide out in this kitchen with the ghosts forever. I would have had to neglect the living to do it.

And the living, all of us, are more important than the dead.

Ribollita isn't traditional at Thanksgiving, but I want to have it on the table anyway. It will mean a lot to me, and to those who aren't with us, if they're watching. I don't know if they are or not. But I figure it couldn't hurt.

Amanda and Brennan and the girls will be here at three o'clock for dinner. At first Amanda insisted I come to their house, but in the end, they let the girls decide. The girls said they wanted to go to Aunt Ginny's. It makes me smile. Midnight is spoiled, with the scraps I've been dropping down to her all afternoon, her belly already full underneath the fluff. Shannon will probably slip her more treats when she arrives. Midnight is a very lucky cat, just like I'm a very lucky human. I've been thinking about bringing another companion home for both of us. I'm sure the shelter would have a black kitten I could name Snowball.

Should I make something more? The counter disappears under bowls and Pyrex already. Spoons I used for tasting have piled up in the sink. Strong, good smells clash with each other, garlic against cinnamon, savory against sweet. Two dressings, Ma's traditional corn bread version as well as the stuffing she made last year for a change of pace, a buttery version with cherries and sausage and hazelnuts. The herb-brined turkey, probably larger than we need, and a challenge to manhandle into and out of the refrigerator. A deep dish of creamy, smooth mashed potatoes, riced and dried to make them thirsty, then plumped back up with warmed cream and butter. For dessert, a mocha cake I came up with one day. In the batter is barely sweetened chocolate and dark, strong coffee. The layers are sealed together with more chocolate, warmed up with a hint of ancho powder. It's mine, no doubt about it, but I was thinking of David when I made it.

I look around the kitchen, count off the courses. Maybe I'll make just a little something more. Cranberry relish, maybe. Too much will be just enough. There are a lot of people to feed.

Gert is joining our family for Thanksgiving. I still see her every week. Sometimes she cleans the house, and sometimes she lets one of the women who works for her do it, and spends the time talking to me instead. I help her come up with recipes and strategies for the women who cook at the temple. She helps me plan for the community garden. Before the winter was over, I found Ma's list of who worked what plots, so I was ready when spring came. And I worked with the rest of the planners to make sure the garden ran smoothly, all through the summer when things were flowering and growing, and into the fall, when we harvested and turned the exhausted vines and stems back into the soil again.

Once a month I go back to Dr. Stewart, and we talk about strategies. I'm modifying my behavior, one day at a time. I'm getting a little better at conversation. I fear it less. I don't exactly smile—I tried that, it was a disaster—but I practice making my brow smooth and my body language open. I searched the Internet for some advice columns about how to do this. I work on not crossing my arms, though I'm having trouble figuring out where to put them. If your hands don't go in your pockets or on your waist, where do they go? Before, I never knew the word *akimbo*. *Akimbo* is on a page with *alacrity, Alamogordo,* and *alarm.*

Amanda calls every day at least once. We don't always talk about important things. But we talk. And sometimes she'll bring the girls over here, or she'll pick me up and take me to her house for dinner. If I go to her house I always take cookies. Parker loves the peanut butter cookies, the kind you stamp an X onto with the tines of a fork, which were her mother's favorite too, when we were little. Shannon's favorite are the lemon cream cheese drops, because she knows how to make them herself. All it takes is a box of cake mix, a block of cream cheese, and an egg. I still help her with the icing, and the oven. While they bake, we look through newspapers for new scraps to paste into her Normal Book.

I don't have to move into Amanda's house to be present in her family. Even though I'm not there physically all the time, I want them to have something that says, *I'm out here. I'm okay. I love you.* I want them to bite into a cookie, and think of me, and smile. Food is love. Food has a power. I knew it in my mind, but now I know it in my heart.

The doorbell rings. My guests are here.

I rest the wooden spoon on a plate alongside the simmering pot of ribollita, turn off the burner, and go to let them in.

GALLERY READERS GROUP GUIDE

the

KITCHEN DAUGHTER

JAEL McHENRY

Introduction

With the unexpected death of her parents, twenty-six-year-old Ginny Selvaggio finds that her safe, sheltered existence has completely shattered. Painfully shy and unsure of adulthood, Ginny seeks comfort in the only place that has ever brought her peace: the kitchen.

But the kitchen has its own surprises in store for Ginny. The scent of her Nonna's rich, peppery soup summons the spirit of Nonna, and she leaves Ginny with a cryptic warning. Suddenly, Ginny is forced to untangle hidden family secrets, all while dealing with her domineering sister Amanda. Ginny comes to realizes that the ghosts of her loved ones can be beckoned back to her kitchen by cooking from their recipes. But she must decide if she has the courage to face the truths they will reveal about her family—and about herself.

Questions for Discussion

1. Ginny undergoes a great transformation through the course of the novel. Compare the early version of Ginny with the woman she is by the end. Do you feel she has changed? In what ways?

2. "Food has power. Nonna knew that. Ma did too. I know it now. And though it can't save me, it might help me, in some way." (p. 45) Do you agree with Ginny that food has power? What did food and the kitchen do for Ginny? Is there something you turn to such as cooking, cleaning, or organizing as a means of coping with your emotions? Or is there a place you go to (as Ginny goes to the kitchen) that makes you feel safe?

3. Many times throughout the story, Amanda appears domineering and high-handed. But do you think Ginny is also quick to judge her sister? Did you relate more to one or the other? Why do you think Amanda feels she has to assume the role of the older sister?

4. Ginny observes, "They say you learn by doing, but you don't have to. If you only learn from your own experience, you're limited." (p. 38) If Ginny had applied this advice outside of the kitchen, do you think she might have had an easier time relating to her sister? Do you agree with her observation, or do you think avoiding mistakes others have made is a different way of limiting yourself?

5. Discussing Elena's death, David remarks that it might have been better if he had never met her. He says, "I wouldn't have ever loved her, and that would've been my loss, but how bad is a loss you don't know about? You can't mourn all the people you could've loved but didn't. You mourn the ones you loved and lost." (p. 245) Do you agree with his statement? Why or why not?

6. Gert warns Ginny not to summon the spirit of Elena, but Ginny doesn't listen. Would you have done the same? Why or why not? If you were in David's shoes, would you want to see the spirit of someone you loved? If Elena had appeared the first time Ginny cooked her dish, do you feel things might have ended differently?

7. Do you think Ginny asked the right questions of the spirits she summoned? What would you have asked if you were in her place?

8. How did you feel about the way Amanda tricked Ginny into going to see Dr. Stewart? Do you think Ginny would have gone to see someone eventually, if Amanda hadn't forced her? Is it a situation where the end justifies the means? Why do you think communication between the two sisters was so difficult?

9 Along with the kitchen, Ginny often turns to the Normal Book to calm herself. She tells David, "See? Normal means a lot of things to a lot of people. You're normal. Don't worry. It's okay." (p. 269) Do you agree with her? Do you think normal is a term that has a single definition, or not? Do you think we try too hard to label people as one thing or another?

10. The theme of appearance, in opposition to reality, is central to the book. What are some of the obvious, and not so obvious, examples

of this idea? What does Ginny come to understand about the way things appear versus the way they truly are?

11. Ginny's father hid a very important secret from his family. Do you feel he was right to keep both his and Ginny's condition a secret from Ginny and Amanda? Do you think by trying to protect her, he ultimately did her a greater disservice?

12. The title of the novel is *The Kitchen Daughter*. Discuss the significance in relation to the story. What does the kitchen teach Ginny? How does trust, both in and out of the kitchen, play a part in Ginny's shifting perspectives?

Enhance Your Book Club

1. Ginny has certain recipes that specifically conjure certain family members. Prepare and bring a dish special to you to the meeting—if the scent could bring a ghost back, who would it be? What's the story behind the dish?

2. Check out author Jael McHenry's SIMMER blog at simmerblog. typepad.com. Pick a recipe or two to try after you've finished discussing the book!

3. Compare this novel to other novels that share themes of food and self-discovery such as *Julie and Julia* or *Under the Tuscan Sun*. How are they similar? How are they different? If *The Kitchen Daughter* was made into a movie, who would you cast?

4. Research Asperger's syndrome and autism and have each member present an interesting fact. Are you surprised by what you learn?

5. Do you have an item that is to you what the Normal Book is to Ginny? Have each member bring their "Normal Book" to the bookclub and discuss!

A Conversation
with Jael McHenry

What inspired you to write *The Kitchen Daughter*? What was the experience of writing a novel like for you?

When I started writing the book, I had just moved to Philadelphia, and I lived just a few blocks away from the Italian Market, which is this amazing area with fruit and vegetable stands, and Italian stores full of pasta and salumi and cheeses. I'd always enjoyed cooking, but at that particular point in my life I really started to get serious about expanding my skills and trying new things, and shopping at the Italian Market gave me great ingredients to play with. The more time I spent there, the more I was amazed by the great sense of tradition and identity. There are these Italian families that have been running shops there for generations, and that really spoke to me, the connection between food and family.

So I started developing this character who loves food and loves cooking, but is completely closed off from the world, a young woman who just can't connect to people. Because food is such a wonderful way to connect, I wanted to create this conundrum, this person who doesn't use it to connect, has never used it to connect. And she couldn't just be shy or nervous. She needed to have a real obstacle, not just something she could "get over" by the end of the book. That's where the Asperger's came in.

As for the writing process, the first draft came very quickly—it took only a few months to write—but there was a lot of rewriting and reshaping to find the core of the story I really wanted to tell. It wasn't easy, but I'm so happy with the result.

How has being both a columnist and a food blogger impacted your fiction writing? Are there any particular websites you draw comfort or inspiration from, as Ginny does from Kitcherati?

I think the more you write, the better you get, and you develop skills in one type of writing that you can apply to another. For instance, for the Internet, your writing needs to be crisp and sharp and digestible. If people have trouble following your point, they'll just go click on something else. My natural fiction style is to write long, flowing compound sentences, but I knew that wasn't how Ginny would think—you have to watch out for things like that in first-person narrative—so my online writing experience came in handy when developing her voice. It's short. Almost fragmented.

As for websites, there are definitely blogs and sites I go to almost every day. Serious Eats and eGullet, I think they're mentioned in the novel, I visit them a lot. They're interactive and discussion-oriented. Among the blogs, my personal favorite for inspiration is Smitten Kitchen. Her photography is just achingly gorgeous.

There are great descriptions of meal preparations in the book, and you yourself are an enthusiastic cook. What is your favorite dish? Is there a story behind it, or a particular memory it conjures?

I have a whole lot of favorites! Nearly all of them are family recipes, so they're important to me because of who made them and where they came from. Pierogi from the Ukrainian branch of the family, Cornish pasties (not pastries, pasties, pronounced like "past" not "paste", they're meat pies with potatoes and rutabaga in a flaky crust) from the English side, rum cake and bourbon balls at Christmas, Grandma's butterhorn rolls, the list goes on and on.

Because my background and Ginny's are different, it didn't make sense to use many of my own family recipes in the book, but I did sneak one in there: the biscuits with sausage gravy are a McHenry classic. Either my mom or my dad will make them at least once whenever the family gets together. I grew up on that gravy. Ooh, and potato puffs. That's what I used to have for my birthday when I was a kid, fondue and potato puffs, which are mashed potatoes mixed with cream puff dough and then fried. Incredible. And now I'm hungry.

Your heroine Ginny suffers from Asperger's syndrome, though she doesn't realize it for the majority of the novel. What made you decide to write her this way? Was it difficult to delve into the mind of someone who sees the world in a very different way than most? What kind of research on Asperger's was required to make her believable and multidimensional in your mind? Was there a reason you chose Asperger's as opposed to another developmental condition?

As I said a little earlier, I knew from the beginning I wanted Ginny to be closed off from the world, to have an obstacle that kept her from connecting with people. At the time I was just becoming aware of Asperger's syndrome—I'd met John Elder Robison, actually, that was part of it—and I wondered if it might fit the story. Then the more I found out about Asperger's, the more I realized that I was already writing Ginny with many of the characteristics of someone on the autism spectrum. Then when I did more extensive research, including reading a lot of first-hand accounts, it became really important to me that Asperger's be part of her identity and her story. When I was looking for an agent, actually, several of them told me the novel would be easier to sell without it, but I'm really glad I stuck to my guns.

Was it difficult? Absolutely! Writing in Ginny's point of view was a huge challenge, because so many of the usual narrative techniques were just completely unavailable. She doesn't look at people's faces. She can't read body language. She isn't going to say "Amanda looked angry" or "I could tell he didn't mean it" or any one of a thousand other things that would have been natural in some other character's voice.

Since Asperger's manifests differently in different people, I had to make choices about her particular instance, and what she was capable of, and how much she couldn't do because of Asperger's, and how much she couldn't do just because she'd never tried, or been allowed to try. As part of the process, I read a lot of first-hand writing from people with Asperger's, like Gavin Bollard's "Life With Aspergers" blog, and a great book called *Women From Another Planet?,* which is a series of essays written by women with autism and Asperger's, talking about love and work and family and all aspects of their lives. I learned as much as I could about the spectrum, and I picked a point on that spectrum for Ginny to inhabit, along with deciding on all her other characteristics—her sense of humor, her physical appearance, her family relationships, her fears and hopes and strengths, all that.

The book opens with the line: "Bad things come in threes." Do you believe that's true?

Honestly? I don't. I believe we're always trying to make order out of randomness, and that's where that saying came from. But it's something Ginny would believe, because she needs rules and patterns. So that was always the first sentence of the book. That came very early in the process. I always wanted to kick the book off with that contrast, that she lumps those three things together. Most of us would consider death the most traumatic thing possible. But for Ginny, being surrounded by strangers who are actively focusing on her, wanting to touch her and talk to her, that's almost as traumatic.

Who or what inspired the recipes you chose for each spirit that Ginny brings to life?

The recipe inspiration came from all sorts of places. In some cases the characters drove the recipes, and sometimes it was the other way around. I wanted a Cuban character because I wanted to include a recipe for picadillo, and I read this fascinating interview with a Jewish-Cuban woman, and that's how Gert came to be. Along the way the scene with the picadillo came out and Gert's role evolved into something else, with the burial committee, helping bring Ginny out into the world. Most of the other stories are simpler. Elena is from Peru because my husband loves aji de gallina. The biscuits and gravy, like I said earlier, is a family recipe of mine. The 12-minute egg instructions are funny because I don't actually cook eggs, I don't like them, but I knew I'd heard somewhere that 12 minutes was the magic amount of time. Then I was talking with my mom about boiling eggs one day and she mentioned "12 minutes" and I thought, "Oh! Right. That's where I heard it."

What else is there? Right, the ribollita, the very first recipe. I wanted something simple, and it's a simple peasant dish, so it would be comforting and she would have all the ingredients right there to make it. And the brownies, there are so many great brownie recipes out there but I really wanted my own that was unique to the book, and I absolutely love salt with chocolate. So I just started playing around. I wanted them dark and not too sweet and salty like tears. Luckily, my critique group was available to eat my experiments.

Many authors find that their characters are extensions of themselves, in one way or another. Do you find that to be true? Are any of the characters in *Kitchen Daughter* based on people you know?

In a lot of ways, everything about Ginny's life is the opposite of mine. For one thing, I get along with my mother really well! Always have. So that relationship was hard to write, especially that big argument in the kitchen, because I just have no experience with that kind of tension. I did draw heavily on my life, but not in the way you'd think—it's the places, not the people. I was living in Philadelphia when I wrote the book, in one of those gorgeous old houses on Portico Row right next to Pennsylvania Hospital, and you totally see that in the writing. When Ginny looks up Broad Street and stares at City Hall, or she walks along Spruce or Pine looking for the antique bootscrapers next to the brownstone stairs, that's the most of me you see in the novel. You'd think it's the cooking, but I don't even cook like Ginny cooks. I've never followed a recipe letter for letter in my life. (Well, not until I tested the ones I was going to put in the book.) I'm much more improvisational in the kitchen, and even when I do cook from a recipe, I'll nearly always change something.

In many ways this is a sister story, as the complicated relationship between Ginny and Amanda is central to the development of the novel. Do you have a sister? If so, did you draw any parallels between your life and the relationship between Ginny and Amanda?

Again, kind of the opposite. No sister. I do have an older brother, but he is very cool (Hi, Derek!), and has never tried to run my life the way Amanda tries to run Ginny's. Like the tense relationship between Ginny and her mother, the tense relationship between Ginny and Amanda is something I don't have experience with. I had to stretch to get it right. But the circumstances of the story really drove it—if a person is used to taking care of things, it's not unlikely that they'll perceive a family member as one more thing that needs taking care of, especially in a time of crisis. Even though she's the antagonist, on some level, Amanda's right—can Ginny really take care of herself? How can anyone know for sure?—so I really enjoyed the complexity of that relationship, and I hope it drives a lot of good conversations between readers.

One of the most significant ideas in the book is the idea that there is no such thing as "normal." Is that a mantra you live by? What gave you the idea for Ginny's Normal Book?

You know, I do believe that. I enjoy reading advice columns, and that's a true thing, the idea that people always want to know if their feelings or their husband's behavior or their sister's ultimatum is "normal." And whether it's "normal," whether it happens to everyone else or not, that's not important. What's important is that it's happening to you. The Normal Book grew out of that, the idea that the advice columnist is this judge of sorts, the stranger who people ask for a ruling. Across the excerpts of the Normal Book you'll see a pretty wide range of where "normal" comes into play. I just felt like that would reassure Ginny, and it's true, that "normal" to one person is "abnormal" to another and that's why it's a largely useless distinction.

Are you planning to return to Ginny and this cast of characters in your next book, or do you feel like their story is finished? If so, where do you think you'll go next?

I've gotten really attached to Ginny, but I think the arc of this book is the crux of her story. These few months are where everything changes for her. So if I do explore more of this cast of characters, it would probably be in short stories and not a whole novel. Each of these people—David, Gert, Amanda, and certainly Ginny's parents—has a rich history we only glimpse in this book, so I may come back and tell other parts of those stories someday. Right now I'm working on another novel with a first-person narrator and she is very unlike Ginny—bold, shifty, a born storyteller—so I'm exercising totally different writing muscles on that project. But it's another story of transformation and magic, so I think readers who enjoyed *The Kitchen Daughter* will find some familiar ground in it.

Who are your writing influences and what are you currently reading?
I have three all-time favorite books: *Lady Oracle* by Margaret Atwood, *Middlesex* by Jeffrey Eugenides, and *All About Braising* by Molly Stevens. Of those three, Atwood has definitely had the most influence on my writing (though Stevens has had the most influence on my cooking, and as far as cookbooks go, *All About Braising* is remarkably well-written.) I'm always impressed with writers who find ways to break the rules. Both Atwood and Eugenides are brilliant at that.

What I'm reading right now, it's the same type of thing—it's Jennifer Egan's *A Visit From the Goon Squad*—it just amazes me when writers take a giant leap into the unknown and it somehow works. This book has a whole chapter in PowerPoint. PowerPoint! And it works, because it's the character's voice, it's the character's thought process, and the writer has done a brilliant job of making herself invisible. It sounds weird to aspire to invisibility, but that's always my goal.